CHASING DIRT

BRANDT LEGG

By Brandt Legg

Chase Malone Thriller

Chasing Rain
Chasing Fire
Chasing Wind
Chasing Dirt
Chasing Life
Chasing Kill
Chasing Risk
Chasing Mind
Chasing Time
Chasing Lies
Chasing Fear
Chasing Lost

As always, this book is dedicated to
Teakki and Ro

Vinci Books

vinci-books.com

Published by Vinci Books Ltd in 2025

1

Copyright © Brandt Legg 2019

The author has asserted their moral right to be identified as the author of this work in accordance with the Copyright, Designs and Patents Act 1988. This work is a work of fiction. Names, characters, places and incidents are the product of the author's imagination or are used fictitiously. Any resemblance to actual persons, living or dead, places and incidents is entirely coincidental.

All rights reserved. No part of this publication may be copied, reproduced, distributed, stored in any retrieval system, or transmitted in any form or by any means, including photocopying, recording, or other electronic or mechanical methods, nor used as a source for any form of machine learning including AI datasets, without the prior written permission of the publisher.

The publisher and the author have made every effort to obtain permissions for any third party material used in this book and to comply with copyright law. Any queries in this respect should be brought to the attention of the publisher and any omissions will be corrected in future editions.

A CIP catalogue record for this book is available from the British Library.

Paperback ISBN: 9781036705237

Printed and bound in Great Britain by Clays Ltd, Elcograf S.p.A.

Chapter One

September in Paris. Sunlight filtered into the apartment through high, slender windows. It was one of those long, narrow, century-old Paris flats that would've been called cramped and dingy anywhere else, but in the City of Light, even the ordinary was often romanticized.

Chase Malone, once a celebrated tech billionaire, stood in the stale air of the closed space, wishing he were someplace else. As was his habit, he'd taken a mental inventory of objects that could be used as weapons and, more important, all the avenues of egress available. This place had few exits.

He had recently become part of an underground movement known as "The Cause," or to those who understood its mission more intimately, "WOLF."

In a back room off the kitchen, Chase watched as a man he'd just recently met counted cash—a stack of Euros totaling more than one hundred thousand dollars. The money Chase had delivered would be used to fund controversial operations of the group, including protecting and supporting whistleblowers and bribing officials for critical information.

"Mind if I open the window?" Chase asked. "A bit stuffy in here."

The man nodded without slowing his counting.

He had reluctantly joined WOLF at the urging of his girlfriend, Wen Sung, a former spy for MSS—the Chinese intelligence service. Chase wished she could have come with him, but she was elsewhere in the city, assisting in a WOLF operation. They were to meet in Lac Inférieur, Bois de Boulogne park, very soon.

It had taken him longer to find the apartment than he'd expected, so he was anxious to go. *I might be late to Wen,* he thought, checking the time on an antique wall clock. *However, there should still be plenty of time to make our train to Amsterdam.*

A violent crash shattered his thoughts. Chase, who had been on the run for nearly a year, didn't wait to find out who had kicked in the front door before he was squeezing out the window and dropping onto an ancient, rusted fire escape.

Can I make it down two stories before whoever busted in gets to this window? he wondered, looking for anywhere else to hide. Turns out the answer was no. Before he was halfway down, bullets ricocheted off the metal steps.

Without looking up, Chase leapt off the rickety platform, landing on the roof of a city bus that was cruising up the busy street. As his pursuers continued down the fire escape, one of their team, who'd been covering the sidewalk in front of the building, followed him on foot. Chase, now lying flat on top of the moving bus, watched as the man jumped onto the hood of a parked Mercedes, ran up the windshield to its roof, and then onto the top of a delivery van that was driving near the back left side of the bus.

Jumping from the van to the bus, the man pulled out a pistol, but before he could fire, Chase lunged at him. The two of them wrestled and struggled as the bus picked up speed. Chase jammed his elbow into the man's face—a trick he learned from Wen, an expert black belt fighter, that always produced a profusely bloody nose. However, the man continued fighting, seemingly oblivious to the injury. After dealing several hard blows to Chase's rib cage, he freed himself, and was able to aim his weapon again. Chase used the momentum of the bus turning to slide back toward the attacker and hooked his foot between the man's legs, causing him to fall backward. Blaring horns added another distortion to the minutes and actions that Chase felt couldn't be real.

I've got to get the gun, he thought, grimacing at a weapon he never liked and rarely carried, while throwing himself across the man's body before he could recover, thrusting his knee into the man's solar plexus and grabbing for the gun with both hands. The bus bounced over a pothole, allowing the man to pistol whip Chase's forehead.

Chase kicked his leg desperately, and miraculously his foot connected into the man's shoulder. The momentum left the two separated. An instant later, both were on their feet. The bus, now on a busy four lane boulevard, momentarily slowed as a changing traffic signal allowed more vehicles to enter the flow. The man now had an easy shot.

Like a scene in an action movie he would not want to see, the unpretentious billionaire dove onto another bus driving in the opposite direction. Barely getting a grasp, he dug for his beloved multitool, flipped the pliers open, and pinched its teeth onto the half-inch ridge of metal running along the edge of the bus' top. Before the man could react and adjust his aim, Chase was too far away.

Panting and shaking, Chase watched as the frustrated man jumped down off his bus. *He'll never catch me,* he thought, pocketing his multitool and turning to see if there was anything ahead that would stop his bus. Instantaneously, he threw himself flat against the roof a split second before it entered an overpass that would have knocked him off the bus into traffic.

Six minutes later, no longer hearing a cacophony of urgent horns, Chase jumped off the roof at a bus stop and walked the final three blocks to the park. Their routine had always been to meet at parks, or other easily accessible public places, before heading to their true destination. Chase sat on a tree-shaded bench, pretending to read a small book, while watching for Wen—or anyone else who might have followed.

They had talked about the possibility of having a small boat ride if neither of them were delayed. A lake in a Chinese park had been their special place when they'd first met and promised themselves to each other forever. They had been to Bois de Boulogne park separately, and were excited about sharing the experience. Wen had spoken enthusiastically about the Musee Marmottan Monet. She'd loved the impressionist's paintings since first seeing them as a child in her Chinese art classes. Chase had hoped that after the boat ride through the Parisian forest, they could sneak a visit to Le Chalet des Iles restaurant on the island in the middle of the lake, where he'd secretly made reservations as a surprise for Wen.

However, that was all before the man on the bus. Now, they would have to do what they always did—run.

"You got here early," Wen said, finding him twenty

minutes later. "Any trouble?" She eyed his bleeding forehead.

"We had visitors at the drop," Chase said.

"They found us again." She scanned the area. "We better go."

He nodded, frustrated that, more often than not, they didn't always know who was after them.

Chapter Two

Chase and Wen exited Lac Inférieur, Bois de Boulogne park, just as a bus was approaching. "This one's going to the train station," Wen said. "We should take it."

"I've had enough buses for one day," Chase said. "Let's get a cab instead."

"So the meet up was compromised, and the funds did not make it," Wen asked rhetorically, once they were in the taxi. "How could they have known?"

Chase shook his head. He'd been asking himself the same question since getting off the bus.

"I'll have to call Margot."

Chase knew she meant as soon as the short ride was over. Margot Ariesen was the leader and founding member of The Cause. A decade earlier, her husband had been jailed after disclosing corruption among Europe's largest defense contractors and the French and British governments. There were no whistle blower laws to protect him, and three months into his prison sentence, he'd been killed in a suspicious accident. In their grief and outrage, a group of his friends began what later grew into WOLF. Margot was a fierce advocate of people's rights.

"You tore your coat," Wen said.

"I'll get a new one, and I'm not the one who tore it. At least it wasn't my fault."

Wen smiled. "But I gave you that one." Chase had a habit of getting his clothes torn, cut, blood stained, and even punctured by the occasional bullet.

He smiled, squeezing her hand. "Get me another one?"

Chase paid the driver as they pulled into the taxi rank at Gare du Nord. The massive station, the busiest in Europe, had first opened in 1846.

"Lots of police," Wen said, automatically surveying the huge space as they entered the main concourse. "The French are always concerned about terrorists."

"For good reason. They get hit often," Chase said, checking the time on his phone. "Are you going to call Margot now?"

"I was going to wait until we're on the train," Wen said. "We're taking Thayls, high-speed to Amsterdam, platform seven."

The crowds swirled in many patterns. Wen pulled out her phone to call the leader of WOLF.

"I can't wait to hear her theory on how they found the safe house," Chase said. He'd always been apprehensive about The Cause, believing they were too radical, too revolutionary—too dangerous. However, Wen was committed to the group, who had helped her escape China and the MSS.

"The breach may have nothing to do with WOLF,"

Wen said. "Whoever it was could have been after us. *We* may have compromised The Cause."

Just as Margot answered the call, Wen disconnected. "Trouble two o'clock," Wen said to Chase as she slid the phone into her pocket. "Not a good place for a gun battle."

"Split up?" Chase asked, knowing the protocol.

"Good luck. See you at platform seven." Wen casually walked toward the lavatories.

Chase reached into his messenger bag, as if looking for tickets, but instead brought out a gun, careful to keep it concealed in the sleeve of his coat.

In positioning the gun, Chase had let his guard down only for an instant, but it had been enough. An attractive woman bumped into him at the same moment a man grabbed his gun hand and relieved him of the weapon. Before Chase could protest, the three of them, with him sandwiched in between, headed for an exit. Each of his "new friends" had a gun stuck in his side. He scanned the area for Wen, hoping she had not suffered the same fate.

I can't let them take me out of this building, Chase thought. He glanced at them, to be sure he had not seen them before, and to look for weaknesses.

"Your cooperation is appreciated, Mr. Malone," the man said in a French accent. "No harm will come, I assure you."

"Of course not," Chase replied. "Why don't you let me buy you lunch at The Etoile du Nord? Chef Thierry Marx is wonderful. It's inside the station, near platform nineteen."

"It's only open in the evenings," the woman responded with laughter, as if he'd made a joke. "Perhaps another time."

"The restaurant *upstairs* is not open now. However, the brasserie downstairs is actually open all day. My treat."

"Amusing, Mr. Malone," the man said. "But we'll pick up something on the way."

"The way?" Chase asked. "Where are we going?"

"No more talking," the woman said sternly, jabbing her gun harder into his side.

A couple of minutes later, they exited the main terminal. Chase knew it was now or never.

Chapter Three

About thirty yards ahead, Chase spotted two men waiting next to a large black SUV. They were obviously his destination. He looked around, desperately wanting an idea, a plan, some way out, that didn't include two bullets in his gut. The area was busy. He considered screaming for help, but decided that was likely to get some innocent bystanders shot as well as himself killed.

They were about twelve yards from the SUV. Chase, knowing he was going to die anyway if they got him inside the vehicle, decided this was the moment. He would fake tripping, which would get him to the ground, and—assuming they didn't shoot him in the process—as they were getting him back to his feet, he could use the leverage to bring them down, where he would at least have a chance to get one of their guns.

Just then, Chase's phone rang with an obscure ringtone, *Persecution of the Masses* by Shiro Sagisu, from the *Shin Godzilla* soundtrack, that he recognized as a signal from

Wen. It meant she could see him, she was coming, be ready to act.

"What's that?" the man asked, alarmed.

"It's my phone. Mind if I get it?"

"Don't even think about it."

"I'm pretty sure it's my parole officer. If I don't answer, I could get in real trouble."

"Forget it, funnyman."

The phone stopped ringing.

"It's okay, he'll probably send the FBI looking for me. My ankle bracelet will tell them exactly where we are. Don't worry about it. I'll give him a call later."

The man looked down at Chase's feet, as if looking for the electronic ankle bracelet, but kept moving.

Chase abandoned his tripping plan, instead putting himself in a Zen zone, trying to anticipate what his partner would do, listening to every sound as if they were clues.

They were about ten feet from the SUV when Chase heard approaching vehicles, even before he saw the flashing lights. A second later, his entourage noticed. People all around them were stopping, curious, not wanting to miss what might be happening.

"See?" Chase said. "They really get crazy when I violate parole."

"Shut up!" the woman snapped as the man pushed them all faster toward the SUV. The men waiting at the vehicle had also noticed and jumped in the front seat, leaving the back door open, obviously planning a quick getaway.

Multiple police vehicles appeared. Behind them, Chase saw two fire trucks. Five feet from the SUV, he began to wonder if Wen was going to make it in time. The man gave Chase a shove toward the vehicle.

Wen flew in from the other side of a burgundy van parked behind the SUV. In one motion she nearly picked up the woman, sending her sailing into the open back door, and kneecapped the man. Chase kicked his former captor in the face as the man went down.

Wen pulled Chase away. "Come on!"

They slipped past a shuttle bus and crouched behind a row of parked commuter cars. Police surrounded the SUV, guns drawn, screaming at the occupants in French to surrender their weapons and come out with their hands on their heads.

"What's going on?" Chase asked, wanting to hug her, but knowing it would have to wait.

"I called in a bomb threat as soon as we split up."

"You didn't even know they were going to grab me."

"I knew we'd need a diversion, one way or another. We were running into a hornets nest."

"How'd you know about the car?" he asked as they ran through the vehicles toward the terminal, careful to keep below the roof lines.

"As soon as I saw them take you out of the building, I looked for their getaway car. It was easy to spot. I called the police again and told them the bomb was in the black SUV. Even gave them the plate number."

Chase was used to being impressed by Wen, but this was a story he looked forward to telling his mother, brother Boone, and very close friends. Most of their stories could never be shared. "Where to now?"

"Platform seven," Wen said. "We can still make the train to Amsterdam."

"What if there are more?"

"There are always more," Wen said, kissing him quickly

on the lips. "However, today, all the ones that were here at Gare du Nord are in police custody."

Wen dumped her gun before they reached the baggage X-ray, metal detector, and passport check at the entrance to the platform.

"I've already gotten rid of mine," Chase said. "Earlier, a nice couple assisted me with the process."

"Do you miss them? Were you flirting with the woman?"

"We were going to have lunch at The Etoile du Nord."

"Ah, chef Thierry Marx," Wen said. "They declined?"

"Apparently they don't know his work, and in any case, they were late for an appointment with Préfecture de police de Paris," Chase said in his best French accent, which wasn't very good. Both knew that humor was their reality check.

Chase and Wen found the first class section and sat facing each other in the single seats. "Let's see if we can make it to Amsterdam without you getting into any more trouble," Wen said, watching a man carefully as he passed.

Chase looked at her, wondering if the passenger was another problem.

She shook her head. He leaned closer to her and held her hands.

For the remaining three hours before reaching Amsterdam, they were content and grateful to speak with only their eyes . . . creating a time filled with silent laughter and immeasurable love. And yet, in between those moments, Wen ran through every conceivable scenario for who could be on the train, or waiting at the final stop.

When and from where will the next attack come?

Chapter Four

The train ride had been wonderfully rejuvenating and uneventful. Chase and Wen were even more careful than usual on the way to their flat. Only after Wen was certain they hadn't been followed did they go home. Long ago they had realized that they could not read and unwind as others were able to do. Even with the pleasure of being in their much loved penthouse flat, overlooking two canals, a part of each of them was always alert, constantly listening, their instincts revved on high . . . ready . . . waiting . . . wondering.

Although Wen kept drought-resistant plants and cactus, which she trimmed, removed old leaves from, and doted over, they could go for months without care, as she had them on a self-watering device. The flat was alive with as much greenery that could be sustained one way or another as possible because the greenery rejuvenated her when she could not be outdoors, and in some inexplicable way, having plants everywhere made her feel safer, even though she didn't understand why.

Chase fixed them a light meal and then sat down, setting himself to cleaning and oiling his multi-tool.

"Why do you love that thing?" Wen asked, leaning over an abnormally tall Australian shrub.

"It makes me a superhero."

A few hours later, Chase's phone woke him from a nap. He looked out the window before answering. Whenever an unexpected call came, even from someone familiar, he had developed the habit of assessing his surroundings before answering. Such had become his life on the run.

"Something you'll want to know about," Dez said. His longtime friend and business partner was one of Chase's links to his old life, to the 'real' world. The two had met in college, formed the company Balance Engineering, and gotten rich together, developing three breakthrough technologies centered around artificial intelligence—RAIN, SEER, and fAIr. Dez, an African American man, was one of the smartest people Chase knew, and in the not very diverse Silicon Valley, he was widely known and respected. The tech community had rallied around Dez when he lost his leg in a terror attack. Since then, he'd been pursuing ALAI - Artificial Limbs controlled by Artificial Intelligence —working on ways to make amputees, paraplegics, and quadriplegics able to function and walk again. The interface had been based on the super "Rapid AI" that Chase and Dez had developed.

"Do you remember about a year ago when Lars Krauss of Gravacon tried to license fAIr?" Dez continued. "They wanted to use our AI technology in optimizing Gravacon's agrochemical products and process?"

Chase thought back on all that had happened in the last year—most of which had been spent running for his life. His hand absently reached for the multitool in his pocket, but found it empty. He hadn't given Krauss or Gravacon a thought since their heated phone call back when Chase was still living a normal existence as a top tier tech investor and businessman. "Of course I remember. The guy was a jerk." He scanned the room until his eyes landed on the coffee table.

"Still is," Dez said.

"Why are we talking about him? Don't tell me he's asking us to license fAIr again? I couldn't have been more clear." The fAIr system—Free Artificial Intelligence Recapture—was a quantum-based AI program that reinvented itself as users applied it to their process or business systems.

"No. He's already been using it for at least six months."

"He *what*?" His sudden shout of disbelief brought Wen running from the other room.

"He purchased Sun & Earth Farms, and has been using their license."

"Sun & Earth is the largest organic producer in the world—what the hell would *Gravacon* want with them? The two companies are polar opposites!"

"Exactly. He bought them just to get their fAIr license."

"Have legal send them a cease and desist letter. He can't use Sun & Earth's license for Gravacon." Chase walked over to the table and reached for the multitool, but Wen snatched it up just before he got there.

"I've already talked to legal, and he *can* use their license."

"What? There's *nothing* we can do to stop them? Who screwed up that original agreement?" He grabbed at Wen, but she escaped, gleefully waving the tool in the air.

"Apparently it wasn't a screw up, there's just no legal way to prevent Gravacon because the companies have some sort of merging structure for whatever they're doing. If we restricted it in the way that could've stopped him from using it, it could stop any of our other clients from using it how they need to use it. Therefore, that's why that language was omitted from the licensing agreements."

"I don't care. Sue them anyway. We can get a restraining order, tie them up for a while." Chase squinted and frowned at Wen.

"There's nothing we can do. Anything like that will just get thrown out and open *us* to a countersuit."

"Then I'll call Krauss."

"And what? You think you're going to change his mind? You said yourself he's a jerk." Dez checked the security cameras. Balance Engineering's headquarters had recently moved to San Jose, California, but the large, lighted name on the side of the sixteen-story glass and steel building read "OAKTON OPTICS," and that was also the only way the address was listed anywhere. It was as if Balance Engineering, like its primary founder, Chase Malone, no longer existed. But it did. Dez oversaw the day-to-day operations of a small team of exceptional engineers who maintained SEER and fAIr, the only two "products" the company still had. "Anyway, I only found out when Ed Weston called me."

Weston had been the CEO of Sun & Earth, prior to the sale to Gravacon. They both liked him.

"Okay, I'll call Ed as soon as we're done," Chase said. Wen dropped the multitool into her backpack and smiled coquettishly at her silly looking partner, dressed in nothing but bright orange boxers. "How's the exoskeleton leg working out?" Chase still felt guilty because Dez had lost his leg when one of the people, trying to stop Chase, blew up Dez's boat.

"Progress, but I've been so wrapped up with getting SEER back online . . . " The secretive company's most secret project was SEER—Search Entire Existence Result—which utilized advanced photonics quantum information processors to run deep learning, AI, quantum algorithms with virtually every data point in digital existence to predict the future with stunning accuracy.

"Remember what my dad always said, 'Know your priorities.'"

"I know," Dez said. "I'm trying to do both, and the exoskeleton is very promising. In the first trials, I was able to run a mile faster than I ever could when I had a leg."

"That's amazing. Glad to hear it," Chase said enthusiastically. "Wen will love that news." He looked up to wink at her, loving every piece of that Asian mystique, but she wasn't there. He paused to check on her. "I've got to go. I'll let you know what Weston says."

"Do that. At least this time we're only talking about battling lawyers instead of agents and assassins."

Chase decided not to tell him about their morning in Paris.

Chapter Five

Chase went looking for Wen, assuming she'd gone to a nap in the bedroom. All he found was a note.

I've gone to finalize the weapons deal.

Chase pounded a fist into his other hand. "She shouldn't have gone alone," he said out loud. She had left his multitool beside the note.

The transaction had been arranged through WOLF, and would provide Chase and Wen with the supplies they needed—a small cache of weapons, passports, local currency, clean computers, burner phones, etcetera, wherever they would need them around the world. It was a straight deal that she could handle herself, but it was also an arms deal, and, to him, that always sounded dangerous.

He continued reading the note. She told him to meet her at noon in Amsterdam's Jordaan area, just west of the Amsterdam Central train station and was bordered by the Brouwersgracht, Prinsengracht, Leidsegracht, and Lijnbaansgracht canals. Wen loved the scenic neighborhood, filled with art galleries, shops, boutique restaurants, and bars. He left their penthouse a few minutes later.

Once on the street, he called Ed Weston, the former CEO of Sun & Earth Farms.

Weston had started Sun & Earth Farms from scratch out of his house in Eugene, Oregon. Back then, not many people talked about "organic," and few had ever heard of genetically modified organisms and genetically engineered seeds—GMOs and GEs. He leveraged the company into a half-billion dollar force in the industry—the largest organic food producer in the US. Chase had licensed fAIr shortly after, and the sophisticated program had helped increase crop yields significantly.

"Chase, good to hear from you again," the charismatic Weston began. "You sort of fell off the face of the earth. I envy you that. I'd like to do the same myself, if I were a little younger."

"Is that why you sold?" Chase asked, walking past a cafe drenched in the tempting aromas of baked goods and chocolate. He made a mental note to send his mother, Daisy, a case of Verkade dark chocolate bars. A self-proclaimed chocoholic, his mother had said, for as long as he could remember, that Verkade Dutch chocolate was the very best in the world, but was not available in the States. He knew she'd be thrilled.

"No, I sold because the business was hard, and my health was suffering."

"I'm sorry to hear that. Are you okay?"

"I'll be fine, but the stress . . . " He hesitated. "We were doing pretty well, until all the consolidation, the big conglomerates, started buying our competitors. General Mills bought Cascadian Farms and Annie's Homegrown. Kellogg took Kashi. Kraft, Coke, even Hormel have all purchased stakes in natural food. Suddenly it was harder, our market share started shrinking, credit got tighter, and when Gravacon came with their generous offer, at first I thought it was like making a deal with the devil, but Lars Krauss—you know, their CEO . . . "

"Oh yeah, I know Krauss."

"Well, he and a big team came in, told me they wanted to create a whole world dominating organic approach, something about easing regulatory on other products. He said that they had seen the success of organic, and wanted to make sure the two approaches could coexist."

"Sounds like a PR stunt." He passed a book shop with a table outside displaying used books. One jumped out at him, *The Last Librarian*, "Intriguing title," he muttered to himself and made a mental note to buy a copy another time when he wasn't so "occupied."

"I thought that, too, yet with all this great vision . . . I really thought it was going to be a wonderful thing, and with my health issues . . . anyway, I guess I got conned."

"Krauss doesn't care about the environment," Chase said matter-of-factly.

"Sorry your fAIr program got caught up in this. It was an amazing thing for us. We were able to increase yields, cut water consumption. The data told us how much to plant, when to change crops, everything! Your fAIr can change the world for organics."

"It's not your fault. The guy is a real snake. Gravacon doesn't care if they poison the world, as long as the next quarterly profits top expectations."

"That's the thing, though. I really think in spite of all that he's doing, he wants to end world hunger."

"You give Krauss more credit than I do, but even if you're right . . . end hunger at what cost?"

"Ultimately it doesn't matter whether or not Krauss is a bad guy, a scam artist, or Gravacon is the worst company in the world, it's gotten way more serious than that."

"I can't imagine," Chase said, stopping on a small bridge and leaning on the railing, still devastated that his invention was helping what he believed was one of the world's worst corporations. A dead bunch of flowers floated by, followed by an empty plastic water bottle.

"Gravacon is less than a week away from gaining worldwide approval of its new GMO concoction."

"This is worse than what it's already doing?" Chase asked, a slight feeling of alarm prickling through him.

"It's so much worse. I think it could *end* organic food forever!" Weston didn't realize he was almost shouting.

"*What*! How? Why?" Chase continued on, turning a corner and noticing a man in a blue blazer, dressed a little too nicely for the weather. Wen had taught him to always look for the person who either seemed out-of-place or overly "normal." Both were signs of surveillance, or a hit.

"You need to talk to somebody other than me. Someone on the leading edge of all this who really understands the science. I'm not that smart, I'm just an old backpacker who wanted to eat clean, healthy food instead of the junk we could get back in the day. But there are these two women—Dr. Kali Garodia and Dr. Paloma Boulet. They're researchers in Belgium at the University of Antwerp."

Chase glanced around and still saw Blue-blazer, but a little farther back. "I'm in Europe, so I could . . . "

"You need to see them yesterday."

"Okay, but I've already talked to legal. I can't stop Krauss from using fAIr."

"Chase, he's gotta be stopped, and not just from using fAIr. Wait till you talk to the scientists, you'll see. Krauss thinks he's going to solve one of our great problems." His voice rose, filled with fear. "What he's really going to do is destroy the water, the soil, our chances . . . "

"A real food fight," Chase said, trying to lighten the drama.

"It's about so much more than food," Weston said breathlessly. "I can't talk about it on the phone, but Kali and Paloma will explain. I can't stress the urgency enough."

"Like I said, what can I do?" Chase could tell Weston was agitated, even scared, but didn't understand what he expected him to *do*. He turned another corner.

"I'm just a fading old hippie. I've made a large donation to the University of Antwerp, but otherwise, Krauss has already gotten the best of me."

Chase turned back and saw Blue-blazer had also turned the corner. "I'll check it out, but—"

"I've heard rumors about some of the things you've done since you disappeared. If they're true, I know you can do something."

"And if they're not?"

"Then the universe is about to get a lot darker."

Chase ended the call, ducked into an alley, and ran.

Chapter Six

Chase emerged from the alley, cut across another street, and then jogged to an intersection. A route that was the long way around, but he seemed to have lost Blue-blazer, still unsure if he was an actual tail. His next call went to Gravacon's seventy-three-year old CEO, Lars Krauss. He walked along a canal, waiting for the assistant to put him through.

"Chase Malone, the ghost of Christmas past," Krauss answered. Industrial noise hummed in the background. "I'd heard a rumor you were dead, or I might've been expecting your call."

"Did you really acquire Sun & Earth Farms just for their fAIr license?" Chase asked, passing a mother trying to catch her little boy's red helium balloon before it floated out of reach. Leaning over a railing, Chase grabbed it at the last second. The woman smiled and thanked him.

"It's a good company. There are some synergies—more than you might expect. There are many ways to feed the world."

"I can sue you," Chase said as the boy let the balloon go again.

"I'm sure you've already spoken with your attorneys, and, as you know, Gravacon is no stranger to lawsuits. We have one of the best legal teams in the world, and we're always bringing on new attorneys. Your case might be a quick training exercise for them. I say, if you're so inclined, *do* it." Krauss walked through an enormous factory filled with millions of seedlings sprouting in various colors and depths of dirt.

"How do you justify what you do?" Chase asked angrily, but smiled as the woman just managed to catch the balloon and avoid tumbling into the canal. The little boy seemed delighted by the whole adventure.

"I have nothing to apologize for," Krauss said, sounding indignant. "I am trying to stop world hunger. Can you think of a bigger problem facing humanity?"

"Maybe poisoning the ecosystem and contaminating the water table across the globe?" Chase suggested, checking behind him. "Because *that* seems incredibly important."

"Gravacon isn't doing those things," Krauss said. The lights above him in the factory suddenly went dim and twenty feet away a new row illuminated. "Don't believe everything you read."

"Because you've faked the research, bribed scientists, probably even silenced critics by any number of means." He continued on at a clipped pace through another intersection.

"Your accusations offend me. Particularly coming from a man who is a quasi-fugitive. Perhaps we should ask you— is *your* conscience clear?" Forty yards away, strobe lights blinked in a frenzied sequence above thousands of trays of green plants, their leaves the size of coins.

"You're avoiding the issue. Does making a few more dollars on the quarterly reports justify crushing another family farm in favor of bigger corporate artificial food factories? Is efficiency worth what your poisonous chemicals and genetically modified seeds are doing to the ecosystem? To the environment?"

Chase noticed Blue-blazer had caught up to him again, about a half-block behind, but he no longer wore the blazer. There was no longer any doubt the man was after him.

"It's not about the money," Krauss said. "It's never been about increasing our stock price, or adding revenue to the bottom line. I'm not a greedy man."

"Really?"

"I grew up poor, hungry—something *you* wouldn't know about. I almost died of starvation. A painful, wanting emptiness that you—growing up in the American suburbs—could never comprehend. Your idea of hunger was finishing the last bowl of Cap'n Crunch and having to wait an hour or two for your peanut butter and jelly sandwich."

Chase couldn't argue. He'd grown up in a comfortable, albeit hard-working, middle class household.

"Do you have a clue what the taste of nothing is? What the wretched, raw taste of poverty is like?" Krauss continued, moaning his words. "There are eight hundred and thirty-eight million, fifty-nine thousand, eight hundred and seventy-nine hungry people in the world *right now*, desperate, starving, malnourished, many wondering if they'll even wake up tomorrow. Mothers unable to feed their children . . ."

"I suppose you only care about them."

"Yes!" Krauss snapped as he climbed a set of concrete steps to another level of plants. His stomach hurt, it had for a while, something he decided was sympathy pain. "That's what I'm trying to fix. Damn you and your holier-than-thou attitude. Who placed *you* on the podium?"

"Talk about espousing superiority." Blue-blazer still trailed Chase, who had decided to stay on the busy street and avoid his destination—at least for now—but he checked his watch, not wanting to be late for Wen.

"Does being right ever get tedious for you? Don't answer, I already know! You have no idea what our chemicals do. No one does. Any report to the contrary is biased and inconclusive. Yeah, we may be doing some harm, but we don't know that the earth can't handle it, absorb it, and fix it. The best scientists don't know what it can filter. I don't know, and you don't know."

"*That's* reassuring."

"I can tell you this, evolution is a damn slow process. We sped it up by genetically modifying the seeds, making them do what would take thousands of years otherwise, for an ecosystem that isn't prepared for seven billion, eight billion, ten billion people."

Chase saw Blue-blazer faintly reflected in a corner shop window.

"Saint Krauss, going to save us all." Passing a flower shop, he noticed the light of an open entrance in the back.

"How dare you! I am a noble man attempting to make a lasting change. Damn right I'm trying to save people. And what are *you* doing, Chase Malone? You are doing *nothing*. Thirty years after you die it will be difficult to find a hundred people who remember your name. One hundred years after you die, there might still be a handful. Another fifty years, there'll be none. Because you aren't doing anything other than writing computer programs. People might use your programs to effect real change, but *they* are the ones doing it, while you will be forgotten, lost to a wasted life."

Chase realized his hand was trying to crush the phone. He felt a stinging truth in Krauss's words as he dashed out the back of the flower shop and headed in the opposite direction he'd been going. Chase wanted to call Krauss a liar. He didn't believe they weren't driven by profits. Everything Gravacon did was in the pursuit of control—dominating more markets, killing off competing companies, lobbying, which was actually bribing politicians to let the corporation literally get away with murder. There were estimates that Gravacon had caused thousands of cancer deaths, a number which could swell into tens of thousands in another decade, as the poison in their formulas slowly found its way in an infinite loop of the food chain, destroying people's health and DNA.

Instead, "Screw you!" was the most eloquent response Chase could manage.

"You're a weak, little man, Chase. Don't get in my way."

Chapter Seven

Krauss ended the call with Chase, far more furious than he had let on. After quickly checking his computer, he learned that Erhard Krieg, head of Gravacon's Security and Safety division, was on site. Krieg's group was charged with identifying and mitigating threats to the corporation that could not otherwise be successfully defended against by the legal department or outside attorneys.

Krauss summoned Krieg to his office. "The Tower," as workers called Krauss's private office, rose sixty-six feet above the sprawling Gravacon headquarters campus, located on the outskirts of Cologne, Germany. Krauss loved the view. In the distance he could see the famous Cologne Cathedral, the Rhine River, the Colonius Tower, and the Hohenzollern Bridge.

A two-foot high clock with digital readouts in various colors ran along the ceiling. The numbers, changing constantly, presented current total world population data: seven billion, seven hundred fifteen million, six hundred twenty-one thousand, five hundred and seventy-eight, seventy-nine, eighty, eighty-one, eighty-two, eighty-three, eighty-four, eighty-five . . .

Undernourished people in the world right now: eight hundred and thirty-eight million, fifty-nine thousand, nine hundred and forty-nine, nine hundred and fifty, nine hundred fifty-one . . .

People who'd died of hunger today: forty-nine thousand, three hundred fifty-three, three fifty-four, three fifty-five, three fifty-six . . .

People who'd died of hunger this year: eighteen million, six hundred eighty-six thousand, one hundred and one, one hundred and two, one hundred and three . . .

There were other numbers, including tons of food wasted in the world, money spent feeding pets, money spent on ice cream, candy, cigarettes, on and on, but the big numbers, the ones in red that kept Krauss up at night, were the people dying, and the nearly one in eight who were undernourished, and the ticker showing a child dying every twelve seconds due to malnutrition and starvation.

Krieg walked into the tower as if he were angry. He wasn't at all, or at least no more than usual. He just looked that way. In fact, he had a general pirate-like appearance. Krieg had lost an eye in a fight long ago that he claimed he couldn't remember, and had worn a black eye patch ever since. But it was more than the patch. Although only forty-two, his face had an aged, pinched look, as if he were a scrappy sailor who'd spent too much time at sea. He always had a difficult time eating much, consumed by guilt at the state of the malnourished world.

"What is the issue?" Krieg spat, knowing that he was

only asked to the tower when something serious needed attention.

Krauss took a sip of water. He didn't care much for Krieg, always felt like the temperature dropped as soon as his head of security entered a room. The man actually gave him the creeps—"creepy Krieg," he sometimes called him behind his back. However, it could not be denied that Krieg was very effective, and a company like Gravacon needed a man like him.

"Yes," Krauss said. "There is somebody I need you to keep an eye on." If Krauss had a sense of humor, he might've laughed at his inadvertent faux pas. *Keep an eye on*, to a man with one eye. He tossed Krieg a flash drive, never wanting an electronic trail of communication with matters such as these. "You can review the files later. However, this man, Chase Malone, is threatening the company. I'm not certain what his plans are . . . but he must not be allowed to succeed."

Krieg studied Krauss. His boss was a determined and accomplished man in his early seventies, thick gray hair, distinguished, if not dower. He admired his toughness and focus. "Is Malone to be eliminated?"

"Too soon to say, but I'm afraid that will be the eventual outcome. It will depend greatly on your reports, and his stupidity."

"Is he a stupid man?"

"No, I'm quite certain he is not."

Chapter Eight

Chase walked up to the street-side terrace of Winkel 43. Wen was addicted to their apple pie—its smooth, yet crumbly crust filled with thick chunks of caramelized apple and served with thick dollops of whipped cream, delighted her.

"Sorry I went alone," Wen said as soon as he sat down. "I ordered you a piece." She pointed to a fresh wedge of pie. "You're not mad?"

"No," Chase said, looking over his shoulder.

"Were you followed?"

"Yes, but I think I lost him."

"Who?"

"Don't know."

"In Paris, the men back at the safe house," Wen began, "did you hear them speak?"

"Yes, French."

"Are you sure they weren't Americans?"

"Yeah, I know Americans."

"And this one?"

"He hasn't introduced himself yet."

Wen got a to-go box for Chase's piece of pie. "We had better leave."

He told her briefly about the calls with Weston and Krauss as they walked south on Noodermarkt, and then took a left onto Westerstraat. The beautiful neighborhood of historic homes and galleries was Wen's favorite in Amsterdam, and normally she would have liked to linger, especially on such a lovely afternoon, but she sensed trouble close.

"Where are we going?" Chase asked.

"Back to the flat."

"Isn't that against our rules?"

"Rules are made to be broken." She winked. "I want to see if anyone is watching the place."

They took a right onto Prinsengracht along the canal. Wen took out her phone as if she were going to make a call, but instead held it so that she could see behind them through the camera.

"Lean in and kiss me," Wen said. "So you can look in the camera."

"That's him," he said, giving her a quick peck. "Earlier he had on a blue blazer."

"It's hard to tell who he works for," Wen said.

"Too soon to be anybody from Gravacon."

She eyed him. "You think Krauss will send people? It must have been quite a conversation."

"Hundreds of billions at stake."

"This Blue-blazer may be with the same organization as the men in Paris. We've got to assume they're connected to this morning's money drop."

They crossed the canal, still maintaining a casual pace,

not wanting to alert their pursuer that they had spotted him again.

"The cash was going to the Cause," Chase said. "I don't know if those men were after the money, or even knew about WOLF."

"Then why were they after you?"

He shook his head. "Margot seemed shocked, right?" Wen had called the leader of The Cause from the train thirty minutes after their first call abruptly ended.

"Yes."

"If they wanted the money, why go after me? I left the Euros."

"Blue-blazer is alone?"

"I saw no one else," Chase said. "And I lost him."

"Apparently not very well," Wen mocked.

"What I'm saying is, I think if we get to the right spot, we can lose him."

"There's a section ahead where that might be possible." Once across the bridge they headed down Keizersgracht. "But I'm not sure we want to lose him," she said. "I'd like to question him, find out who he's working for."

"He might not be working alone," Chase cautioned. "We could be walking into a trap."

"Story of my life." Wen gestured toward a shop entrance and they walked into a spacious showroom filled with blown glass, beautiful swirling colorful creations of every imaginable size and shape.

"It'll be a shame to have a shoot-out in here," Chase said.

Wen gave him a disapproving look, then glanced out the large storefront's window to confirm that the man was still following, using the vantage point to determine if he had anyone else with him. "He seems to be working solo," she said.

Chase was pretending to admire a red and yellow paperweight full of air bubbles—at least he thought it was a paperweight. If it hadn't been priced at two hundred and eighty euros, he might've bought it to throw at Blue-blazer.

Wen knew that it would be unusual for the MSS, or the CIA, to send a single operative after them. Her frustration was clearly evident on her face as she told Chase they should go back out onto the street. Wen, usually excellent at profiling a person, deducing a situation, anticipating what would happen in any given scenario, had been perplexed for months because they had been continually pursued by people they could not identify or attribute to any specific organization.

"Who the hell is this guy?" Chase asked, mirroring Wen's thoughts as they exited the shop. A breeze carrying the scent of coffee, cherries, and buttered popcorn wafted through the air.

"Today we are going to find out," Wen said, determined.

Chase was about to say, "That sounds risky," but before he could get the words out, he'd already predicted her response would be, "Everything we do now is risky," so he let it pass.

"Half a block that way," she gestured with her eyes, "there is a small antique shop set at the back of a cluttered courtyard. If he follows us in there, we'll get him. Hope you don't mind being the decoy."

"I'm always the decoy," Chase joked. "When is it your turn?"

"As soon as you learn martial arts, Darling," Wen replied. "Also, getting a little better at shooting would help."

They strolled into the courtyard as if shopping, but Wen worried the man following them had already guessed they were setting a trap. She made sure he could see them lingering for a moment. Chase remained in the courtyard, admiring what appeared to be a large old Gypsy cart priced at 4800 Euros. Wen hid inside the entrance behind a lattice filled with flowers.

It took longer than they expected, but eventually the man showed up. He stood near the entranceway, remaining on the street for a moment, never quite close enough for Wen to grab him. After spotting Chase, he casually continued down the street. Undeterred by Blue-blazer's decision not to enter the courtyard, Wen instead became emboldened, springing out of her hiding place and following him down the street. She knew Blue-blazer would not be going far.

He turned around, not expecting her to be there, just as she shoved him into a doorway, sending him tumbling over a short wrought iron gate, and pouncing on top of him as his head hit the slate paving stone.

Chapter Nine

Wen held the struggling man down and searched him for a weapon. There was none.

"Dorvadilla!" he yelled. "Dorvadilla."

"Who are you?"

"Simon, I am Simon Belfort."

"Who sent you?" Wen demanded.

"I said Dorvadilla! I am hunting King Dorvadilla," he said. "Margot sent me."

Chase appeared, standing above Wen.

"He claims he's with WOLF," she said as Chase helped her up.

"Did he give you the code?"

"He's been yelling Dorvadilla, but I can't remember if that one is still current."

"It is," Simon said, exasperated. "In Scotland, during the 2nd Century BC, King Dorvadilla decreed that an ox would be given to anyone who killed a wolf. Therefore, I am hunting King Dorvadilla."

"Do you know if it's the current one?" Wen asked

Chase. Simon stayed on the ground, seemingly afraid Wen might kill him any second.

"If you can't remember, I sure can't," Chase said.

"Oh, come on! Call Margot. I have the stupid code right."

Wen texted her. A few seconds later, Margot called.

"Go ahead and get up," Wen said to Simon after listening to Margot. "Why didn't you tell me you were sending someone?" she angrily asked the WOLF leader.

"I told you when we spoke earlier that I would send someone to help," she said. "He was supposed to shadow Chase to make sure no one was following him."

"Not a smart idea," Wen admonished, having no idea he would come that quickly. "I could have killed him."

Margot apologized.

"What are we supposed to do with him?" Wen asked, now belatedly recalling that during their call on the train from Paris, Margot had volunteered to give them someone from The Cause to assist in finding who had taken the Euros from the Paris flat and gone after Chase. It was likely someone trying to stop WOLF—which could be anyone. The organization had quietly amassed a long list of enemies as it built a secret worldwide base for a people's revolution.

"He lives in Amsterdam. He's smart, and willing to help, just please don't get him killed."

After the call, proper introductions were made. Simon, with short brown hair, and baby blue eyes, could have been Chase's brother. The two of them were actually the same age. Simon quickly gave them his background as they all walked back to the apartment. An American, he had spent two years in the Peace Corps after college, then become a nurse, and married a woman from Holland. Each week he worked three twelve-hour shifts, which allowed him to be free the remaining four days.

"We hope to have kids soon," he said.

"Why put all that at risk?" Chase asked.

"I'm passionate about The Cause," he said. "I'm not doing anything that can get me killed. But someone has to change things. The world is a mess, and our generation is the most connected, the most technologically advanced, and the least likely to do better than our parents . . . and also the most surveilled." He gestured toward a camera. "Big Brother."

While Wen and Simon kept an eye on the street, Chase picked up things at the apartment, including their "Go-Gear," a small bag of various passports and cash. Wen made a call to have "groceries delivered" to Belgium. They needed the "groceries," their code word for weapons, gear, etcetera, sooner than Wen had anticipated, but it would not be a problem. They were paying well for the service, run by former CIA and MI6 agents. They'd already made an appointment with the Antwerp scientists, as urgently requested by Ed Weston.

At Amsterdam-Centraal Station, Wen received a call from Nash Graham, a math savant keyed into the intelligence community who had helped them in the past, and was now also working with WOLF. Graham, known as "The Astronaut," had been introduced to The Cause by Wen, and was attracted to their mission of rooting out corruption in the world, something he had long hoped to see after working with most of the major intelligence agencies around the globe. There were a handful of 'astronauts' known, but Graham was, most likely, the best. The CIA had coined the term "Astronaut" because the brilliant savants were so far "out there" in their ability to understand and process complex data.

At their first meeting, the Astronaut had explained to Wen that his brain was wired differently. He could tell the day of the week on any date named for the past two thousand years and could recite the number Pi carried out to nearly a million digits by memory. Equations normally requiring a calculator or computer were easy for him. If asked "fourteen to the eighth power," he would instantly respond "one billion, four-hundred seventy-five million, seven hundred eighty-nine thousand, fifty-six." He saw numbers as an extraordinary array of infinite colors. He once told Wen that if he did not answer the equations flying through his mind, he would land in a place where numbers stopped making sense, a dark and random world where he would be lost, and where he would go mad.

The two of them had, for reasons neither could articulate, developed a deep and immediate bond. He'd made her a special, untraceable, atom transistor-based computer called the Antimatter Machine, which Wen and Chase had used several times to access critical, life-saving data. It had been damaged, and now the Astronaut was working to rebuild and improve it for them. She asked him for help with Gravacon, and he gave her an update on the status of his work on the Antimatter Machine.

Graham, like Chase and Wen, always stayed on the move, trying to keep ahead of those wanting to use his unique talents and awesome brain for nefarious purposes. However, unlike Chase and Wen, the Astronaut always knew who was after him.

Chapter Ten

Once Krieg reported that Chase Malone had made contact with the Antwerp scientists, Krauss knew the crisis was real. He must find out what Kali Garodia, Paloma Boulet, and their team were working on. His spies and surveillance had already told him they were trying to prove diseases could be cured from the microbes in dirt, but that would be easy to discredit. Yet the scientists were apparently attempting some kind of unifying theory known as the String-Continuum. There were recordings of them talking about how the String-Continuum would destroy Gravacon.

"Our priority is to uncover the String-Continuum," he'd told Krieg. "Nothing is more important."

Krauss wandered through the outdoor testing facility located adjacent to Gravacon's Cologne headquarters. Soon Gravacon's chief of agricultural chemistry would be giving him an update on their latest successes, but first he had to make a call that could not wait.

Amine, the President of the Democratic Republic of Congo, greeted Krauss in thickly accented English, a language they could both speak. "My friend, it is wonderful to hear from you at this time," Amine chuckled coolly.

"I wish I was calling with happier news."

"What is wrong, my friend?" Amine asked, his voice filled with concern.

"I'm afraid there is someone who does not want Congo to become food secure."

"Who is this person?" Amine countered, gruff and defensive.

"Before I tell you his identity, I should warn you, he is a powerful man with more resources at his disposal then those of your fine country."

"It is not my care if this man is dangerous as a pride of lions, and richer than all the kings . . . if he is standing in the way of Congo reaching independence, then I will find this man, and fight him. I do to make sure this man cannot stop us. So please, my friend, tell me who this is that means us such harm."

The Democratic Republic of Congo had been wracked by civil war and revolution for decades. As a result, it was one of the poorest nations in the world, dependent almost entirely on food imports to feed its people. The corruption which had plagued many in the African nations had been particularly cruel to the Congolese. Amine, who had come to power via a coup d'état, was a ruthless, but fair man, in the way only those living in embattled African countries might understand.

"In his own mind, the man means well," Krauss said. "He believes that our Agro chemical process, which will enable you to grow the food to feed all your people, and even have an excess to export, is a bad thing. This agitator thinks the chemicals that allow this process to work and give Congo food security, will harm little frogs, and insects."

"But this is not so. And even if it were, it would not matter. What is a frog? What is a bug? They mean nothing when my people are hungry." His dark eyes narrowed to distant trees outside a small window in his sparse office.

"He is also concerned that water can become contaminated."

"The water is too deep. Whatever we spray on the ground and the plants will feed the plants. It cannot reach the deep water." He stood and walked to the window.

"Of course not," Krauss said, looking at the plants—more than one hundred thousand of them—around him. "I merely want you to understand where he is coming from, why he is doing this."

"But he does not care about Congo, about my people . . . he does not care. He is like many rich Westerners who think they know what is best for Africa, and they can take what they want from Africa. These people, like this man, are . . . how do you say? Hypocrites. It is okay for them to have used chemicals, oil, to cut down trees, to do whatever they needed to do to grow their nations, feed their people, become secure, independent countries, but when little places like Congo tries to stand up and pull on its boots and take care of itself, to act like a man, they shoot us down. They say no." His hand clenched after opening the window and inhaling deeply.

Krauss brushed his hands over the shiny green leaves as if they were fine silk. "You are right."

"This man, you say he is powerful, with many resources. Your words mean he is a Westerner like I speak of, is he not?"

"I'm afraid he is. And his arrogance has blinded him."

"Tell me his name, my friend. Please, tell me his name."

"If I do this, I cannot know what your intentions are. I'm in a difficult—"

"My friend, tell me, can this man stop you from helping us stop the hunger in the Congo?" Amine's eyes turned to a photo on the wall of his dead father.

"Yes. I believe he intends to, and is capable of stopping us from helping you, which means he will also stop us from assisting many others in Africa, Asia, and throughout the world."

"I will take care of this, my friend, please do not worry. You need never know another thing about the situation. I will make this problem go away for us. Please do not slow down the timetable. My people are starving. Our time is very limited." Amine also knew the threat of rebels removing him from power grew each day. The cycle of poverty, hunger, corruption, and uprisings would continue again and again, further hampering those poor countries from ever being able to find their way out. "The name?"

"Chase Malone," Krauss said, then proceeded to give him all the details he had on the billionaire.

"Thank you, my friend. When next we speak, we will talk about more pleasant things than Chase Malone."

Chapter Eleven

Once they were all on the train, Chase and Wen questioned their new friend, trying to get a sense of his skills and intelligence.

"WOLF might seem like a noble idea, but you do realize The Cause's leader, Margot Ariesen, is a dangerous woman," Chase said to Simon.

Wen remained silent, waiting for Simon's reaction.

"No," he said. "WOLF works in the background. Almost no one knows they exist. It's members are unknown, even to each other, thus the code." His blue eyes flashed—obviously they had gotten him far in life.

"Dorvadilla," Chase said in a teasing tone. "But don't you think that kind of secrecy, her power, can be misused?" They kept their voices low, glad the fourth seat was empty.

"Margot wants to see global equality, for us *all* to share the world's resources, benefit from humanity's work and technological advances," Simon continued. "She sees corruption as the greatest threat to those goals." He looked suspiciously at a man in a dark suit as he worked his way down the aisle.

Chase nodded.

"You were a billionaire," Simon said. "Maybe you still are. I remember reading about your advanced AI program, and then you just disappeared." He stared piercingly into Chase.

"Did I?" Chase asked, masking his surprise that Simon recognized him. "I'm right here."

"You dropped out," Simon pushed. He leaned in closer to the rogue billionaire, who acted at least ten years his senior. "*Why?*"

Chase looked at Wen. She just smiled.

"I became disillusioned with the world, the greed and corruption, but mostly with the misuse of technology."

"Isn't the misuse of technology connected to greed and corruption?" Simon asked.

"Yes, directly related," Chase said.

"Then why do you say Margot is dangerous?"

"All revolutionaries are dangerous."

"I guess so," Simon agreed. "But it depends on which side you are on—the status quo, or the change."

"True. But you said earlier that you weren't doing anything that could get you killed."

"Yeah."

"WOLF is a revolution—peaceful or not—and revolutions don't always end well, especially for the revolutionaries."

Simon looked suddenly hesitant. Scenes of his wife echoed in his heart, how she had said similar words.

"Before I left China," Wen began, "I could see the looming threat that China's communist government was having on the world, and how many countries were becoming more like our oppressive leaders. Surveillance is only a tool to control us. The world is becoming less free. They have built a mass surveillance state. People don't realize they monitor every keystroke you type while surfing the internet, they have every email, every call . . . Why?"

"Edward Snowden said, 'No system of mass surveillance has existed in any society that we know of to this point, that has not been abused,'" Simon said.

"It was built to be abused," Wen said. "The Cause had a China chapter actively recruiting. They now have thousands, maybe tens of thousands of members in China."

"People who will peacefully change the world through resistance, protesting, boycotting, and awareness," Simon said, reciting one of WOLF's initial pitches at new recruits.

Wen smiled. She and Chase knew that The Cause also had a secret militant arm.

They talked for a while longer before Simon said, "If you'll excuse me, I need to find the badkamer."

"What?" Chase asked, confused, as Simon walked up the aisle.

"He's going to the restroom," Wen explained since she spoke fluent Dutch.

"He's okay," Chase said.

"If a bit naïve," Wen said.

"Isn't everyone that young?" Chase asked.

"He's our age," Wen said, laughing.

"Is he? I feel so much older."

"Life on the run," Wen said, her expression turning somber.

"We've made a long list of enemies," Chase said. "Who was it in Paris?"

They reviewed the possibilities—MSS, Mossad, NSA, almost any of the major intelligence agencies around the world, at least twenty-eight multinational corporations, an anti-tech militia, several individuals, and others known and unknown. The constant exercise of trying to figure out the identity of their pursuers was making them crazy.

"Hard to stop them if we don't know who they are," Chase said.

"But we will," Wen replied with an expression that made Chase almost feel sorry for their enemies.

After the short trip—the high-speed train had traveled one-hundred-sixty-eight kilometers from Amsterdam in just over an hour—Chase, Wen, and Simon arrived at Antwerpen-Centraal railway station. Only Simon had been to the extraordinary station before.

Wen watched the crowds, checked the dark corners, the nooks, and doorways, as she scanned the huge space in seconds, and then began again.

"Beautiful isn't it?" Simon said. "It was built between 1895 and 1905, under orders from King Leopold II, and soon dubbed 'the railway cathedral' because of its opulence and majesty."

"Aren't you the local historian?" Chase said, smiling.

"My wife is really into twentieth century European history," Simon replied, shrugging his shoulders and returning the smile.

"It is gorgeous," Wen said, admiring the glass ceiling and huge arched windows, which combined gave a daylight feeling to the structure. The interior also had the appearance of being an ornate exterior facade like those found on grand cathedrals. "I see how it got its nickname. Just wonderful . . . and massive."

"Prettiest in the world," Simon continued. "Twenty types of stone and marble were used to construct it, designed by one of the most renowned architects of the day, Louis Delacenserie."

"How do you remember this stuff?" Chase asked.

"It really impresses my wife."

Chase laughed.

"No surprise that this place survived repeated bombings during World War II," Simon continued. "There's even a noticeable bend in the roof, a lasting scar that multiple restorations couldn't remove."

Wen continued the search for threats, but missed the biggest one.

It had taken Erhard Krieg only two hours to drive to Antwerp, Belgium from Cologne, Germany. Krieg, who was personally overseeing the assignment with an associate, spotted Chase, traveling with another young American and a Chinese woman, as they exited the station.

Krieg had ordered electronic surveillance on Ed Weston, the former CEO of Sun & Earth Farms, since well before the acquisition by Gravacon. It didn't take long for one of Krieg's assistants to flag the phone call from Chase to Weston in which the research at the University of Antwerp was discussed. The legal team was also alerted, since the Antwerp scientists were already a major irritant for Gravacon. Krieg was troubled that his highest priority,

Chase Malone, had crossed with a former key person of interest, Weston, raising a red flag in Antwerp. All necessary resources would be brought to bear.

Antwerp, Belgium's second biggest city, straddled the Scheldt River and the Westerschelde estuary, which connected it to the North Sea. Its port was the second largest in Europe and, in addition to being known for its diamond trade, Antwerp was a research center, with many universities and colleges, including the University of Antwerp. Founded in 1852, the school had excelled in medicine, health, and biomedical sciences. Its research departments were among the best in the world in drug discovery and development, ecology and sustainable development, and infectious diseases.

Chase, Wen, and Simon adjusted to the quieter and brighter atmosphere of the street. It was an eight minute cab ride from the train cathedral to their destination at the Antwerp University Hospital, but Krieg already knew this, as well as exactly what building they would be visiting.

Chapter Twelve

Ed Weston was a major donor and enthusiastic supporter of lead researchers Paloma Boulet (a two-time award winning French whiz of a woman whose lean, tall, sculpted body was that of an athlete) and her lab partner, Kali Garodia (the dark haired and bronze skinned beauty who held honors in many countries for her contributing expertise in the scientific field). Both had been told to expect the American billionaire by an engaging phone call from Weston, knowing they'd hit it off. Both Wen and Chase liked the two scientists right away. Almost immediately, Chase realized the two women were about to change his and Wen's life in very many ways.

"How much did Ed tell you about our work?" Paloma asked in a boisterous, accented voice that was a beautiful mix of French and Algerian, from where her parents had immigrated during her childhood.

"Not much, just that we needed to get here today and that Lars Krauss and Gravacon are threatened by what you're doing here."

"Ahh, he leaves the dirty details to us," Paloma said with a raucous laugh. Chase had read an assessment of her that said the soil scientist could sometimes be resistant to rules. He liked rebels, so that didn't bother him. He thought her thick, curly brown hair might also not be subject to rules. He felt immediately comfortable with both women.

"We work on two things," Kali, an immigrant from India, said with a lyrical Hindi accent. "We've taken all the research on hydenosyn, the chemical that makes up Gravacon's main product, known as OrgriSource. It's also in the consumer version called *GET-EM®*."

"It causes cancer," Paloma interrupted. "There is no doubt about it. We have twenty-nine human studies that show it conclusively." Chase knew she was passionate about her work, and in her dark eyes, he also saw a woman who would fight against any injustice, no matter how small—a trait he shared.

"Of course, Gravacon has even more studies to discredit those," Kali said.

"But theirs are flawed, corrupted, and unreliable," Paloma added.

"There are people all over the world cataloging the many ill effects to health and the environment caused by hydenosyn," Chase said. "That's the main reason I would not license fAIr to Gravacon in the first place."

"We know that," Paloma said, looking at him so intently it almost made his knees buckle. She knew far more than he had imagined.

Kali launched into a long monologue about the health issues caused by Gravacon's chemical. Chase could already tell she could talk endlessly about serious and complex matters, and he enjoyed her habit of always punctuating pauses with a radiant smile, no matter the topic—dire or light. He knew, from reading her bio, that Kali's pursuit of medical research was born out of watching so many people suffer during her childhood in India, but most tragically, her younger sister.

"You're right, it is no secret how bad hydenosyn is, although you must admit it's astonishing that they still allow this product to be used all over the world, and particularly in the United States," Paloma said. "It seems only a small percentage understand how horrifying this compound is, because not only are the farmers still using it, but homeowners go through gallons of *GET-EM®* just to keep the weeds out of their perfect lawns . . . lawns that they water and fertilize so they will grow lush and green, so they can spend time cutting, edging, and trimming, so they can water and fertilize, so they can cut them over and over again."

Kali smiled, then laughed infectiously. "Sometimes Paloma goes off topic." Her long black hair, slim frame, and gentle nature made her seem younger than the fifty-four years Wen had read to him from her bio.

"Sorry," Paloma said with an exaggerated apologetic face.

"I was saying our greatest work is in the microbes. The dirt that almost nobody, other than farmers, gives a second thought about, is the Holy Grail, what medical science has been searching for since Socrates."

"What?" Wen asked.

She smiled again. "The magic pill . . . the cure to *all* the great diseases can be found in a handful of dirt." She smiled again.

"Is that true?" Chase asked. "How can that be?"

Paloma led them over to a graph-laden wall with

pictures and arrows, small diagrams, and writing that, overall, looked like a huge collage. Kali pointed to it as she spoke.

"We've long known that many plants and even parts and secretions from small animals, birds, and insects hold medicinal properties, but where does all life begin? What makes up those plants and animals, and us?" Kali became animated, as if she were telling a young child an exciting bedtime story about a princess who escapes from a castle. "Everything comes from the dirt! The microbes in the soil are alive. That means the dirt *itself* is alive."

"That life, inside dirt, is the actual origin of all living things on the planet," Paloma said, leading them to a computer where an assistant was told to bring up a short docu-video they'd created to show the potential of dirt and the entire program

"And the dirt contains the antidote for all things," Kali said.

"We have limited funds," Mutsu Sato, the twenty-seven-year-old lab manager, began, turning from his computer to interject. He had just pulled up the video. "But what we have, we use a long way. We do cover expenses for a large team of volunteer students who have traveled the world to bring in samples."

Three years earlier, as a grad student, Mutsu had transferred from Kyoto University in order to work with Paloma and Kali after reading one of their papers on the potential of microbes in soil to heal. He had been a follower of Dr. Ohhira, the Buddhist monk turned microbiologist who created an incredible probiotic from soil (actually decomposing plants), that healed him from an awful bout of food poisoning. Because he played Mozart in the lab when he created the microbes, Mutsu convinced Kali and Paloma to do the same.

"Samples?" Wen asked. "Of what?"

"Dirt," Kali said. "Mutsu manages the collections."

"It's more complicated than just digging up any old dirt from your backyard," Paloma said. "Not all dirt is the same, and the world is very big."

"How do you know where to get your samples?" Wen asked.

"Different scientists have classified it in different ways, but we use the nine Schultz eco-zones, and within those there are many sub regions, which we call bio zones."

"It's all very precise with GPS. We've been trying to get samples from every bio zone within each eco-zone," Mutsu said. "Should I show them?"

Kali looked at Paloma. She nodded. Chase, Simon, and Wen followed the bespectacled Asian youth to the end of the lab. He put a key into a lock and opened the door, revealing a large storage closet, its shelves stacked with hundreds of clear, one-quart glass jars, each with a small typed label.

Chase quickly calculated the number of shelves by the number of jars on each shelf. "There must be four hundred jars in here," he said. "You've been busy."

"There are still quite a few missing," Paloma said. "We're cataloging and analyzing each subset of soil, and we haven't even begun to discover all the cures."

"However," Kali began, "we have enough to know we can cure most cancers, Alzheimer's, dementia, diabetes, and many others."

"That's incredible," Chase said. "Have you published?"

"No, we're a long way from publishing. First we must

finish collection, cataloging, analyzing, crosschecking, the common denominators—"

Paloma interrupted. "It's a *huge* undertaking. And there are many microbes that are unique to each sample. It's extraordinarily complex, as you might expect."

"And the problem isn't just *that* workload, it's hydenosyn," Paloma said. "Hydenosyn sterilizers the soil and kills all the microbes. In Gravacon's attempt to make greater profits, allegedly to eradicate world hunger, they are destroying the very means to end disease forever."

Chase looked at Wen. The enormity of these discoveries and Chase's part in creating the technology that was once again being used for harm, filled him with guilt and anger. He tried, as usual, to focus on the teachings of Buddha. *Let go of the guilt*, he thought. *Let go of the anger*. Yet it was difficult, considering how many people would die.

Kali could see Chase was upset. "As Paloma said, it's ironic that hydenosyn causes cancer and at the same time kills the only thing that could cure it." She smiled. "But all is not lost. We can still win."

"How?" Chase asked, digging his hands into his pockets, gripping the multitool.

"Look at this," Kali said, pointing to a screen displaying the results of a microscopic attack of microbes against cancer cells. "The tiniest microbes from a little bit of dirt are conquering mighty and dangerous cancer cells."

"Where did that soil come from?" Chase asked.

"Don't you see? It almost doesn't matter. The earth is covered with microbes contained in the soil."

"But that particular sample came from New Zealand," Mutsu responded.

"If those little microbes from the dirt can win against those odds," Kali said, with a big smile, "so can we." Kali had a certain way with her smile and positive thrust that made Chase—and Wen, he later learned—want to ask her what she does to have such positive balance.

"It'll take a miracle to stop them in time," another lab technician said.

"Dirt is the miracle," Kali said. "We've discovered the secret to health and longevity. This is no accident. Dirt can save us all."

Chapter Thirteen

Ryan, a twenty-five year-old grad student, had been working for the Antwerp Research Center for more than two years, collecting soil samples from across the globe, often in obscure locations, but he never considered the work dangerous. His father, a Greenpeace activist, and mother, an environmental lawyer, had helped him secure the position with ARC, a private and public partnership based at Antwerp University in Belgium. Large parts of his childhood had been spent in exotic locations, and even when home in the States, his parents had always told him stories of their trips and exploits around the world from before he'd come along.

The geeky looking, buffed out jazz aficionado loved his work, not just because he believed in the environmental movement, but he also craved travel and meeting new people—two requisites of the job. His adventurous spirit and easy-going personality made him a perfect choice. Paloma Boulet, the lead scientist, and Mutsu Sato, who managed the massive program, were his contacts at the University, and both considered him a favorite among the forty-one grad students working to obtain soil from specific areas.

He'd already collected samples from all nine eco-zones, and countless sub regions bio zones, for the original round of research. Now they were close to confirming the next cycle. Whenever he got tired, or bothered by the sweltering heat he sometimes had to cope with, he'd remind himself that ARC wasn't just working on helping the environment, it was also mutual relationship of letting the environment help us. Ryan couldn't believe he'd been so lucky to get to participate on a project of this importance. "I'm going to be part of history," he would tell himself in those moments of exhaustion.

Many times he thought of his two grandfathers, whom he had adored. One of them died of cancer, the other's body had worn out too early. The microbes that he was working to find and research might have saved them both, and given him more years with the men he'd so loved and admired. On long, tedious drives, pursuing containers of dirt, he'd think of their tenacity in life, and all the people everywhere who'd lost someone they cared about who should have lived longer, healthier, happier lives, if they had known what nature could provide. Ironically, it had been one of his grandfathers who'd told him when he was just a boy, "*The cures for every disease exist somewhere in nature, and we simply have to find them. The bark of a tree, the saliva of an Amazon tree frog, certain flowers, a type of seaweed . . .* " Although his grandfather had never actually thought of the dirt as having all the answers, as it turned out, he hadn't been far off.

Ryan turned his truck down a long, open road, the flat prairie of Argentina passing in its simple scenic beauty— miles of cattle ranches, dairy farms, and seemingly infinite fields full of crops.

The lowland Pampas region was a vast, fertile plain. He wasn't far from the low Ventana hills, about an hour outside the city of Bahía Blanca, having already collected another sample closer to the Atlantic coast. He hit the brakes when a fox, which looked more like a coyote, ran in front of his car. The small, furry creature stopped abruptly, and looked directly into the wild and exhausted eyes of the young student. Ryan's heart beat rapidly. The gaze moved him radically in a deep part of his mind. The fox's wise, penetrating stare lasted seconds before it skittered away. Ryan put the car into gear and slowly moved on.

What the hell was that about? he thought, totally rejuvenated by the encounter.

Finally, he reached the 32,000 acre Poncho Verde Ranch, where Mutsu had actually obtained permission for him to take a sample. That made his job easier. Only about a quarter of the sites they visited were authorized. It didn't seem as if taking the equivalent of a quart-jar worth of dirt was a big deal, but some folks were funny about trespassing. Many of the samples came from national parks or other protected public lands, but most were from private property.

He parked, used GPS to make sure he was in the acceptable zone, and bent down near a stream bordered by a row of evergreen shrubs with light purple stems and thick, waxy leaves with smooth edges. The white flowers and yellow berries were a giveaway.

It's a Yerba Mate plant, he thought, knowing its leaves were used to make a beverage called "mate," and that overharvesting in the wild had brought it to near threatened status. *A good spot to take a soil sample.*

Kneeling on the ground, he cleared an area, turned over the top layer with a small hand spade that had been sterilized and sealed in a vacuum packed plastic bag, dug deeper, and filled the container.

Suddenly, he saw a shadow and jerked around. A tall, imposing man wearing a black leather cowboy hat, holding a shotgun, glared at him. "What the hell you think you're doing?"

"Just taking soil samples," Ryan said. "I have permission to be here."

"I didn't give you permission!"

"I'm sorry, is this is your land?"

"No."

"Then why—"

Before Ryan could finish his question, the man hit him hard in the face with the stock of the gun. He fell face down in the dirt, unconscious, and might have recovered with a broken nose and a horrible headache if the man hadn't shot him in the back of the head.

Chapter Fourteen

Chase, Wen, and Simon continued to absorb as much information as they could from their eager teachers in the Antwerp University lab. They were stunned by the potential of the microbes to cure diseases.

"Unless Gravacon destroys the dirt," Paloma said.

"We'll figure out a way to stop them," Wen offered, as if it were a promise.

Chase had been about to utter the same words, but more as a question of how to overcome the challenge. He had taken his multitool out of his pocket, his nervous habit of opening and closing the pliers making a clicking sound that caused Wen to shoot him a *Stop that!* glance.

"What day is it?" Paloma asked, eyeing the silent exchange between Chase and Wen.

"Monday," Mustu replied, amused that someone so brilliant rarely kept track of the days of the week.

"The votes are taking place Wednesday."

"What votes?" Chase asked, pocketing the multitool.

"Gravacon has lined up votes around the world," Mutsu

began. "The big ones, including the European Union, United States, Brazil, Argentina, India, and most African nations, take place on Wednesday."

"For what?"

"They've had their paid-for politicians introduce legislation that would invalidate any and all court rulings that prevent GMO and GE crops from being planted, or sold, into the food supply. It also creates a precedent-setting limitation on judicial review of genetically-engineered crops, allowing them to be planted without governmental oversight, or safeguards, in places that protect environment, and health of farmers, and the public at large. And, perhaps most outrageous of all, it grants Gravacon immunity from prosecution and lawsuits arising from their GMO and GE seeds, as well as products made with hydenosyn, such as GET-EM® and OrgriSource."

"How can they *do* that?" Wen asked.

"Money talks," Paloma said. "They've bribed everyone and buried the language in bigger bills. Hardly anyone knows it's happening."

"And even if they did," Mutsu added, "people just don't believe the risks."

"No one knows about the potential to cure cancer, dementia, Alzheimer's, reverse aging, substantially extending life expectancy . . . " Kali pulled up a chart on her computer. "Look at all the increases in these diseases over the past hundred years."

"What's caused that?" Simon asked.

"There are a many factors. However, the number one cause is the dirt. As we've depleted the microbes in the soil and relied more on herbicides and pesticides, which have killed off so many microbes, our health has suffered. Not to mention the explosion of consuming processed food."

"No microbes there," Paloma said.

"So what can we do?" Chase asked.

"We need more proof," Paloma said. "Dirt from every eco-zone." She pointed to a chart.

1. polar/subpolar zone
2. boreal zone
3. humid mid-latitudes
4. arid mid-latitudes
5. tropical/subtropical arid lands
6. Mediterranean-type subtropics
7. seasonal tropics
8. humid subtropics
9. humid tropics

"And specific bio-zones within them," Mutsu added. "The rhizosphere is a narrow region of soil that's formed partially by root secretions and related soil microorganisms —root microbiome. This area holds countless bacteria and other microorganisms feeding on sloughed-off plant cells, in addition to proteins and sugars released by roots. This nutrient cycling leads to disease suppression in plants, and the same can occur in humans. These communities of microorganisms also produce allelochemicals. It's like a plant-soil feedback loop."

"You lost me," Simon said.

"All it means is we need dirt," Paloma said. "And in the past week, we've had several of our collectors disappear."

"What do you mean 'disappear'?" Chase asked.

"A while back, some of them started to get roughed up. In the fall, we instituted strict protocols for checking in, and they were all really good about it," Mutsu added. "Two weeks ago, Steve didn't check in. It's been a week since we heard from Eric and James, and in the last forty-eight hours, four more have failed to contact us."

"We're terribly concerned about their safety," Kali said.

"And at the risk of sounding insensitive, we still need the dirt," Paloma said.

"Do you believe Gravacon would harm them?" Chase asked.

Paloma looked at him angrily. "Of course they would."

"I'm afraid to believe that," Kali said, "but where *are* they?"

Chase knew all too well what corporations were capable of doing in the pursuit of billions of dollars, and he also believed, in spite of Krauss's talk of ending world hunger and saving humanity, he saw people as commodities. "I agree with Paloma. Krauss will do anything to achieve his goals. The pending legislation and looming referendum deadline only add to Gravacon's desperate urgency."

"Maybe they've just detained our people until after they get their laws passed," Mutsu said. "I'm hoping that on Thursday we'll hear from the seven missing."

"We can still stop those bills from passing," Paloma said. "However, we don't have enough samples to complete our work."

"I don't understand," Chase said. "How hard can it be to prove they sterilize the soil with OrgriSource?"

"That's the easiest thing to prove," Paloma said. "But it isn't enough to stop them. We must show the *benefits* of the microbes that are destroyed. That is all that matters. If the microbes are made sterile, and nobody thinks they can do anything against disease, no one will care, because the soil will still grow crops."

"What about the chemicals causing cancer?" Simon asked.

"There are numerous studies that verify that," Kali said. "But Gravacon has just as many studies disputing it. Proving something causes cancer is a very challenging business. It can take decades to prove, and almost that long to get through the courts.

Announcing the data, publishing our work showing the beneficial microbes and what they do, will have the most impact. It's really our only chance to stop Gravacon."

"I still don't understand," Chase said, pointing to the cabinet containing hundreds of dirt samples. "Aren't those enough to make your point?"

"We can show individual microbes," Paloma said, "that will illustrate *potential* benefits, but we don't have time to do full trials, and so, the only hope is to show them what we believe . . . " She pointed to a large monitor displaying a sophisticated 3D graphic.

He looked at the image, stunned. "I don't believe it! That's . . . "

"Yes, it is," Paloma responded proudly. "We call it the String-Continuum."

"Incredible," Chase and Simon said simultaneously.

"Can you prove that?" Wen asked.

"We need the missing pieces to complete it, but yes. Once we have those, we can demonstrate it conclusively."

"The one roadblock may be in the United States," Mutsu said. "We might not get all the way because many of the microbes in the American soil have been destroyed by continued use of chemicals."

"There is some duplication in France and Luxembourg," Paloma said. "So we are still extremely hopeful we can complete the String-Continuum."

"One of the missing collectors had key samples from France and Luxembourg," Mutsu said.

"If we complete the String-Continuum," Paloma said, "no one will ever be able to deny what the dirt can do."

Wen, ever sensitive to the energy of any location, felt as if this entire building, and everyone in it, was holding their collective breath, as if on the very edge of a precipice. She wished she could dismiss the feeling, but knew, from many past experiences, that it was a clear, yet intense, premonition, demanding her attention.

Chapter Fifteen

Tryhon Amine, President of the Democratic Republic of the Congo, waited in an old warehouse. The corrugated metal roof and rusty prefab walls made the building hot, almost stifling. The space had an odor of oil and dead mice.

Amine was used to the heat and smells of Congo. He had known little else in his forty-seven years. Educated in a rebel school and raised in a remote area of the country, he somehow managed to get to the University in Uganda, and then returned to fight in various rebellions and civil wars. Amine came to power as part of a coup, with the support of Colonel Kabongo.

The two men shared a deep love for their country, and a desperate hope to save it, and their people, from the constant poverty, hunger, and turmoil that had plagued it for so long. Amine had been in power for nearly fifteen years, and much of that time he had faced continuous wars in eastern Congo, as well as internal battles with rebels, whose forces were supplied and trained by the hostile governments of Congo's neighbors, specifically Uganda and Rwanda.

The Constitution of the DRC required him to step down in a little more than one year. The pact Amine had negotiated with Gravacon would be the cornerstone of his legacy, a chance for his country to finally have food security. An agricultural based economy would lift his people out of poverty, giving them the opportunity to truly be a strong, independent nation.

The colonel arrived with a small entourage—battle-hardened and armed with AK-47s, knives, and grenades on their belts. The lean, muscled men exchanged smiles with Amine's bodyguards. They all knew each other. Some were trusted, others not as much, but familiarity and a shared history in struggle was a deep, bittersweet bond.

Amine hugged the Colonel and explained the situation.

"Why does this man, Chase Malone, want us to not grow our own food?" Colonel Kabongo asked, removing his beret and wiping the sweat from a lean, delicately boned face. "Does he sell food?"

"No. I do not think he seeks to profit from our trouble. That I could almost respect. He believes the chemicals are bad for the soil, harmful to the environment."

"Do not the Americans use these same chemicals to grow their abundant crops?"

"The very same."

"I do not understand." He placed the hat back on his cropped hair and knelt down, scooping up a small handful of dry dirt.

Amine handed the colonel a thick file folder. Kabongo stood, dusted his hands on crisp, newly pressed fatigues, before flipping through it. "He is a white man. Is he racist?"

Kabongo asked rhetorically, believing any white person was racist to varying degrees.

"Aren't they all?" Amine said. The men around them laughed.

"Where is this man?" Kabongo asked.

"We have some information from our friends that he might be in London at the moment, but he may be soon heading to Turkey."

"Will our friends be able to tell us where he is tomorrow?"

"I think so. When can you leave?"

"Immediately. I will kill this man," Colonel Kabongo quipped. "And anyone else who brings harm to our country.

The president looked at the colonel as he put a heavy hand on his shoulder. "This is an important mission my brother. We are close to delivering our people from the hardships and horrors of our history, and now one man tries to stand in our way."

The militant returned the gesture. "It is done."

Amine and Kabongo hugged, patting each other affectionately on their backs. "Be strong," Amine said.

"You too," Kabongo said, knowing the challenges facing the president, the risks that would be even greater in the absence of the colonel.

Rather than picking his most trusted men, who he preferred to stay behind to watch over many serious situations at home, the colonel chose men who were great fighters, and excellent shots. Aboard the plane, flying to London —Chase's last known location, they received a call from the president with new information. Kabongo instructed the pilot to divert the plane to a small airfield in France, where a helicopter would be waiting.

"We have friends in France," the president said. "They will help you. Everything is being arranged."

"This data, it is accurate on his whereabouts?" Kabongo asked.

"In spite of many sightings around the globe, and data pointing to more than a dozen other destinations, our friends in Washington assure Malone is in France."

"Then Chase Malone will die in France."

Chapter Sixteen

Bull, a world-class hacker, and member of the Cause, walked into the lab with an un-lit cigarette in her mouth and a six pack of her namesake energy drink. She'd been working with WOLF ever since Chase and Wen had rescued her from a deal gone bad with Russian mobsters.

"Hey, Bull," Simon said. The two of them had worked together several times. "What are you doing here?"

"Margot asked for volunteers to help Chase and Wen."

"And you were the first to step forward," Wen said, hugging her.

"Yeah." The normally gruff, wiry young woman, melted around Wen. Already upset to be working in daylight, the hacker with spiked blonde hair moaned when she saw the big red sign declaring absolutely no smoking.

Chase smiled.

Mutsu came over and introduced himself. They were both in their early twenties, and anybody paying attention could see the Japanese student was immediately smitten by her. Bull saw it, too.

"Listen Fukushima, the last dunce who fell in love with me is dead now. I'm bad news. Keep your mitts off. Strictly professional. Can you handle that?"

Mutsu, surprised and embarrassed by her bluntness, nodded, then bowed slightly. But in his fluster he answered, "No," when he meant to say, "Yes."

"No?" Bull said, flicking her fingers into his chest. "You can't handle that? How did you get this job? Don't you have to be smart to work here?"

"Yes, I mean yes to I can handle it, and yes to—"

"A girl just tells you to take a hike, and it's not clear enough for you?"

"Yes."

"Do you want me to write it down? Maybe you need it translated into Japanese or something."

"No, no I mean yes. I'm sorry. No."

"Whatever, Fukushima." Bull laughed. "Just try not to walk into a wall every time you see me." She blew him a kiss, which confused him entirely.

Bull set her drinks down, and unzipped her oversized messenger bag. "What's with the Mozart music?"

"Oh, yes, you know him?" Mutsu said obviously pleased she recognized the great composer. "His magnificent music calms the soil spirits while we work in the lab." He wrung his hands together while talking to her and raised his eyebrows and voice in nervousness.

"Okay, Fukushima, if you say so."

"What's that?" Simon asked as she pulled out a black and silver piece of equipment about the size of a regular camera tripod.

Bull held a single finger to her lips. She turned to Simon. "It's just Red Bull, want one?"

Simon shook his head confused.

Bull scribbled on a note, *Margot wanted to sweep for bugs. This will find them.*

The device, they would later learn was affectionately referred to as "The Exterminator," would detect all RF, FM, UHF, WiFi, and cellular signals, as well as other frequencies. In addition, the exterminator would do infrared detection. It didn't take her long. Using hand gestures, she indicated a listening device had been located. Ten minutes later, after a full sweep of the rooms, the machine found a second transmitting microphone.

It has to be Gravacon, Bull wrote on a piece of paper. Wen agreed.

Wen, who'd been following Bull during the process, began making small talk while writing a note informing Kali and Paloma that the lab would have to be moved silently and quickly within the next few hours.

Wen and Paloma left the lab and took the stairs to the floor below, where they huddled in an urgent conversation in whispered tones. "I'm telling you, if they have people watching and listening, they're prepared to obliterate your work," Wen said while looking out the window for Gravacon people. "We must get the soil samples out of there immediately."

"We do off premises backups of all the analysis, sequencing, test results, etcetera, so if the computers are destroyed, we'd still be able to recover all our work," Paloma said.

Wen shook her head. "That's fine, but it's not just erasing files that they are after. They want to know what you discovered, how much proof there is, how far you've gotten."

Paloma closed her eyes in exasperation and worry. "The dirt. We've got to get the dirt out."

"Krauss knows how destructive their product is, and they don't care because they think their goals are more important than any others." Wen spotted the van. "Do you see that?"

"Yes."

"They're in there monitoring every word you all say. My bet is that this evening, once it's dark and more of their people arrive, they'll attack the lab."

"So we have to completely dismantle?" Paloma asked. "The computers and everything?"

"Just the equipment you need to keep working, and the dirt. Nothing else matters, right?"

"I guess not," Paloma said, instantly trying to calculate how they could possibly get everything done now. Already, she'd planned to work late into the night processing the latest samples and trying to complete the String-Continuum.

"Now isn't the time to guess. You're a scientist. Think of anything in that lab that could help them stop your work. And then we must take it out."

"But if they're watching the building, they'll see us."

"You're right. That would be too risky. Do you know of another space inside this building, as far from your lab as we can get, where we could safely store the dirt and the drives temporarily?"

"Maybe . . . I think there's an office on the first floor. One of the professors has left the university, and his replacement has not arrived yet. At least, the last I heard, maybe next week."

"That will have to do."

Soon a plan was formulated to evacuate the samples, the main computers, and other equipment to an office space on the lower level, knowing that if they attempted to take materials out of the building, they would be spotted by whoever was watching them.

Chapter Seventeen

WH Watkins, wearing a leather safari hat, looked a little like a young Indiana Jones—except with a goatee. In his late twenties, he'd been collecting dirt samples for more than two years, and adored his work traveling the world. He parked the old Land Rover in high weeds and checked his GPS. Congo was one of the riskier assignments, but he'd been in the country, collecting, once before.

The local guide, who'd come with him, would stay with the vehicle, or it might not be there when he got back. WH hiked to the field through the woods, enjoying the brief break from the strong African sun. He knew the only reason these trees had been left was to shield the Gravacon fields from the road. They didn't want anybody to know what they were spraying there, or the size of the crops. It was a typical practice he'd seen in many countries, especially in Europe and America.

Mutsu had warned him yesterday, when he last checked in, that now seven collectors were missing. Even before getting that distressing news, WH would have been extra careful. The job he loved was fraught with risks—trespassing, exposure to Gravacon's toxic chemicals, unsafe areas in remote parts of third-world countries, hired hands attempting to prevent his collections efforts, and now the disappearances.

Walking in the woods took WH back to his years growing up in rural Scottsville, Virginia, where he still lived, along with a collection of nine jeeps in various states of repair, and a two-cylinder Honda-600 sedan. He recalled camping trips with his buddies, not long after he'd gotten his driver's license. Even at sixteen, he'd had three jeeps. WH started working at a small chain of hardware stores when he was nineteen. He learned about gardening, selling fertilizers, and seeds. He knew the importance of his mission.

WH collected a good sample and headed back to the Land Rover. He continually checked behind him; every noise readied him for an attack.

The guide had been letting him drive, as WH couldn't get enough of banging the vintage vehicle along the winding dirt roads. He was careful because he knew there were rebels in the area, but the adventure of it all made him feel like he was actually driving through Raiders of the Lost Ark. Paloma had said the dirt in parts of Africa was special —"beyond priceless" her exact words.

After almost three hours of dry, dusty roads, WH was still having a blast and feeling as if he'd just gotten behind the wheel. He was glad they had plenty of water, as the landscape had grown considerably drier.

"Where did you learn to speak English?" WH asked the guide as they drove through a section that reminded him of the scenic roads of Nelson County, back home in Virginia.

"I taught myself, with people like you," the guide

answered. He couldn't have been much more than twenty. "It is not so hard a language. I like it better than Japanese."

"You speak Japanese?"

"Not too much, not too good," he said and then proceeded to rattle off a few sentences in Japanese.

"That's very good," WH said. "What did you say?"

"It means: Too hot. Where are the gorillas? What kind of bug is that?"

WH laughed. "Do you get many Japanese visitors out here?"

"Oh yes, second only to English speakers, you know, Americans, British, Australians." The guide turned around to check the road behind them.

"What do the Japanese do out here?"

"Safari. Only with cameras, no guns."

WH nodded, swerving to miss a wild doe-like animal. "How much farther?"

"Just up here two more clicks, maybe. Slow down, please Mr. WH, the road gets very bad from the big farm trucks."

"It doesn't seem much would grow here," WH said.

"Not used to. But after they spray, it does." The guide stared into the sideview mirror.

"Yeah," WH said, knowing the impoverished nation needed the food, but wondering about the long-term damage.

After a few minutes of silence, the guide pointed to a faded sign with several gorillas pictured in peeling paint. "Congo is the home of gorillas safaris," the guide said. "I can take you."

"Maybe another time."

"Gorillas very important here."

"What about other industry? Jobs?"

"We have a lot of crime now with corruption, but our

president is very determined to make things better. Maybe he can do this, maybe not." The guide glanced at WH, a concerned look on his face.

"Do you believe him?"

"I hope I believe him. My country needs good things . . . it has been very, very hard for a long time."

"I hope so, too," WH said.

"Thank you," the guide said, smiling. "Next site very close now."

When they arrived, WH got out his GPS to make sure of the coordinates. Paloma was very specific that samples needed to be taken within a certain range. Some had been as small as a ten-foot radius, others several miles wide. He wondered again how she determined where the soil should come from, since her explanations only left him more confused.

WH collected the dirt, labeled the container, and jogged back to the Land Rover. The guide was nervously standing by the vehicle.

"Everything okay?" WH asked.

"No worries," the guide insisted. "Next stop much closer. You play more American rock 'n' roll." Earlier, he had liked hearing songs by David Bowie, Pink Floyd, and the Beatles. Even though WH had explained that this was all British rock 'n' roll, the guide continued to call it American rock 'n' roll. "Like Elvis Presley, very good." WH preferred country music, but as they drove through the Congo countryside, listening to Dark Side of the Moon, he had a feeling that he would remember this surreal episode as long as he lived. Finally, after little more than an hour, they arrived at the next site. This time there were people nearby.

"Anything to worry about?" WH asked the guide.

"No, no," the guide replied, watching the men closely. "Go get your dirt."

WH took the sample, repeating the process he had done nearly a hundred times, labeled and sealed the lid, but when getting up, noticed a man inching closer. He headed back to the Land Rover as quickly as possible. Once there, the guide was already in the driver seat.

"I drive this time now, WH, okay. I drive, you be passenger. Ikimacho!"

WH could see fear in the guide's eyes, but decided this was not the best time for questions. He simply nodded, climbing in with the sample still in his lap. The guide pulled away quickly. WH turned around and saw, through a cloud of dust, that several men with guns had gotten within fifteen feet of the Land Rover.

"You said something back there in Japanese," WH said, when the men were no longer in sight.

"I say 'Ikimacho' because I could not think in your language for a minute. It means 'Let's go.' Those men were *very* bad."

Chapter Eighteen

Krieg lifted his eye patch and rubbed the sunken eye socket. It always seemed to hurt when he was under stress. In the back of his mind, as soon as he heard that Chase was heading toward a meeting with Kali Garodia and Paloma Boulet, he had hoped it would not amount to much, but, of course, he was too smart for that. As he listened to their conversations, it was clear that two of Gravacon's biggest nightmares had now converged. He called Krauss, knowing the report would infuriate him.

"How did this happen?" Krauss demanded.

Krieg left an associate to monitor further conversations inside the van while he walked across the campus, smoking a cigarette. He took a long drag before he answered. "Ed Weston." He knew what was coming next, so paused to sit on a bench next to a large circular reflecting pool with a statue in the middle that looked like a tall man carrying a child. He wanted to smash it into the water.

"Malone together with Boulet and Garodia?" Krauss blasted. "I told you we should've taken care of Ed Weston *months* ago. Do you recall me telling you that he was going to be a bigger problem? But for some reason, you didn't think so."

"We can handle this."

"Damn right, *you* can handle it. This is now *your* mess to clean up. I don't care how you do it, but don't let this become a bigger hell-storm than it already is."

Krieg finished his cigarette and walked back to the van. It had been a lapse in his judgment to let Weston go. Krauss had wanted him killed as soon as Weston began complaining about Gravacon's practices. Weston was specifically upset that environmental assurances he'd been given when selling Sun & Earth Farms weren't being met.

Krieg, a methodical man, certainly had no problem with killing people, it was part of his job; an honorary heritage, no doubt. His grandfather had been a member of Hitler's SS. While other Germans went to great lengths to hide their past, he was very proud of his grandfather. Krieg liked to think that if he had been alive during the war, he would've happily served in the SS as well. Something in him had always secretly admired most everything about the Schultzstaffel, Hitler's protection squadron. Originally just meant to be bodyguards, they constantly expanded, some in the Secret Police (Gestapo), others into the very elite SD (Sichierheits diets des Reichsführers) created by Heinrich Himmler in 1931. The SD became the intelligence agency for the SS, the Nazi Party, and, of course, Hitler himself.

Krieg knew that he would have been in the SD because they were the best and most powerful. He often reminded himself that he was entitled to have that status, even now.

Except for Ed Weston, certainly a thorn in his side.

His eye ached. *Why had I miscalculated?*

However, Krieg believed that there needed to be a good

reason for an execution. He didn't care about people. He believed they were simply a commodity, but he did believe in what he called "prudent procedures." If Krauss had ordered him to kill Weston, it would have been done without question. Yet, Krauss had asked his opinion, and Krieg believed Weston would not become a major problem for Gravacon. Furthermore, if he died after airing his grievances, it would likely raise suspicions. A questionable death of a major Gravacon critic would be a greater risk then a disgruntled former CEO whining that the deal didn't go the way he expected.

Krieg was right, he knew it. Had Malone not shown up, nothing would've changed. But you can't live on what-ifs. The fact that Weston sent Malone to Boulet and Garodia, seemingly an innocent gesture, resulted in a mistake Krieg could barely swallow. After hearing the conversation, all of that was moot, the threat was real, and it needed to be eliminated.

He took his time getting back to the van. Nature didn't necessarily relax him, but it eased eye tension, as he could look out and not measure the lack of depth having only one eye afforded.

"I'm calling Krauss," Chase said.

"Is that wise?" Kali asked.

"We'll find out."

"Listen to me," Chase began as soon as Krauss picked up. "I know the scientists in Antwerp notified you about their findings."

"What are you talking about?"

"The microbes in the dirt, the cures for diseases that

hydenosyn, the main ingredient in *GET-EM®* and Orgri-Source, destroys."

"*Alleged* cures," Krauss said indignantly. "If I had a dollar for every time some quack scientist, or fringe doctor, claimed to have a cure for cancer or Alzheimer's or something, I'd be a whole lot richer than I already am."

"These aren't *alleged* cures—these microbes actually *kill* the viruses. They can wipe out the diseases," Chase said. "I'm begging you to stop marketing and using hydenosyn, at least until they can finish the research."

"Ha! Are you joking? You want me to shut down tens of billions of dollars on something you just admitted was only research. They haven't *proven* anything. Show me peer-reviewed published papers in leading medical journals, patient survival rates—not just speculation, fantasy, and wishes—and I'll give it to our scientists for their review. But otherwise, quit wasting my time."

"I'm sorry you grew up hungry. But if someone who had been molested as a child decided that in order to make sure no one else ever got molested, they would do something to make everybody else sterile and impotent, would that make sense?"

"No," he said with authority. "Hunger has nothing to do with your foolish molesting analogy. Nearly a *billion* people in the world are undernourished." The numbers ticking along the ceiling of his tower office caught his eye. "Millions are dying every year—but I'm sure *you* had a great lunch today."

"You can still address hunger. We just need more time." Chase knew he was losing. He sounded like a wounded child.

"Forty-nine thousand, four hundred thirty-six people will die of hunger *today* . . . How long do you want me to wait? One day? A week? A month? Maybe a year, or two. Do you think those hungry, dying people would agree with you? Go play in the dirt, and let me know when you have something real. Meantime, I'm going to save millions of lives, and make a billion more better!" He ended the call.

Wen told Chase to take a deep breath. She'd been raised a Buddhist, and had introduced Chase to Buddhism not long after their first meeting. Attracted to the non-violence, meditation, seeking balance, the elimination of suffering, and the general lack of dogma, he'd named his company Balance Engineering as an homage to the philosophy.

"How does a man like Krauss get that way?" Chase asked rhetorically.

"Breathe."

He opened his eyes to speak, but read Wen's eyes.

"Breathe," she said, once more.

Some who knew Chase well in the tech world, had given him the nickname, "The Buddhist Billionaire." Chase never liked the title. At times like these, meditating was more difficult, and also more important, than ever.

He turned from the scientists, from Wen, from the dirt, shut his eyes, relaxed his tight fists, and loosened his jaw.

Such corruption, such greed.

He breathed.

It's unfair. How can the world be so cruel, how can we be so off balance?

He rolled his shoulders and arched his back, stretching the tight muscles.

Damn it, what can I do?

Chapter Nineteen

"Let's sue Gravacon," Simon said, as if it were a new idea, after Chase told them about the call. They'd decided to leave the listening devices in place so the people listening wouldn't know they had been discovered. Whenever possible, they continued anti-Gravacon talk to seem natural.

"We could go after Gravacon with lawsuits all over the world, but there isn't time," Paloma said.

Wen and I can go to France, Chase wrote on a note, then checked the time. *We can get there with enough daylight.*

"Excellent," Paloma said. She sent the coordinates to his phone.

I'll be happy to go to Luxembourg first thing in the morning, Simon scribbled on the back of an old envelope.

"Perfect." Paloma nodded, knowing those samples were critical to completing the String-Continuum.

Chase and Wen headed across campus, careful that they weren't being followed. A man, probably a professor, or a doctor, talking on his phone, distracted Wen for a few moments before she decided he was not after them.

"I'm not sure we should leave Kali and Paloma with those Gravacon security goons out there," Chase said.

"They're just going to continue monitoring," Wen said. "We'll be back early in the morning and she needs the dirt. It's the only chance to stop Gravacon from getting those approvals." She looked at her phone. "The Astronaut just sent this." She showed Chase a photo of Krieg. "Gravacon head of security."

"Looks like a pirate."

She grimaced, reading Krieg's bio. "His grandfather was a bigshot in the SS."

"I'm not surprised Krauss hired a Nazi to run his own Gestapo." Chase realized both his hands were in tight fists again. Instinctively, he reached for his multitool, as it served like a worry stone. Holding it relaxed him. "Still think it's okay to leave Kali and Paloma?"

Wen looked over her shoulder as a couple of "students" jogged toward them. Her first impulse was that they weren't a threat, but she readied her Glock under her windbreaker anyway.

Krieg, back in the van, overheard one of the lab assistants ask Paloma about where Chase's and Simon's samples would be coming from, so he could put the data into his formulas. Paloma, deep in equations relating to the String-Continuum, answered without realizing. Krieg immediately

Chasing Dirt

contacted freelancers they'd used before, based in a town near where Chase and Wen were headed.

"We'll handle it," the man said to Krieg. "No worries."

Krieg had already had half a dozen "sample collectors," killed. Chase and Wen were just two more hash marks. *They mean nothing. Normally,* Krieg thought, *I'd do them myself, but I have to stay here to erase this problem.*

He phoned Krauss and reported the progress, telling him the plan.

"I don't want to know this stuff, okay?" Krauss said, even though he knew the line was secure. "Why aren't you going yourself?"

"The more complicated operation is the lab. Too much damaging data here," Krieg said.

"Good," Krauss said. In spite of his earlier outburst, he thought Krieg was the best in the business—ruthless, smart, and definitely scary. "You'll take care of the dirt?"

"Tonight, the samples will be destroyed." Krieg knew Krauss would understand that Paloma Boulet and Kali Garodia would also be destroyed. After the call, Krieg ordered more people to the rural area of France where Chase and Wen were headed.

Mutsu, recovered somewhat from his innate shyness, went on to nervously explain to Bull where the data sources were for computer sorting. She got right to work. He stumbled over his words and apologized for mixing things up.

"Don't worry, Fukushima, I know you're only pretending to be a dunce so I'll pay attention to you."

"No, I really am . . . I mean."

"You're kind of cute, but I'm out of your league. Plus, I'm a vampire, so beat it."

Later, she went out on another cigarette break. Bull liked the landscaped campus, but would rather it be nighttime. When her phone rang, she half expected it to be Mutsu. Instead, it was Chase. He asked her if she could get into the Gravacon mainframe servers.

"Are you joking? Or just trying to insult me?"

"It's a fair question."

"No it's not. The fair question is *how long* will it take me to get into Gravacon. Not *if* I can do it. Geez, do I have to teach the whole world manners and proper etiquette?"

"Okay then. Let me know when you're in."

"What do you need, once I'm in?"

"I don't know, but I'll know when I see it."

"Sometime, when I get in a super secure server, it's a one-off. Meaning they hunt you and shut you down. So if you're not around . . . unless you're gonna spend the night here."

"Can't you just start downloading?"

"Well, yeah, but depends on how much data they have . . . they're a pretty big operation. Could be petabytes."

"Get all you can, but focus on hydenosyn and lobbying efforts."

"Gotcha. Give Wen a kiss for me."

Bull would have to juggle the Gravacon hack between tracking the samples, volunteer's eco-zones, bio zone data, and lab results. She put in thirty minutes after the call before her nicotine demon summoned her again. Bull had just exhaled what she considered to be lifesaving smoke when Mutsu appeared, startling her.

"Dude, what is your problem? Are you like a stalker?"

Mutsu turned around to look behind him, thinking she

was talking to somebody else. In the process he bumped into a signpost, knocking his glasses off. Bull caught them before they hit the ground.

"Fukushima sure was the right name for you." She laughed. "You're a walking disaster area." She handed his glasses back.

"I thought I could show you around the campus, while you poison smoke, smoke yourself."

"Do you use that line on all the girls?" she asked, making her face into an incredulous expression.

"No. You're the first."

"I don't doubt that," Bull said, blowing smoke directly at him. "I'd rather just sit here and smoke, or poison myself, whatever."

He nodded, staring at her for a moment . . .

"*Alone*," she said, winding her eyes.

"Yes," he said, turning and once again knocking into the signpost, but this time managing to keep his glasses on. Bull shook her head as she watched him go back into the building.

Chapter Twenty

As they bounced over the uneven, rutted road, WH managed to put the soil sample onto the floor of the backseat with the others. "Are we okay?" he asked.

"Yes, yes, everything okay now."

WH wasn't sure it had been a convincing response, but after the guide turned up Elton John's *Goodbye Yellow Brick Road*, he decided to let it go for now. WH had been in dicey situations before, but none that left him with the sickening feeling that was growing in the pit of his stomach. He hoped the guide knew what he was doing, and reminded himself of all the prior occasions which had just become good adventure stories to share with Mutsu, Ryan, and the other sample takers. Paloma never liked to hear the dangerous tales, so instead he always told her about the beautiful scenery and the friendly people he'd encountered. WH knew they were in trouble just as Elton John finished the song.

I'm going back to my plough

Chasing Dirt

Back to the howling old owl in the woods
Hunting the horny back toad
Oh, I've finally decided my future lies
Beyond the yellow brick road

WH noticed a pickup truck barreling up behind them. Even before he could say anything, the guide had accelerated, pushing the Land Rover faster than it should safely travel on those roads—and WH would use the term "road" loosely.

"Who are they?" WH shouted, nearly hitting the dashboard after the Land Rover went in and out of what appeared to be a dry lakebed in the middle of the 'path'.

"Everything good, WH, no worry."

"Then why are you driving like crazy?" he yelled above the rumbling motor and crashing branches.

"No trouble, as long as I drive crazy."

"How much trouble is no trouble?"

"Very, very much trouble, too much trouble, but I not let them catch us." The guide reached under the front seat, pulling out a revolver and dropping it on WH's lap. "Can you know how to use this?"

WH *did* know how to shoot. Back home he was a gun owner, but not a hunter. Just targets, cans and bottles, fun stuff. And he'd certainly never shot a *person* before. WH took the gun in his hands, spun the cylinder, surprised it was a Smith and Wesson, disappointed it was only a thirty-eight caliber. "Yeah, I can shoot, but I don't want to."

"Maybe you no have to. I keep driving fast."

Chase and Wen talked constantly on the drive to the large farm in France where they would take samples.

"Krauss is dangerous," Chase said. "He's so obsessed with ending world hunger that I think he'd be willing to annihilate half the world's population to save the other half."

Wen, savoring the scenic French countryside, a place she'd never visited before, wasn't really interested in discussing a delusional megalomaniac. "He won't matter if we get enough dirt to show what the microbes can really do."

"But you heard Paloma. It may not be possible with so much soil permanently damaged in America."

She continued to absorb the scenery as they passed a vineyard, at least a few hundred acres, vines thick with dark grapes. "What about using fAIr to recreate the missing sections from America?"

"And I thought *I* was supposed to be the brains of this outfit," Chase said, enjoying being a passenger for once. Typically he drove, because he loved it, and because they were often being pursued, and, although Wen had been trained in evasive driving tactics, he had a natural ability for connecting with a vehicle and making it do things that others could not. Wen called it "impossible driving." His skills behind the wheel had saved them many times. "You're right," he continued. "The fAIr program can take the String-Continuum and work backwards."

"Paloma and Kali already know where it's going, they just need to prove it."

Chase smiled. "And fAIr can fill in the blanks."

"It might be enough to convince the scientific community."

"And change the world," Chase said softly, at the same

time realizing that Krauss had probably already come to the same conclusion.

"What is it?" Wen asked at his sudden silence.

Chase came out of his somber thoughts. "Somebody is going to revolutionize the way we use and view dirt in the next twenty-four hours. If it's us, it'll mean Krauss is dead, and if it's Krauss, it'll mean we're . . ."

Chapter Twenty-One

Tess Federgreen, the head of Corporate Intelligence Security Section, looked at the call waiting for her, frowned, then smiled. "CISS," (pronounced with a hard 'c') one of the most secret divisions within the US intelligence community, had been formed as a joint operation of the CIA, NSA, and FBI. Its mandate, to prevent war between corporations, would surprise many, if it were public. However, even members of the House and Senate Intelligence Committees were routinely kept in the dark about the existence of CISS.

In the moment before she accepted the call, a hundred scenarios streamed through her mind. Chase Malone would never reach out to her unless something serious had happened. With him, it could be anything from a pending nuclear disaster to an invasion from space. She pulled up his file, although it was really unnecessary. She'd made a study of Chase, having several times, just in the last eighteen months, spared his life.

"Well, Chase Malone, I never thought I'd hear from you again," Tess said. "But I also had a feeling that I would."

Tess, a no-nonsense forty-something-year-old, had risen through the ranks of the NSA with an impressive list of Washington contacts, and knew more than her share of secrets. With long hair, sometimes blonde, sometimes any number of other shades, and intense eyes the color of wet jade, she often came across as prettier than she was, and could easily be as seductive as she could be intimidating.

"I'm not calling because I *want* to," Chase said. "I'm calling because I need a favor."

"And you're not even going to try to sweet talk me first?" Tess said. "How disappointing." A master with strategy and presentation, Tess had a talent for reducing complex situations to quick, flash-card answers.

"We've been through too much for anything other than straight talk," Chase said, remembering all the times she'd been anything but straight with him. Tess had become the most powerful woman in the intelligence business by using her unfailing ability to play people, and by anticipating, based on accumulated scraps of information, hidden patterns, using the big picture months or years ahead of the crowd.

"What do you need?" she asked, as if already exhausted with the conversation. CISS, always in the middle of juggling a dozen crises, had become the dominate agency in the US intelligence arsenal. Tess had been with CISS from the beginning. A highly decorated CIA official, she'd been recommended by the Director of National Intelligence and head of the CIA, then appointed by the president. CISS had been formed after a World Economic Forum report showed that only thirty-one of the top one hundred global economic entities were countries, with the other sixty-nine being corporations. The shocking trend, expected to continue, meant that in the next fifteen years, ninety-five conglomerates would dominate the list, with only five countries remaining. A secret government study concluded that a shift from nation states to corporate states made the likelihood of major conflicts, or "wars," erupting between companies, or corporations and countries, highly probable, as the world entered a new phase of decentralized power. CISS's mission, by any means necessary, was to keep the peace, or, at the very least, make sure the "right" side won.

"Are you familiar with Lars Krauss?"

"CEO of Gravacon."

"That's the one."

"Lars Krauss, age seventy-three, born Würzburg, Bavaria, height five-foot-short . . . " She continued rattling off facts and figures about the man.

"I hope you're reading that from a screen, because if you have that kind of stuff *memorized*, you're scarier than I think."

"You flatter me."

"Can you tell me what his grades were like in elementary school?" Chase asked sarcastically.

"If you give me a minute to switch screens," Tess replied, quickly bouncing the verbal ball back to him. "I sure can."

"The EU, US Congress, and several other countries are about to pass legislation that would essentially give Gravacon the ability to use patented seeds in conjunction with pesticides and herbicides, formulas that are also patented for nearly one hundred percent of the available farmland. This would give them unprecedented control over the agricultural output of most of the world."

"I'm aware of the legislation," Tess said. "We've been following it. However, Gravacon is a *foreign* corporation. Are you sure you're not over dramatizing the situation? That's certainly not the intent of the legislation."

"Do I have a history of exaggeration?" Chase asked.

"What would you like me to do?"

"Well, if it's up to me, I'd want CISS to destroy Gravacon and arrest Lars Krauss."

"He's not an American citizen."

"When has that ever stopped you?"

"You misunderstand what we do here at CISS. We're trying to keep a level playing field for the corporations."

"Exactly. This will give them a monopoly on food."

"Where are you right now?"

"That doesn't matter."

"I can see you still have the Astronaut placing your calls."

"You only know that because you've been trying to trace it."

"You want my help, but you don't trust me?"

"That's right."

"Fair enough. But you know I can't destroy his company—"

"Yes you can."

"Assuming I'm not *going* to destroy it, you must have some other idea of how I can help you in this situation."

"It isn't about helping me. Believe me, you do not want Gravacon to have this much power, a German Corporation."

"What if the legislation doesn't pass in the US?" Tess asked.

"He's getting EU approval the same day. It's slated to be voted on in the Senate, it's already approved in the House. The president is expected to sign it."

"I know all this."

"It's also been approved in virtually every African and South American country. He's working on the deal right now with the Asian Federation. Can you stop the US, EU, Asia, or all of them?"

"Won't that only be a delay?"

"A delay might be enough."

"What are you working on?"

"Same as always."

"Trying to save the world from greedy, corrupt people who misuse technology?"

"Something like that."

"Something exactly like that." Tess looked at another screen, silently cursing that the Astronaut was staying a step ahead of the best tracking software in existence. "I must admit, you're uniquely qualified for the role."

"Someone has to do it."

"How's Wen?"

"Wen is wonderful."

"Good. Say hello for me. I'll be back in touch after I look into some things."

"Thanks."

"And, Chase, try not to cause another international incident that I'm left to clean up."

Chapter Twenty-Two

A tree, that could have been a Dr. Suess monster, almost swallowed the Land Rover as the road descended into some kind of marshy-lowland that didn't seem to belong in that part of Africa.

"Bandits?" WH asked, looking back at the still pursuing pickup truck.

"I not think so, at least not regular bandits," the guide said.

"Then some sort of special bandits?" WH asked, bracing his hand against the dashboard. The high speeds and road conditions reminded him of the old wooden Rebel-yell rollercoaster back home at Kings Dominion. Out the rear window, he could see the pickup truck gaining on them. "Seriously, what makes them different from other bandits?"

"Bandits don't bother company I work for. They taken care of by the owners so that we bring in money for gorilla safaris."

"But we're not *on* a gorilla safari."

"They don't know you pay my boss for guide service, everyone leave us alone. My boss very powerful."

"They might be after the dirt."

"Why do they want dirt? Why do *you* want dirt? There is dirt everywhere. Congo is made of dirt."

"I don't think they want me to have the dirt." A large rock ripped through the undercarriage as they crossed a creek.

"It's just dirt, who cares who has dirt? I think you crazy man to come down here, not look at gorillas, but go to risky areas, just to take some buckets of dirt."

WH recalled Mutsu's warnings and wondered if he was about to become another victim, like the seven sample takers who were missing. He'd gotten some threats, even had a few close calls, but this was much more ominous.

Gravacon has been playing rougher lately. They're one of the most hated companies in the world, but would they really kill over dirt?

"Is there a place we can go?" WH asked. "Get some help, maybe find the police?"

"Police here aren't like America. They same as me, as the bandits—wherever there is money to be made, that's what the law is."

Bullets grazed the Land Rover. WH crouched down in the front seat, counting on the thick steel body to protect him. The guide was doing a miraculous job of keeping the Land Rover at full speed while still staying on the road, but his driving skills weren't going to be enough.

"You have to shoot back!" the guide shouted.

"Why? I'll never hit them. We're driving too fast, it's too damned bumpy."

"It will not matter if you hit anything! They need to know we have gun, and we shoot back. Do it before they shoot out the tires!"

WH leaned out the side of his window, aimed as best he could, and fired. Incredibly, he actually hit a headlight—although the sun was still high in the sky, so it didn't seem to matter. Yet suddenly the distance between the two vehicles widened.

"Hey, hey!" WH said. "I hit them!"

"Good job, James Bond. They farther back now. But don't celebrate too much. I don't think they need headlight for a long, long time," the guide said as the hot sun shimmered a heat mirage on the dusty hood of the battered Land Rover. "We turn up here. It's bigger road, much smoother. We go faster."

"But they'll go faster too, right?"

"Yes, but only for a while. If we make it far enough to Gobas Village, we will be out of their territory."

"And they'll just stop following?"

"They have to, or they be killed."

"Let's go."

"You must shoot them when we turn. Shoot and aim for the driver."

"I've never killed anybody."

"You won't kill him. If you get lucky and hit again, that'll be enough to make the space between us bigger."

WH had been fighting the urge to vomit ever since the pickup truck had first appeared. Now he wasn't sure he could continue to win that battle.

"Here we go," the guide said as they took a hard right. For a moment, WH thought the Land Rover was going to tip over.

"Shoot! Shoot!" the guide yelled.

WH waved his gun in the general direction of the pickup truck and fired two shots. One of them hit the windshield, causing it to crumble, flying back into the passenger area. WH had no idea where he hit the windshield or how, but he could see that both men were still completely alive as they brushed away the glass. However, the passenger returned fire immediately. The Land Rover had already pulled farther ahead, and none of the shots connected. The guide was going almost twice as fast on the more improved road. Ten harrowing minutes later, they passed Gobas Village, and, sure enough, the pickup truck stopped.

Chapter Twenty-Three

Chase scooped the final soil sample into the collection container, surprised something so important could be that easy, and put them into his pack with the others.

Wen jogged toward him. "There's a plane coming!"

He scanned the sky. "I don't hear it."

"It's approaching from the west, probably still behind that tree line," Wen said. "Could be nothing, but it's a small single-engine, and I'm not in the mood to get shot."

"I'm rarely in the mood to get shot." Chase winked. "But that never seems to make a difference to the ones shooting at us."

Wen took out her MP7.

"You're serious," Chase said.

"Just to be safe."

They began jogging up the dirt road toward the gate where they had left their car.

"The plane will be here long before we get to the car," Chase said. They'd had to walk a long way to reach the specific spot, according to the GPS coordinates Paloma had given them. Unable to risk not being able to get the sample, no one had asked permission from the property owner. They figured trespassing was bad enough, so hadn't broken the gate.

"Here it comes now," Wen said. "It'll be quicker to cut across the field."

The plane, a yellow crop duster, crested above the tree line, then began a fast descent.

"He's coming right for us," Chase said.

"It's a crop duster, but it doesn't look like he's hitting the fields at the right angle," Wen shouted breathlessly. "There were fields not far from one of our MSS training areas . . . crop duster's always come in-line with the crops. But he's going perpendicular."

"That doesn't mean he won't drop hydenosyn all over us."

"It's too slow running through the corn," Wen said. "We've got to get into that cut field."

Chase broke into a full run as soon as they cleared the last row of corn. "We're too far away from the car. Let's hide in those trees!"

"He can still spray us in there."

"At least we'll have some cover."

"I may be able to shoot that plane down," Wen said, tripping on a rock, but recovering before she hit the ground.

Wen's boldness and confidence had long ago stopped surprising Chase. However, he was still impressed that she would attempt to shoot down a plane with a submachine gun.

Suddenly, the plane was upon them. Chase looked over his shoulder, running as fast as he ever had in his life. It appeared as if the pilot intended to smash into them. "He's gonna cut us up in his propeller!"

"Get ready to drop when I yell! If he doesn't want to crash that plane, he won't be able to get low enough."

"How do we know the pilot doesn't want to crash? And how do we know he's not going to dump hydenosyn?"

The plane's motors were so loud, even if Wen had answered, he couldn't have heard. All around them, dust swirled in the dry field, creating a disorientating storm, the plane, flying less than ten feet behind them, and only a few feet above the field. Chase took one last look back and then dove flat into the dirt a full two seconds before Wen. He slammed hard onto the packed earth, knocking the wind out of him, then looked up, gasping. From his angle, it seemed as though the plane propeller was going to cut into Wen. She had timed her drop dangerously close. When she landed, he could have sworn one of the plane's tires burned into her back, and was surprised scraps of her clothing weren't flinging around the propeller. The crop duster pulled out, flying into a wide turn. Chase crawled and stumbled toward Wen, knowing the plane would be back for them in seconds.

Chapter Twenty-Four

Tess Federgreen walked through a wide door at the end of a corridor, deep within CIA headquarters, in Langley, Virginia. Although the spy center was only about a twenty minute drive from the CISS building, it seemed a world away. Tess, along with the CIA director, and several other high-ranking intelligence officials, had just come out of a meeting regarding Gravacon's influence in Africa and South America. Undiscussed during that briefing were similar issues with the corporation's growing power within the United States and Europe.

Africa and South America were already hotspots in the ongoing geopolitical chess match between the US and China. There were hundreds of operatives on the ground, plans and contingencies, and actions would be taken. The reason the US and EU had not been mentioned was because they were caught up in the more complicated world of corporate corruption and blurred national interests. Profits for American multinationals had, for years, taken precedent over national security issues. With that backdrop, Tess had to navigate the hellish waters of Washington policy and the lobbyists who crafted, bought, and manipulated it.

"Are you a go for tonight?" the director asked her as they passed through a secure area and continued down the corridor.

"Do you really want to know?" she asked, her cowboy boots clopping on the polished linoleum floor, sounding like the ominous footsteps used in the old radio serials from decades past.

He took that as a yes, and grimaced. Although technically her superior, he didn't really have power to stop her plan. Only the president could, and neither of them dared tell him. Even having the conversation with the president could lead to the end of his political life. No, Tess was on her own with this one, a move he didn't agree with, but knew must be taken.

"You're a tougher man than me," he said as an aide jogged up behind them.

"Excuse me, sir," the aide said to the director.

"What is it Davis?"

"Just got word that Amine in the DRC is asking about Chase Malone."

The director looked at Tess. "Another ball to juggle."

She smiled, but swallowed hard. This was the last thing she needed. Especially now. Her highly illegal and incredibly difficult mission was already underway, and now Africa was reaching into things. "Where did it come from?" she asked the aide, sounding as if she were talking about a stray dog wandering into a picnic.

"Inside source."

She looked at the director, clearly irritated.

"It's Africa," he said, sounding almost defensive, as if the fact that the Democratic Republic of the Congo was located in Africa explained why the CIA was cooperating with an oppressive regime—which was now entangled with US internal affairs.

Tess shook her head. "Bad timing." She turned back and headed in the direction from which they'd come.

"Where are you going?" the director called after her.

"To fix this damned thing before it becomes a complete disaster."

WH, happy to be on a plane back to Belgium with the dirt samples safely in a carry-on bag in the overhead compartment, closed his eyes and tried to forget how close he'd come to dying. Somehow he managed to sleep through most of the flight, something he rarely did. *Fear will do that*, he told himself as the plane made its final descent. He believed in what Kali and Paloma were doing, but he didn't want to die. If things had gotten to the point where his life was in jeopardy, WH needed to rethink his commitment, and he planned to talk with Mutsu about that as soon as he got back to Antwerp.

Krieg accepted a call from a shady informant that Gravacon used. The woman, whose code name was "Dancer," had connections into corporate security networks, the intelligence communities, major militaries, and even US and Russian mafias. Although he'd never met

Dancer in person, he'd authorized more than two million dollars in payments to the mysterious woman. He'd already put out word to her that he was looking for information on Chase Malone and his companion.

"Malone is in France," Dancer said as the conversation began.

Krieg, who had taken the call outside the van, walked the campus, careful to keep the lab building in sight, silently imagining killing the people who stared at him as they passed. He had been used to it for years, yet it still made him angry. *It's only an eyepatch, what's their problem?* "I know he's in France."

"You need to be there."

"Why? I have people on it."

"Those scientists *need* the sample from the Tyler Farm."

"Don't they need them all?"

"This one is a missing link," Dancer said, as if talking to an idiot. "If it were me, I would make sure he didn't come out of there with any dirt, and preferably didn't come out at all."

Krieg jogged back to the van, gave orders for the attack on the lab, and, a few minutes later, a car picked him up.

He would be there in a few hours. *Can I make it in time?* he wondered. *I should have gone . . . Damn Dancer, she always seems to know things.*

Eight months earlier, Dancer had told him that a judge was going to rule in favor of a plaintiff in a precedent-setting twenty-six million dollar lawsuit against Gravacon, and he hadn't listened. He should have killed the judge, discreetly of course—a sudden heart attack, maybe a stroke—but Gravacon's lawyers told Krauss it was in the bag.

It wasn't. And now there were *hundreds* of incoming

suits. Most would go away after the legislation passed in two days, but there were going to be endless challenges to the law, and many of the older suits would continue. He didn't want another repeat, one that could bring down Gravacon just when they were so close to taking control of the food, of everything.

Chapter Twenty-Five

Chase and Wen ran in a desperate race to the trees. Chase stumbled, scraping his arm as he landed in a rough patch of dirt. With the sound of the plane roaring closer, he sprang to his feet and bolted after Wen, trying to make it to cover before the plane found them again.

Even with his longer legs, catching up to Wen was not easy. He reached her just as the crop duster came screaming at them for a second attack, while they were still completely exposed. Wen resisted firing at the plane, knowing she'd never be able to hit it while running and trying to avoid the propeller. She had trained in situations like this—being trapped in the open, boxed-in where there were no walls—but all those exercises had involved people, vehicles, even tanks. This aerial assault was something entirely new and, for one of the first times in her life, she wasn't sure what to do. The deafening noise made rational thinking impossible.

Wen's desperate plan to make it to the trees was a long shot at best. They both dove to the ground at the last second, but this time the pilot fired a machine gun. Bullets ripped across the ground, hitting only feet from them. It was amazing accuracy, since their adversary had to fire out of a window, with a handheld machine gun, while piloting the plane only feet off the ground.

Chase and Wen clawed their way back up, and continued running.

"The chances of one of those bullets hitting us are pretty low," Wen yelled. "The real weapon is the propeller."

"I'm not a big fan of bullets *or* propellers," Chase shouted.

"Look at those trees—far less cover than we thought." As they got closer, the trees turned out to be just a single stand along the fence line. They would prevent the plane from being able to fly right into them, but not give much protection from the machine gun fire or a chemical drop.

"Got any better ideas?"

"I can shimmy up one of those trees and get in position to shoot him while he's chasing you."

"I thought it was *your* turn to be the decoy," Chase said as the plane turned and began to bear down for another pass.

"Do *you* want to try to shoot the pilot while he's chasing me?"

"It might be fun," Chase said, knowing she could out shoot him blindfolded. "But I'm a gentleman. I'll be the decoy."

This time the pilot didn't fire, he did something worse. While flying over them, the fiberglass chemical hopper opened, and what they could only assume was OrgriSource, laced with hydenosyn, dumped all over them.

Wen choked and coughed as she rolled on the ground.

"What does hydenosyn smell like?" Chase yelled, dry

heaving. Their bodies were covered, lungs filling with poison. Chase instinctively tore off his shirt.

"We have to get to the trees," Wen wheezed. Chase got up and helped Wen to her feet. The plane was already circling around again.

They staggered ahead, but weaker, dreading the next strike. Chase coughed. "I think we can still make it."

Scrambling across the final stretch of open field, fighting through wasted stalks of corn, their race with the plane seemed hopeless. Chase tore through a line of brambles over a broken fence. Suddenly, a wide gully they hadn't seen opened before them. Wen flew across it like an acrobat. Chase, still coughing from the chemical inundation, missed the jump and landed badly on the opposing bank.

The plane, forced to pull up to avoid hitting the trees, neither dumped nor fired. While Chase worked his way across the small ravine, Wen quickly climbed one of the trees.

"Are you okay?" she yelled to Chase as he stood.

"Yeah."

"Run that way!" She pointed to the adjoining field on the other side of the trees. "Then turn around and run back this way."

He looked up at her. It was a fleeting glance, but they shared so much in that instant. He might get shot, might get another dose of hydenosyn, might meet the propeller. He ran into the field anyway, the silent *I love you* left floating in the dusty air.

Chapter Twenty-Six

The dirt had to be moved. Without knowing how much time they had, even Kali and Paloma chipped in to get it organized.

Bull and Mutsu helped load containers into the thick cardboard boxes. Mutsu made a list of which samples were going in which box. "It looks like it'll take sixteen boxes," Mutsu whispered.

"I'm impressed you can do such big math problems in your head," Bull said, winking.

"I actually did the calculations earlier and memorized them so I would be able to impress you."

"You did not."

Mutsu laughed. "No, it was a joke."

"Not a very funny one."

"I knew I should have practiced it earlier, so it would have been better funny."

She laughed. "You are funny, in a goofy sort of way."

He smiled, not sure if that was a good thing.

Twenty-four containers were loaded into each box. It

took two of them to pile the boxes onto a dolly. It all had to be done in complete silence. Kali pushed crumpled newspaper between the jars. Then the next box was filled and hoisted on top of the first. All the while, they kept enough normal activity going on in the lab so as not to create any suspicion from the people monitoring them.

Paloma was nervous about the new location for the samples, which had been collected from more than a hundred and fifty countries. Although she had the results and analysis backed up at another location, the original samples were needed to continue their experiments, and ultimately prove the String-Continuum. "Some of these are truly irreplaceable," she told Simon out in the hall as he wheeled the first stack to the elevator. "Please be *extremely* careful."

Once the sixteen boxes were filled, Simon methodically moved them while Bull and Mutsu stood watch on the first floor. A pair of lab workers checked the upstairs hall. Another technician kept an eye on the van from a bathroom window, being careful to not be seen.

"I can't believe Gravacon would actually come in here and destroy all our work," Mutsu whispered. "Moving the samples is making Paloma crazy."

"There's no choice," Bull said. "Before Wen left, she made it very clear that an attack on the lab is imminent. This is the safest place they could find without leaving the building."

"We should call the police," Mutsu said.

"You should trust Chase and Wen. They said no authorities."

"But why not?"

"I don't know, maybe Gravacon has them bribed, maybe it would make Gravacon blow up the whole building

—whatever the reason, Chase and Wen know what they're doing. They saved my life."

"I'm glad they did," Mutsu said, meeting her eyes and then quickly looking away.

"Me too. At least most of the time."

He looked at her, confused. "What you mean? Sometimes you wish they hadn't?"

"I wouldn't expect you to understand. You, with your orderly world. Everything in place. Perfect and planned."

"I'm not like that."

Bull laughed. "You're just like that."

"No, I'm a reckless rebel."

She laughed again and then widened her eyes in silence. "Is that what you think I like?"

He nodded.

"It's not. I'm too reckless, too rebellious myself. That's not what I want . . . "

"What do you want?"

"I don't know . . . peace, stability . . . safe, normal."

"Really?" he asked hopefully.

"Probably not. Mutsu, I'm just a mess. Why are guys attracted to girls who are falling apart?"

"Are you? Falling apart, I mean." His voice filled with concern.

Bull's face grew sad. She nodded, but said, "No. I'm the queen of cool, an effin' skydiver into pools, a coding tramp with no time for fools!"

"What?" Mutsu asked, confused again.

"Nothing, just a song lyric . . . we should get back up."

He kissed her on the lips.

She let him, then shoved him away. "What the hell was that?"

"I'm sorry. I wanted to show you."

"What?"

"That I am a reckless rebel . . . or at least impulsive."

She laughed. "You're not impulsive. You've been thinking about doing that ever since you first met me. You've played that fantasy a million more ways, haven't you?"

"Yes," he admitted.

"And was it as good in real life as you dreamed?"

"Better."

"I bet it was."

"Could you have dinner with me tonight?"

"Could I? Of course I could. But the question is *would* I, and that answer is no."

His face fell.

"Oh, Mutsu. I'm not very tactful, not even a little. I never bothered learning how to be . . . What's the point, people hear what they want and imagine all the motivations and agendas, whether or not they're real. It's not that you aren't a nice guy. It's not even that I wouldn't have a good time with you. You do make me laugh. Nothing much more important than that."

"Then you will have dinner? You like sushi? I know a very good place."

"Yes, I'll have dinner, but not with you."

A confused, hurt expression returned to his face. "Why?"

"Because I like you."

"I don't understand."

"Of course you don't. Because I'm a mess, remember? If I didn't like you, I might take you up on it. Free meal. Some laughs. Good time. Maybe even wind up in bed. You've thought about that, too, haven't you?" She didn't wait for his answer. "But I do like you, so I'm protecting you."

"From what?" He looked around, as if a Gravacon attacker might be there.

"From *me*, stupid. You deserve a good girl." She reached for a cigarette, turned, and headed toward the exit.

"But I don't want a good girl, I just want to have dinner with you."

She laughed, lit her cigarette, took one deep drag, then pushed out the door and headed outside.

Mutsu saw the afternoon sunlight catch her hair before the door closed behind her. The blonde seemed to glow. *She's an angel*, he thought, before going to inspect the office now holding all the samples.

"How is it going?" Mutsu asked a sweating Simon as he entered the office.

"All in," Simon said. "I've got the last six boxes on the dolly. Can you give me a hand lifting them to the table?"

"Let's leave them on the cart," Mutsu said. "Hopefully they won't be here long."

"It's a lot of trouble for some dirt."

Mutsu looked at Simon as if he were a child. "Dirt that will change the world."

Chapter Twenty-Seven

The crop-duster pilot took the bait. Having spotted Chase in the wheat field, he came in for the kill. This time, instead of running the same direction, Chase pivoted and ran back toward the trees. The plane swooped around in a dangerous maneuver, almost clipping the tops of the wheat, flying straight at Chase.

"I've got you this time," the pilot said in French. "My little plane will chop you up!" *But where is your girlfriend?* he thought.

Chase knew there was barely enough time to get to the trees before the propeller got him. Even if he made it, he might take another dose of chemicals, figuring the pilot knew he'd drop to the ground at the last second and would be ready to unload the hopper. But as the plane buzzed closer to the trees, the pilot apparently realized he'd have to pull up, or risk crashing.

As if scripted by Wen, and well-rehearsed, all the players hit their marks and delivered their lines right on cue.

Chase dropped to the ground. The pilot pulled back on the stick, sending the plane skyward. And Wen, a decorated marksman, fired repeatedly, puncturing the plane's fuel tanks multiple times. There was no explosion, no immediate crash, but before the plane could realign for another pass, its fuel had all been expelled. The pilot coasted down in the original field, and by the time his plane came to a stop, Chase and Wen were already almost to him.

The pilot, knowing who he was up against, was out of the cockpit and waiting behind the tail section. He had the advantage of using the plane as cover while they had to rely on nothing but cornstalks in the breeze to protect them. He checked his pockets—two extra magazines, plus a fresh one in his machine gun.

He didn't know where they were. The corn was taller on the ground than it had seemed from the sky. The pilot, slightly disorientated from the forced landing, tried to remember where he'd last seen them. Taking his best guess, he fired into the stalks. A desperate move, but he was feeling a little desperate.

As the machine gun fire tore apart the cornstalks twenty feet from where Wen crouched, she anticipated his next shots would come closer. She crawled as fast as she could down the narrow space between rows, hoping to get near enough to the pilot to take a good shot. Wen also needed to reach the other side of the plane somehow, but if she were him, she would move around the plane to avoid the very thing she was doing.

Chase could not see Wen, but he didn't think she was far away. They'd become separated while running into the corn, which was more than two feet above their heads. In the suddenly silent field, he didn't dare call out to her. Chase watched for a minute, looking for any sign of rustling stalks, but saw nothing. It seemed silly to think someone with Wen's capabilities would not be able to move through a cornfield undetected.

Chase needed to get closer to the plane. He knew she would be doing the same. The problem was he couldn't see it, but he had a sense of where it was based on where the shots had come from. As he moved in that direction, he tried to make sure he could not be seen, knowing their opponent would be watching the corn for any sign of movement, just as he had.

The pilot called for backup. They told him they were already on the way. He suggested they move faster. After the call, he stooped under the plane and began shooting from the other side. Feeling his phone vibrate, he stopped firing and took the call.

Wen reached the edge of the cornfield less than fifteen feet from the yellow plane as the shooting stopped. The pilot was somewhere behind it. She crouched and waited for him to come back to her side. It would take too long to get back around, and he might just move again.

Suddenly she heard him talking and almost panicked, thinking there was someone else with him, but after straining to hear, she could make out enough of his words to realize he was actually talking on the phone. However, what she heard did nothing to ease her mind. His backup was three minutes out. As he described what section of the field they were in, she knew there was little time left to act.

Chapter Twenty-Eight

Krauss read the report from his investigators, slowly sipping a glass of water. If anyone had walked into his private tower office, they would have thought him in a fine mood.

In reality, underneath his calm exterior, the CEO of Gravacon was seething. Krauss wanted to smash the glass in his hand, shoot something . . . *someone.* No one had been able to ascertain the purpose and principle of the Antwerp scientists secret project—the String-Continuum. What he *did* know is that they believed it could destroy his company and, therefore, his chance to solve world hunger.

I'll kill them myself if I have to, he thought. But in truth that was not something he could ever do. However, he did employ people who could, and would. He wanted String-Continuum details as much as he wanted to breathe . . . perhaps more. *What is it? What the hell is it?*

Wen looked at the plane, the acres of crops beyond it, which separated them from their car, and knew it would be impossible to get there without being spotted by the pilot. With only three minutes remaining until they would become vastly outnumbered and outgunned, she formulated a plan, but first she had to find Chase.

The pilot shot another burst of gunfire into the stalks, getting even closer to Wen. At the same time, she crawled between the rows, searching for Chase, knowing he shouldn't be far. However, if for some reason he'd headed away from the plane and continued to move, he could easily be fifty yards away in any direction by now. With little time remaining, she took a chance and called him, hoping he remembered to switch his phone to vibrate as soon as they got separated.

"Where are you?" he whispered upon answering.

"I'm next to the plane, about twenty feet into the corn," she said quietly. "We've got about two minutes until his friends show up."

"How many?"

"Don't know, but many," she answered, never taking her eyes off the plane. "I've got an idea, but where are you?"

"I'm in the middle of a bunch of damn corn."

"Head to the plane."

"I don't know where the plane *is*."

"Head to the road, but stop at least ten feet before you get there, and you'll see it." Through whispered guiding, plus trial and error, they finally found each other. Wen handed her machine gun to Chase. He'd left his weapon in the vehicle.

"You should keep that," Chase said. "You're the better shot."

"I'm going to sneak up behind this guy, but in order to

get across to the other side of the road, I need him distracted. I need you to shoot at him. But far enough away so that he can't hit you when he shoots back."

"The decoy? You want me to be the decoy *again*?"

Wen, ignoring his joke, gave him final instructions. "If you go about ten feet that way, he should be out of range. Fire at the plane, move around—back and forth. As soon as you hear me yell, you'll know he's dead. Run as fast as you can toward the plane. Hopefully we'll get to our vehicle before his backup team arrives."

There was no quick kiss, no "I love you." They each took off in different directions, fighting through the high stalks, while trying not to move them too much.

Even before Wen reached the place where she was going to exit the field, Chase had begun shooting. The pilot returned fire immediately, and Wen believed the plan might work. She got all the way to the edge of the last row of corn and peered out. Unable to see the pilot, since he was still concealed behind the plane about twenty-five feet away, Wen knew as soon as she crossed the road she'd be exposed. Yet there was no time to change plans.

She dashed into the road, her feet only touching the dirt twice before she was back in the corn on the other side. Without ever risking a look at the plane, Wen had expected bullets. Only when she was safely hidden back in the corn did she steal a glance—he hadn't seen her.

Wen pushed through more of the stalks until positioned just behind the plane, only three rows between her and the pilot. She checked the time. If the incoming reinforcements estimate was correct, there were less than thirty seconds before they arrived. Taking one last listen to make sure they weren't already close enough to be dangerous, she flew out of the field like a samurai warrior, the sounds of Chase and the pilot's rapid gunfire exchange covering what little noise she made. Wen went into a soaring leap, landing on the pilot's back. He was dead before he could turn around. Before his body and Wen hit the ground, she yelled, "Chase, move out, now!" Grabbing the pilot's gun and an extra magazine, she was back into the field, running for the car before Chase emerged from his side.

"Get to the car!" Wen yelled, already vanishing into the towering stalks, before he could find her. Chase sprinted into the road and, while barely glancing at the dead pilot, took a precious few seconds to check the hopper tanks before charging into the corn behind Wen. Half a minute later he had caught up to her. The corn suddenly rustled and blew as if a violent storm had swept in.

"Here they come," Wen yelled before Chase heard anything.

"Where?"

Seconds later, he saw it.

"Helicopter!" Wen shouted above the spinning rotors, wind, and rippling stalks. She took the submachine gun from Chase just as the chopper landed between them and the car.

Chapter Twenty-Nine

Krieg phoned his top lieutenant and told him to get to Antwerp.

"I'm on my way to France," Krieg said from aboard a Gravacon jet. "The plan is I'm going to take care of Malone and his girlfriend, then I'll meet you back in Antwerp and we'll destroy the lab."

His lieutenant understood by "*take care of*" his boss meant he was going to kill them. "So you'll be back tonight, in time to do the lab?"

"It shouldn't take that long to pick off those rodents as they run through the field."

"Understood. But if you don't get back in time, are we to go into the lab anyway?"

"Yeah. I'll be in touch, but we need the lab off-line tonight."

"I'll be there."

Soon, Krieg was in a helicopter, flying over corn fields with another Gravacon security officer.

"There's the plane," the man said through the headsets.

Krieg looked ahead and saw the crop duster, then noticed the body lying next to it and silently thanked Dancer for encouraging him to come there. He communicated this to the chopper pilot through the headset. All three of them tried to spot Chase and Wen, but with the corn so high, they could be anywhere.

"Take it down near the car," Krieg said, after seeing the blue Volkswagen Golf parked on the side of the road.

"Good sign they're still in that field," the other man said.

"And they'll be trying to reach their vehicle," Krieg added, readying his weapon.

Chase, laying in the cornfield, looking up at the sky as the helicopter landed, couldn't imagine how they were going to reach their car.

Once Krieg and the other man were out of the chopper, the pilot took it back up to continue the aerial search.

"Go now! Go now!" Wen said, at that moment still crawling like a commando through the stalks. "They know we're not at the car. They'll be looking for us in the field. We gotta get to the car fast."

"Did you see them?" Chase yelled within the thundering chopper noise as he ran.

"Yes, Krieg!" Wen had seen the eye patch, and could have taken a shot, but it would have revealed their location. Too risky, but even so, as she worked her way through the giant plants, Wen already wished she'd taken him out.

Wen had hundreds of hours of training in this exact situation—being pursued by armed aggressors while moving invisibly and running at top speed. She kept her MP7 submachine gun ready to fire as she ducked and watched every direction, sensing with smell and sounds where the enemy might be. She knew Chase would not be able to keep up, but if she stopped to help him, they would both be dead. If she could make it to the car, there would be a chance to bring the battle on her terms. The danger was the damned chopper.

Wen waited for the bullets. She expected to be discovered in a second. *I'm close to the car.* Her mind calculated, automatically registering each knee bend, every elbow slide, so that she could estimate the distance covered—her guess would be accurate to within ten inches for every hundred feet traveled.

The helicopter flew circular patterns less than ten feet above the crops, the rotors pushing down the green, leafy stalks. It went directly above her, and she assumed she'd been spotted.

Chase could not crawl in the military style that Wen could, nor could he judge with any precision how far he'd come or how far was left to go. Instead, he ran in a crouching jog. He also didn't have a gun, and knew he could run into one of the Gravacon men at any moment. Yet somehow he made it to the car before Wen. He hadn't heard gunshots, meaning she was still alive. Wen would never go quietly.

Chase looked into the sky and saw the chopper doing sweeps between the plane and the car. Fortunately, it had just passed this way, and he made a dash from the edge of the corn to the car. Staying low, he opened the driver's door just enough to squeeze in behind the wheel and started the motor. With the helicopter flying so close to the ground, he knew no one could hear the Golf's finely tuned engine.

Wen emerged from the corn twenty-five feet down the road from the VW, and was stunned to see Chase already there. *He's had better training than me because I trained him!* She flattened herself on the edge of the field, still concealed by the mighty maize, and kept counting. Wen knew from tracing its earlier patterns while she was slithering through the field as soon as the chopper went overhead, she would have eleven to thirteen seconds until it came back. She could make it to the car and back five times before it returned, but it wasn't that simple. As soon as she broke from the corn, there was a chance he'd see her.

But even if you do, you'll have to go back and pick up Krieg.

The chopper flew over, she counted to three, and bolted.

Chapter Thirty

Wen didn't even have the door shut before Chase sped away into the fading daylight.

"Miss me?" Wen asked, slamming the door and pushing the button to lower the window.

"Missed your gun."

"That's not nice."

He smiled. "How long until the helicopter notices we're gone?"

"About two more seconds, but then it'll have to go back for the pirate."

"Great. Want to get some dinner?"

"Sure, what do you feel like?"

"Anything, as long as they aren't serving corn."

She laughed. "Dirt still safe and sound?" she asked, patting his pack, balanced between them.

"Yeah. They sure didn't want us to have that. I hope the lab is still safe."

"I'd call, but looks like we're about to have some uninvited dinner guests," she said looking out the back.

Chase checked the rearview mirror, and across the long, flat expanse of farmland he could easily see the chopper lifting out of the cornfield. "I guess he picked up the shooters. Any ideas how we're going to outrun a helicopter, especially once they start shooting at us?"

"Aren't you a professional race car driver? Can't you just drive better than they fly?"

"I knew you'd have a good idea."

Chase already had the accelerator to the floor, but they both knew that in less than a minute, the helicopter would be on top of them, and this was no race car.

"Maybe I should shoot them?" Wen said, but sounded doubtful. "After all, it's easier to shoot from a car on a nice evenly paved road than from a flying blender like that."

Bullets suddenly ripped up the gravel shoulder just behind them.

"He seems to be shooting all right from that blender!" Chase yelled.

Wen returned fire.

"If I'd known we were going to be running from a helicopter," Chase shouted above the engine's roar as soon as she stopped firing, "I would have rented something with more pep than this Golf!"

"Like what?" Wen watched for her next shot as Chase swerved back and forth on the highway while the chopper swayed.

"Maybe a Cessna or a Gulfstream."

The road began to climb.

Bullets cut across the pavement just ahead of them.

"I think, with a little more practice, Krieg might just hit us!" Chase yelled.

"Those power lines are keeping them off to that side."

She pointed across the road. "I bet it's making the pilot crazy."

"Pilots don't seem to like us much today. Do you think that's a French thing, or do they just take trespassing in a corn field really seriously here?" He passed two tractor trailers as the road entered rolling hills and traffic, although still very light.

After another exchange of gunfire, Wen asked him if he could go any faster.

Chase checked the speedometer, pinned at 200kph, which he quickly translated in his head to be about 124 miles per hour. "If my mother was here, she'd tell you that pushing one hundred seventy horsepower and one hundred eighty pounds of torque in this aerodynamic shell faster than one hundred twenty-five miles per hour is next to impossible."

"A simple 'no' would have done," Wen yelled, firing another burst up toward the Gravacon bird.

"Hey, look at that!" Chase shouted as the road continued to grow steeper.

Wen turned forward and saw a tunnel up ahead. "Nice, but we could use something a little longer."

"Still, it'll screw with their fun."

"By all means, screw with their fun," she shouted as bullets cut into the shoulder next to them—the closest yet.

The tunnel was very short. They blasted out of it in about half a second, but a quarter mile later they were in another one, three times as long. Soon another came up, and the helicopter wasn't able to stay on them. Each time, it had to fly over the top and then find them again as they slid around other vehicles.

Wen put down her gun and checked the navigation

system. "Four more tunnels ahead, and the last one is very long," she announced.

"Sounds like a plan," Chase said. The two of them were playing with the same idea. "Remember that time in Vegas?"

"Yeah, but this is different."

"Yet, sort of the same." Chase slowed down to under one hundred for the next tunnel.

Each time they went in and out, the pilot dipped the chopper low, trying to give Krieg a good shot as they came out. However, Chase was now switching lanes and changing up his speed. By the time they hit the next to the last tunnel Chase came out doing sixty, but flew into the final tunnel going seventy-five.

"There!" Wen yelled as they reached the half-way point.

Chase crossed the center lane and hit the hazards. They jumped out and waved two cars through the way they were going and another heading the opposite direction. Then they got lucky and were able to stop a pick-up truck behind them loaded with firewood.

Chase went to the driver and offered him two thousand Euros for a ride. The man was confused, but before he could respond, Wen was in his passenger seat, pointing her gun at him.

"We need your help," she said in French.

"S'il te plaît ne me fais pas de mal," he responded, staring at the money, confused and frightened.

"We aren't going to hurt you," she responded in French.

Chase quickly tossed enough logs out to make room for him to hide. After grabbing the pack full of dirt and his own submachine gun from the Golf, he climbed in the bed.

"Keep the money," she said in French, "but we need to go *now!*"

Wen saw Chase get tucked in under the tarp, then told the man to go. "Allez! Allez!"

They followed a BMW and Toyota Camry, with a couple of other cars behind them. By the time they exited the tunnel, they were going normal speed, and were lost in the clip of vehicles.

Wen saw the helicopter above, but they could never have seen her on the floor of the front seat.

"Keep driving," Wen said in French.

"Okay," the driver said, "please, I do not want to die."

"Just drive normally, and we'll get out soon. Don't worry." Wen knew there was a good chance the man was going to die, but it wouldn't be by her hand.

Chapter Thirty-One

The helicopter flew back and forth from the tunnel entrance to the other side where they expected the VW Golf to emerge.

"They should have been out by now!" Krieg blasted through the headset. "Those cars went in *after* them!" He pointed to two white sedans and a yellow van.

"They must still be inside," the other man said, sounding confused.

"Take it down as low as you can!"

The pilot hovered dangerously above the vehicles while Krieg strained to get a view inside. "I can't see far enough. Find a place to land. I need to get in there."

Sixty feet ahead, the shoulder opened to a small pull off for emergency vehicles. The pilot set it down, and Krieg and the other man jumped out, immediately running toward the tunnel. The pilot lifted up and flew back to the entrance to make sure Chase and Wen didn't exit that way.

The two armed men dodged cars as they raced into the

tunnel. They didn't bother with the extremely narrow concrete walkway on the side.

"There," Krieg said, pointing to cars crawling around an abandoned vehicle he still couldn't identify in the muted light of the tunnel.

"It's the Golf," his companion shouted a second later.

Krieg barked out several German cuss words, and an exasperated yell. He immediately suspected that Chase and Wen were no longer in the VW and had somehow slipped out of the tunnel, but he needed to be sure. With guns ready, Krieg and the other man cautiously approached the car. *This would be a perfect setup for them to ambush us,* Krieg thought, crouching low against the wall, feeling exposed without anywhere to seek cover other than moving vehicles. His finger was one pulse away from pulling the trigger. He wanted to shoot. He wanted to kill.

With each passing second, Krieg knew they were getting farther away. *They aren't dumb enough to be sitting in here waiting for us.* He took his eyes off the Golf for a moment and scanned the tunnel in both directions, searching for them, trying to visualize how they'd gotten away.

Drivers, seeing the guns, panicked, and even before they reached the Golf, traffic jams had built up around the bottlenecks on either side. But, amazingly, no one was blowing their horns. Those who had no way of seeing the armed men seemed to be following the lead of those who could, as if it were just a normal accident or break down.

Krieg approached the passenger door of the parked VW while the other man took the driver's side. After only a moment, Krieg confirmed what he already knew—the car was empty.

"Which vehicles came out of the tunnel first?" he asked the other man as they started to jog back to the exit.

"I don't know, I was only looking for the Golf."

Krieg racked his brain, trying to recall anything about the first half-dozen cars out after Chase's VW went in. He cussed again, knowing they were not going to catch them. Chase had too far of a lead, and they had no idea what kind of vehicle he was now traveling in, or even which direction the pair had gone. By the time they were back in the helicopter, almost twenty minutes had elapsed since Chase had driven into the tunnel. He had the pilot fly ahead for ten miles before deciding to call off the search.

Nearly an hour and a half later, the pick-up driver dropped them off at a bus station. Chase paid him another thousand euros and thanked the now relieved man. Wen apologized profusely, explaining that some people had been trying to hurt them. She credited him for saving their lives.

"Don't worry, we're not taking a bus," Wen said to Chase after the man drove off. "Just in case he decides to go to the police, I don't want him to know where we went."

"So we're walking?" Chase joked.

"No. I checked, and there's a car rental place two blocks from here, but we need to hurry. It's only open for another fifteen minutes."

After getting the car, using one of their many aliases, Wen contacted the Astronaut, who hacked into a vacation rental site and found them a vacant, fairly isolated farmhouse to crash in for a few hours of much needed sleep.

"We should check in with Mutsu," Chase said as they found the little "ferme" down a long, winding driveway.

"Too risky, and too late," Wen said. "It's almost midnight. Let's just go dark for a few hours."

Chapter Thirty-Two

Alone in an old stone cottage somewhere in the French countryside, Chase and Wen tangled in each other's arms under a light blanket. The bed looked like it had been there for centuries, but was incredibly comfortable. Still, they were unable to sleep. Instead, they talked. Not like fugitives or secret agents, but as lovers.

"Did we really wake up in Paris this morning?" Wen said after a sensuous kiss.

"It's been a long twenty-four hours . . . "

"I thought I was going to lose you today," Wen said, only the flicker of a candle allowing them to see each other.

"Something heavy was in the air, and I don't mean what they dropped on us."

The duster had hit them with a fertilizer, not hydenosyn. Chase had seen the label on the hopper's tanks when they ran past the plane. Still not a great substance to be covered in, and inhaling, but after several showers and lots of fluids, they thought they were probably okay.

"I felt it, too," she said touching his face, their lips only inches apart. "Are we pushing our luck?"

"Yeah . . . but what else can we do?"

She traced his fingers in hers, but said nothing.

"One of the reasons we're attracted to each other is that neither one of us can leave something wrong alone when we can make it right."

"The ancient Chinese warriors spoke of two intersecting trails," Wen said. "At one end of the first is life, at the other end of it is death . . . the second path begins at a moment which requires the most care, and all of our concentration."

"Where does the second path end?"

"The awareness of peace," she whispered. "But the two trails intersect at a place where one must decide whether to fight or run, live or die."

"Is that where we are?" His hand pushed softly through her silky hair and found the back of her neck. He gently pulled her closer.

"I don't know. Sometimes you do not want to fight, but also you do not want to die . . . yet often the only way to live is to run."

"We find ourselves in life and death situations all the time."

"Killing the pilot weighs on me," Wen said.

"I know."

"I'm not sure where we are on those paths. Sometimes it's a paradox, or a paradigm. Could we have gotten away without killing the pilot? I don't know."

"I don't see how," Chase said. "We had less than a minute before the helicopter showed up. And we didn't even know it was a helicopter at that point, we thought it was a vehicle full of people . . . We almost didn't get out of there. There were only seconds to get to our car."

"But I got around to the other side. I could have made it to the car . . ."

"You only got there because I was distracting him. Do you really think we could've both gotten across the road without him knowing, if I wasn't firing constantly at him?"

Wen looked at the candlelight as if it might have an answer. "When I was younger, we only had candlelight in the evenings, and sometimes I stared at those flames for hours, wondering what my life would be like, wondering why my father was gone for weeks, and they would not tell me what he did."

Chase knew Wen's father had been in the MSS, but she had only admitted it, painfully, a few months earlier, as if it were still a secret.

"Do you think one day we will have a family?

"You mean children?"

"Yes."

"I hope so. But not until we stop running."

"When will that be?"

"I don't know. First, we have to figure out who's after us, and why."

"And then stop them," Wen said. They both knew they weren't talking about Gravacon. Someone else had been after them for months. They looked at each other, their silence saying the same thing: who and why?

"Maybe we should ask Tess," Wen said. The words were as difficult for her to speak as they were for Chase to hear. Wen didn't trust Tess. She hardly trusted anyone other than herself, Chase, and the Astronaut, but she *especially* didn't trust Tess. She knew Chase didn't either, and he also didn't like her, but both of them did respect her. "Tess has access to every US intelligence network and tool in existence. If anyone can find out who's been following us, it's her."

"I'll have to think about that," Chase said. "And what if it's *her* who's been following us?"

That was a discussion not new to them, always with the same conclusion—if Tess was the one who'd been pursuing them, they would already be dead. Tess had chased them several times in the past, and although they had managed to elude her in the end, their paths continued to cross. CISS had had many opportunities to have them killed. By that reasoning, she was the one person in the world that it seemed was definitely *not* the one pursuing them, and therefore the one they should most trust.

But that pill was far too bitter to swallow.

Chapter Thirty-Three

Chase and Wen had finally fallen asleep in the secluded farmhouse outside Roanne, France. The soil samples were stashed under the bed. They slept deeply until Chase's phone rang.

"It's Tess," he said to Wen as he answered, putting the phone on speaker. She already had a gun in her hand.

"You've got a serious problem," Tess said without saying hello.

"Do you know where we are?" he asked, looking at Wen. Moonlight streamed in through a high window.

"Yes, and so do they."

"Who is 'they'?" It was a question Chase found himself asking far too often.

"Colonel Gervais Kabongo, from the Democratic Republic of the Congo. He's been looking for you. We suspect that he has orders to kill you."

"What have I ever done to this colonel what's-his-name? I've never even *been* to the Congo." He looked questioningly at Wen again, as if somehow she could answer.

"It might not surprise you to learn that the president of the DRC, Tryhon Amine, has negotiated a huge contract with Gravacon to use OrgriSource. And it seems that President Amine views *you* as a threat to that agreement, and therefore a threat to his country."

Wen was looking out the windows, checking the house.

"Okay, but enough of a threat that some general tracks me down, lost in the remote French countryside, in the middle of the night? How did he *find* me?"

"They have connections."

"With who?"

"Hard to say."

"He got my location from somebody in the CIA, didn't he?"

Tess was silent.

"Unbelievable," Chase muttered.

"It wasn't anyone in *my* division," Tess said. "I assure you of that."

"Well, doesn't that just make me feel all warm and fuzzy. Thanks for not selling me out to the African vigilantes."

"Listen to me, it doesn't matter how. The thing is, the colonel is a ruthless man. He is the only reason President Amine is in power and *stays* in power. Colonel Kabongo has killed any opposition—hundreds, perhaps thousands of people."

"Sounds like a nice guy."

"Yeah, and he's gunning for you. If you want to live, get out of there *now*. I've got to go."

"Wait!"

"I hope I'm not too late . . . good luck." The line went dead.

Chase pulled on his pants, shoved the phone in his

pocket, and grabbed the pack with the soil samples from under the bed.

"Do you think she's setting us up, or trying to save us?" Chase asked as Wen came back in the room.

"We'll worry about that question if we're still alive," Wen said, tossing a gun to Chase. "Remember how to use one of these?"

"Yeah, like a camera, right? Just point-and-shoot."

"Want to be the decoy?" Wen asked.

Chase moaned. "I'd *love* to be the decoy." He smiled at her. "What do I have to do? Light the house on fire? Run out in the field with my hands up? Pretend I'm fixing the tire?"

"Not a bad idea, but I had something simpler in mind. You stay in here and try to convince anyone out there that there are still two people in here."

"And you?"

"While you're shooting out the windows, I'll go out there, find them, sneak up on them . . . "

"Then what?"

"You know the rest."

"Is this a multiple-choice? Maybe another plan that involves us finding a secret escape tunnel out of here that leads to a waiting speedboat?"

"There is, but I decided against it, knowing how much you like a challenge. Don't worry, this will be so much more fun," she said, giving him a sweet kiss, then slipping out of the bedroom. "Remember, it only works if they think we're both still in the house," she whispered loudly back down the short hall. "So look like two shooters."

"Do we have a meeting spot?"

"Back here. As soon as it's over, we'll open up that bottle of wine we saw."

Wen slipped out the back, wearing night vision goggles, although the moon was giving off a fair amount of light on its own. Tess had not said how many were coming. Wen did not have any real knowledge of tactics used by the Congo military. However, she assumed several factors—poor nation, overseas mission far from home, they'd be counting on the element of surprise with their CIA intelligence. No less than three operatives, and definitely no more than six. Wen also guessed they didn't possess her level of training, but would nevertheless be experienced and battle hardened.

She scoured the area on either side of the lane that led to the country road where they would most likely be coming from. The former MSS officer smiled, believing that in all cases, even with six of them, she would have the advantage.

What she had not been expecting was the sounds of rotors. *Not again,* she thought. *An approaching helicopter . . . this definitely changes things.* For a moment, she wondered if Krieg had somehow found them, but Tess had said an attack from a Congo colonel . . .

She scanned the area quickly searching for a ground force. *What if it's two attacks.*

Through her goggles, she could find no one on the ground, and after listening to it for eight or nine seconds, she realized it was not a military chopper, but rather a civilian craft. That could still mean Krieg, but the coincidence of two attacks at the same moment in their isolated location was way too coincidental. It had to be just the Congolese.

She had to admit, coming in from the air was a brazen move by a foreign military operating inside France. She recalled the French had some colonial history with the Congo, and much influence.

Perhaps the relationship goes both ways and Colonel Kabongo received some sort of under-the-table permission for this strike. After all, neither Chase nor I are French citizens, and neither of us have permission to be in the country. Both were traveling under false passports.

She hid and waited.

The helicopter landed closer to the house than she would've risked had it been her operation. *The colonel must be counting on his superior firepower and numbers, or else why risk losing the element of surprise?* Wen wondered if their attackers were making a mistake, or if she was missing something. Certainly he didn't know a lethal MSS agent was waiting for them. *He's counting on an easy takeout of a businessman and his wife.*

The pilot and five others jumped out, each carrying AK-47s.

Chapter Thirty-Four

Standing inside Mission Control, underneath the Vienna, Virginia CISS headquarters building, Tess watched the monitors as IT-Squads undertook one of their most dangerous missions since the top-secret agency had been created. The risks weren't due to the fact that the agents' lives were in jeopardy, rather from the highly sensitive nature of their assignment.

Three different Squads were involved. Two of the teams were dressed as US Capitol police. The third team was working in "Cyber City," which was actually located on the windowless third floor of the CISS building. Banks of the most powerful computers and servers available hummed continually in Cyber City. The vast, dark space, lit only by hundreds of monitors and colored-LED indicators lights, resembled a city skyline at night. The CISS "magicians" working inside Cyber City regularly altered reality around the world through the darknet and many other covert channels available to them. Most of the workers in Cyber City had been trained at NSA, and still routinely accessed that agency's vast trove of sources. Their current task—plant enough legitimate data and damning evidence into the computers of key lawmakers to destroy careers.

Tess watched her people, disguised as Capital Police officers, quietly spread out in the "corridors of power" and felt her stomach churn. *If a single one of them gets caught, we'll have a Watergate-times-ten on our hands.* She shuddered. The two IT-Squads were broken into six teams of three. They had to hit offices in three Senate office buildings along Constitution Avenue, north of the Capitol, and three House office buildings along Independence Avenue, south of the Capitol.

Tess looked again at the real-time digital-maps of the complex, showing the teams' progress throughout Russell, Dirksen, and Hart Senate Office Buildings, the Capitol itself, and down to the Cannon, Longworth, and Rayburn House Office Buildings. Staring at the monitors, she had a stray thought that the average American might not be aware how much *space* government requires. The grand US Capitol building did not contain enough space within its historic walls, so during the last century, Congress had expanded the capital complex to accommodate offices for all the US Representatives, senators, and their staffs, committee hearing rooms, meeting areas, cafeterias, and many more spaces for maintenance and facilities management. All the buildings were connected to the Capitol by elaborate underground pedestrian tunnels, some of which actually had railcars to shuttle personnel, senators, and members of Congress to and from the Capitol.

CISS's operation, as precise in its timing as it was dangerous, could only have been designed and ordered by Tess. She watched tensely, knowing the bold action could fail at any moment. The wrong person, a piece of technology glitching at the wrong moment . . . But IT-Squads were unequaled in their abilities. She had faith.

Cameras, long installed in the Capitol subway system, as well as all the other tunnels and miles of corridors in the complex, gave Tess a nearly complete view of the action—or, preferably, the lack thereof. Although she had complete authority to do whatever was necessary in pursuing CISS's mandate, this one would be impossible to explain, and difficult to justify. If there were a problem, somebody would have to be thrown to the lions, and even though typically, in cases such as these, a deputy assistant director or some such underling could usually be made the scapegoat, forced to fall on the metaphorical sword, not this time. Planting evidence, breaking into Senators' offices, this one could easily blow up and require a bigger sacrifice—even someone like Tess herself.

It wasn't even that Tess cared about losing her job. There were days—many of them, in fact—when she would've loved to have just walked away from the stress, pressure, and responsibilities. However, Tess believed fervently in CISS's mission to save the United States of America and preserve its place in the world by being sure that corporations didn't dominate the future in the place of governments. She didn't believe anyone could do the job as well. It wasn't her career that was on the line, it was the future of freedom and democracy.

Tess wasn't naïve. She knew that the freedom and democracy believed in by the average patriot didn't really exist anymore—if it ever had—but she was convinced it was still the best thing out there. This mission was a turning point. Success or failure, a line had been crossed.

The point of no return, she thought.

Chapter Thirty-Five

In her rush to get out of the cottage, Wen hadn't told Chase when to start shooting. Typically he waited for her lead, but in this case, he needed to fire first. She held her breath, upset at the oversight, one she rarely made. Looking at the men surrounding the cottage, then at her phone, Wen had to risk a call.

"Yeah," he whispered, answering.

"Shoot whenever you have a shot starting when you see the first one—which should be any second. There are six," she said. "Love you."

Chase, the bag of dirt still slung on his back, had wanted to ask her a million questions once he saw the helicopter, but clearly she was still going with the original plan. "Don't lose the dirt, and don't die," he told himself. "Not necessarily in that order."

As soon as the first two men got near the door, he fired. He was fairly sure one was dead, and the other close to it, or at least badly injured.

"Not bad for a decoy," he said, only expecting to scare them in a bluff.

Two more had gone around the back of the house, one to each side. It was a routine military operation. None of the attackers seemed fazed or deterred by the returning fire.

Okay, Colonel, now you know you blew the element of surprise, Wen thought to herself while she started counting and estimating steps, distances, bullets, and breaths, calculating every variable. She knew from her training, and her years in the field, that of the eight people involved in the pre-dawn skirmish, five were already dead—they just didn't know it yet. Her job was to figure out who and how, and to make sure she and Chase weren't among the casualties.

Chase fired out the back window, ran across to the front of house, and fired another shot from there. Neither one hit anything, mainly because he wasn't firing *at* specific targets, just trying to make them believe there were two people inside.

Very good, Colonel, you seem to be falling for my elementary trick. Yes, we are both in the house . . . keep going, Wen thought, still not wanting to reveal her position, yet not willing to risk Chase getting overwhelmed before she could strike. Instead of using her gun, she crept behind one of the men. Killing the pilot in the cornfield flashed through her mind, and the moment of hesitation almost cost her. The man turned around, raising his gun. Their eyes met in an instant of fear.

She still managed to snap his neck. The maneuver, much riskier and difficult from the front, was not as clean as usual, yet was no less effective. Wen chided herself for only an instant, she couldn't risk another lapse. *Focus!*

She worked her way back around to the other man, catching up to him just as he was approaching the front door. This time she grabbed his head from behind—took his chin in one hand, the top of his head in the other, and pulled in opposite directions. Death was instantaneous, the action long instilled in her muscle memory. The result was always effective. Wen crouched down next to the fallen body and pushed the button on her phone to reach Chase.

"What?" he asked, out of breath.

"Come out the front door right now."

As luck would have it, he was actually close to the front door when she called. A moment later, he was with her.

"Come on." They ran toward the helicopter.

"Where are the others?"

"Two in the backyard," Wen whispered, climbing in and sitting behind the controls of the helicopter.

Chase ran around to the other side and got in.

"Keep the door open, you may have to give us cover fire," Wen said quietly, clicking buttons and taking the chopper airborne. "If they see us before we're high enough."

Colonel Kabongo and another man emerged from the front door of the cottage and ran across the grass, shooting up at the helicopter. Chase returned fire. The other man dove for cover, but Kabongo stood there as if impervious to bullets and continued to shoot.

Several rounds strafed the side of the craft, but didn't bring it down. Wen kept flying, and a second later, they were safely out of range.

Chase put on the headset and said, "You were right, that was more fun than a boat ride."

Colonel Kabongo, surrounded by the bodies of his fallen comrades, stood on the ground, furiously looking up at the helicopter. He had blown his best chance. But he swore it would not be his last.

Chapter Thirty-Six

At three A.M., the US Capitol was nearly deserted, but there were always stray staffers working late, or early, pages trying to catch up, and, of course Capitol Police on patrol. As usual, Tess had taken everything into account, and the complex was not a hostile environment—no one would be shooting, and her people were the best pros out there. She expected it to go according to plan.

Part two would begin six hours later, when coordinated FBI raids would visit those same offices and find what the IT-Squads had left there for them. Of course, the FBI agents were not in on the scheme. They would, unwittingly, provide the authentication and corroboration that Gravacon had bribed many for the votes to ensure passage of their controversial bill.

Tess studied another screen where four more IT-Squads were working on a similar operation against the legislative branch of the European Union. There would be evidence planted in Brussels, Belgium, and the hackers up in Cyber City were spinning their own spells across EU Parliament, and EU Commission offices in Luxembourg City and Strasbourg, France. A full IT-Squad virtual-attack on the Council on the European Union, Parliament of Australia, the federal government of Brazil, National Congress in Brasília, and six other nations.

It's all a desperate last attempt, and none of it might work, Tess thought. *Such is the corruption, and the power held by the corporations now.*

Tess stiffened, watching a real Capitol Police officer getting too close to her people.

A Mission Control technician warned the IT-Squad. "Capitol Police officer about to enter your hallway."

"Team Leader, we are fully exposed."

Tess held her breath. The officer was checking doors. Everyone froze. The communications chatter went silent. If the officer entered the office where the IT-Squad was working, there was a plan called "Armageddon." The officer would be subdued, bound, gagged, and blindfolded. If it went bad, they would kill him, but that was to be the last recourse. Next, the office would be trashed—a failed burglary—and the first step of a cover-up would occur. Tess realized she'd been holding her breath as her head began to hurt.

The Capitol police officer's every step seemed to echo like a judge's gavel.

"He's a lieutenant," the technician announced. "We're pulling up his file now."

Tess hoped he wasn't married. She looked for a ring, but the image didn't allow that much detail. Before the technician could reel off the officer's details, he passed Congressman Wallace's office with hardly a glance at the door. Tess exhaled, but there was a long way to go.

Several more close calls later, as the last operatives

exited a senator's office, the fates turned on Tess. Three IT-Squad members were moving down a long corridor in the Russell Senate office building when another Capitol Police officer, this one a captain, came upon them. The captain looked at them, puzzled, and smiled slightly. "What's going on?" he asked, wondering why three sergeants would be in the Russell building at three A.M. Then, as if realizing he didn't recognize any of them, his expression twisted from confusion into something closer to panic or fear. The captain, a seventeen-year veteran of the force, didn't know all twenty-two hundred sworn personnel in the Capitol Police Department, but he knew most of them, and was pretty sure he could recognize the rest.

Just as he was about to touch his radio, two of the squad members seized him. The trained officer didn't even have a chance to react before the CISS operatives had him bound and gagged with a hood over his head.

Chapter Thirty-Seven

Paloma and Kali had each barely slept four hours in the last thirty-six. They'd only left the lab the prior night because they'd been afraid that thugs would come in to destroy it. When they arrived at five A.M., they happily discovered nothing had been touched and Bull was already there.

"Bull, did you sleep here?" Kali asked.

"Yeah, I didn't want anything to happen."

"You could have been hurt."

"Maybe, but I worked security in high school. I'm pretty resourceful."

The two scientists looked at each other. "Thanks," Paloma said, "but don't do that again. We've got enough people missing already."

Kali smiled, but it was not her usual happy expression. Instead, it was the kind of forced smile that attempts to hold back tears. Mutsu and the other workers began streaming in. Everyone showed up early, knowing this had to be the day.

After coffee cups were filled, the lab cranked back into

high gear. They worked as if the Gravacon voting deadline was a gun to their heads, and they believed—metaphorically speaking—it was exactly that to all of humanity. They'd been crunching and extrapolating numbers through millions of individual points of data. Each of the hundreds of soil samples presented hundreds of thousands of equations and possible solutions. Thanks to Chase, fAIr was now being utilized in the quest, which took considerable pressure off the other artificial intelligence programs they'd been using. The massive streams of information had crashed their system on multiple occasions, but fAIr allowed them to do thousands more processes every second, and everything was going faster, so much faster, yet they still didn't know if it would be fast enough.

"Will you finish today?" Bull asked Mutsu. She had disabled the listening device so that it still registered as being on, but only broadcast a high pitched noise and unrecognizable garbled bits of conversation.

"It's proving more difficult to complete the String-Continuum without the missing data," he said, holding his gaze on her a beat longer than necessary. "Paloma had hoped that AI could create the missing microbes, but we really need the samples from France and Luxembourg."

"Why are they so important?" She leaned in close, not necessarily on purpose. She strangely felt comfortable around him, without actually realizing it.

"Because America has destroyed so much of the microbes in their soil with chemical pesticides, herbicides, and fertilizers, there's already such a big hole in the data." He inhaled deeply, quietly. The high-tech, high-octane wisp of a girl absolutely captured him.

"We have to plug in our own variables," Paloma said,

joining the conversation as she returned to her station. The three of them stood next to a screen.

"We can't put in anything we aren't sure of," Mutsu said.

"We know what has to go there, and we know it's right," Paloma added.

"But until we have proof," Kali interjected, "it'll never stand up to peer reviews."

"We don't have time for that," Paloma said, advancing her argument that they should go ahead and announce the String Continuum without the complete data from the samples.

"We need *proof*."

"It won't matter. By the time they start testing, we'll have the proof."

"But what if we don't?" Kali asked. "It'll jeopardize everything."

"Once the world sees what we have, everyone's going to come at this," Mutsu said.

"It's impossible to know what they will do with that hole," Kali added. "After everything we've been through, we can't lose it now."

"We're going to lose it if we don't stop Gravacon," Paloma said, her tired voice rising with impatience.

Mutsu held up his hands. "The decision can wait until later in the day," he said. "Let's see what else fAIr can do, and if more samples come in that will begin to fill in the picture."

Bull winked at Mutsu.

Mutsu spent the next few hours trying to track down the missing collectors and looking for ways to quickly obtain additional dirt from still untapped areas. In moments of pause, he also worked on getting up the courage to ask Bull out to dinner, breakfast . . . a midnight snack, even a cigarette—although he didn't smoke. Maybe he'd start.

Bull helped where she could. Her computer skills were the best in the lab. Everyone seemed to need her help, and she had picked up the fAIr interface faster than anyone, now that Chase was gone.

When Bull first looked at the screen and saw the same thing Chase had recognized in their work, she was shocked. "The String-Continuum . . . I mean, did that form naturally out of the samples?" she asked Paloma.

"It sure did, once we figured out the order."

"But that's . . . it's . . . it's like a miracle."

"Yeah," Paloma whispered, caught up anew in the awe of what they'd discovered.

"How does that happen?"

"Nature, baby," Paloma said. "Same way we're here breathing, thinking, talking."

"But this will change everything," Bull said. "Won't it?"

"I sure hope so."

WH walked into the lab unannounced. Both Paloma and Kali ran over and hugged him. Mutsu, who had just gotten off the phone, practically jumped into his arms. "Where have you been?" the lab manager asked in a tone mixed with irritation and relief.

WH had been one of the first three collectors to go out

in the field, and had long been everyone's favorite. When he hadn't checked in originally, they had all been afraid he'd also disappeared. Taking off his backpack, WH pulled out the samples he'd collected.

"You got them!" Paloma said, pure joy in her voice.

"Getting them was easy," WH said. "Getting them out, that was the hard part." He proceeded to tell them the story of being pursued by the gunmen.

"You're lucky," Mutsu said. "I just received word, a few minutes ago. . . Ryan is dead."

WH's eyes turned soft for a moment, then hardened. "How?"

"Very few details. He was in Argentina. Apparently a gunshot."

"Damn, damn, *damn*," Paloma said. Kali shed quiet tears.

"They shot him!" WH said, disgusted. All the collectors had known each other and been friends, but WH and Ryan had been particularly close. WH had trained Ryan when he'd joined the group.

"It's clear that they're after the dirt, trying to stop our collection," Paloma said.

"The six others still missing are in grave danger," Mutsu said.

"Possibly already dead," Paloma said angrily, her eyes filling.

"Gravacon is going to have to pay for this," WH said through gritted teeth. "Tell me we're going to stop them. Tell me we've completed the String-Continuum."

"We're close," Paloma said. "These samples will be a huge help. As you know, Congo has special soil." He'd been sent back to Congo because the samples there had come in with such incredible quality, they had needed to double check additional regions.

"The dirt may hold the secret cure to our worst diseases," WH said, "but I want to bury Krauss in it."

Chapter Thirty-Eight

Tess wiped a dot of blood from her palm as the nail from her pinky broke skin. She was happy the captain hadn't been killed because that would be a whole new can of disaster to deal with, but now they had to get him out of the Capitol building without running into any other legitimate officers.

Thank God it didn't happen in one of the offices, she thought. *That would have blown the integrity of the mission.*

Even when authorities tried to figure out who had been in the building and why, they would be unable to trace it to a specific office. However, the timing of the FBI raids would complicate things, cause suspicion, and she'd have to try to deal with that.

One of her assistants waited until Tess glanced her way before asking, "Who are we going to call?"

This was a difficult issue. Tess knew that the Capitol Police were a unique organization; a federal law enforcement agency charged with protecting the United States Congress within the Capitol, the District of Columbia, and anywhere else in the United States or its territories that members of Congress, their families, and staff needed protection. The Capitol Police answered only to Congress, not to the president of the United States, Department of Justice, or anyone else in the executive branch, where most of Tess's power and connections originated. Nevertheless, the Capitol Police worked closely with the FBI. She would be on the phone as soon as the director was awake.

Tess turned to her assistant, hesitated a moment, and then said, "Get me Senator Evans." He was on the Senate Select Committee on Intelligence, and had done favors for Tess in the past. However, this one would be the biggest so far. Tess didn't believe that some pressure from the FBI would be enough to cover their tracks. The chief of the Capitol Police was a very politically savvy man, and would immediately be suspicious if major FBI raids took place hours after the abduction and disappearance of a Capitol Hill captain. Tess would need Senator Evans to shut this down, knowing this was the type of career-ending situation that most politicians would run from.

Her assistant looked at her, surprised. "Why would he get involved?"

Tess had encouraged subordinates to voice opinions, and had chosen this particular assistant from the CIA because she was a highly intelligent, logic driven person who wasn't afraid to take chances and bend rules in order for things to work out in the end. However, at times like these, Tess needed more patience than she possessed, and having to debate her answers was not going to happen.

She took a deep breath. "I think I can make the senator an offer he can't refuse," Tess said, without her normal bravado, while turning back to the screens. None of that would matter if they got caught again. *What the hell was that*

Chasing Dirt

captain doing there anyway? she wondered. They had the duty rosters. He wasn't even supposed to be in the Russell building. He should have been in the Hart Senate office building, and off at two A.M. "Get me the file on the Capitol police captain we've got in custody. In fact, get me everything."

The assistant knew that by "everything," Tess meant even his NSA footprints. Within an hour, they would have every email and phone call this guy had made in the last decade. They could go deep—browser history, shopping, everything meant everything. The assistant knew the captain might have had a perfectly innocent reason for hanging around ninety minutes after his shift, and being in the wrong building, in this case, the wrong place at the wrong time. But she also knew very well that in Washington, simple explanations were often anything but.

Chapter Thirty-Nine

Chase and Wen ditched the helicopter in a small field. They had arranged for Simon to meet them in Verdun, one of the countless little cities that straddled the Meuse, a major European river that runs from France to the North Sea through the Netherlands and Belgium.

After hiking for about twenty minutes, they found him waiting in front of a service station, as planned.

"I don't know why I'm picking you up," Simon said, offering them Dragées, sugared almonds, while telling them that Verdun had been famous for the candy since the year 1200. "Wouldn't it have made more sense to go by helicopter?"

"We were down to fumes," Wen said.

"Hey, these are pretty tasty," Chase said, eating the almonds and realizing he didn't remember the last time he'd actually eaten. He tried to think of a joke about eating eight hundred year-old candy, but his brain wouldn't cooperate.

"Not very healthy," Wen said.

"Almonds are healthy," Simon said. "We can't head

straight back to Antwerp. Hope you don't mind a slight detour. I've still got to get the soil samples from Luxembourg. I just spoke with Paloma—they *really* need Luxembourg. That dirt and the stuff you got are pretty critical to the series, so we *need* to get it."

"Fine with me," Chase said. "As long as you drive and I sleep."

"You're going to sleep in a car?" Wen asked, knowing he almost never could.

"When I'm this exhausted . . . "

"How far out of the way?"

"I knew you'd ask," Simon said smugly. "Not far at all. I don't think it'll take us much more than an hour longer."

"Are you okay to drive, if we sleep a little?"

"Absolutely." He decided not to tell them about Ryan's death until they woke up.

"Keep an eye out for trouble," Wen said before drifting off.

Simon watched the rearview, but nothing unusual caught his attention. An hour later, he woke them.

"We're about ten minutes from the sample site."

Immediately, Wen checked the side mirror, then turned around and looked behind them.

"All clear," Simon said. "I've been keeping an eye open."

"Can we stop for some breakfast?" Chase asked from the backseat.

"After the sample site, we've got to roll through the old town of Luxembourg City. There's all sorts of bakeries and cafés. We could get something there," Simon said. "Getting the dirt shouldn't take more than five or ten minutes. According to GPS, it's not far from the road, along an old stone wall."

They had a short discussion speculating how the sample

sites were chosen. Kali and Paloma had tried to explain it to all three of them on different occasions, but none of them really understood—something to do with various soil types. They had all memorized the major ecotones, biomes, and soil orders. They could each chant—temperate grasslands, tropical rain forest, temperate forest, boreal forest, tropical savanna, desert shrub, tundra, alpine, wetlands, ice, and soil orders Alfisols, Andisols, Aridisols, Entisols, Gelisols, and so on—but they didn't really *get* how the puzzle pieces fit. Yet the String-Continuum showed them that it did all fit in a way that could only be described as miraculous.

"I get that the quality of the microbes the soil contains can't be seen with the naked eye," Chase said, "but the French sample is plain brown. It looks dead."

"Paloma told me that some of the world's most fertile dirt, including black soils with high organic content in the American plains, is now devoid of useful microbes thanks to Gravacon. How fertile the soil is performing doesn't necessarily equate to how healthy it is," Simon said. "Ultimately, there are thousands of subtypes, and the soil can vary a lot, even from one side of a small farm to the other."

"Aren't you the expert," Chase teased.

"Apparently I was paying attention when Paloma was explaining things yesterday," Simon said.

"I was, too," Wen said. "What amazed me was that the breakthrough cures are a composite. With various microbe strands from different parts of the earth connecting and blending with others from all different regions, it's not as simple as just feeding some microbes from the dirt in Ukraine to somebody and their cancer would be cured. It's the blending . . . "

"And somehow those two brilliant women, along with a lot of help from artificial intelligence, have found a way to put it all together," Chase said. "Mind boggling. Literally earth changing!" He reached for more almonds. Wen pulled him away from them with a kiss.

They arrived at the location, and since another sample-taker had been there before, Simon had photos on his tablet showing them the precise locations. They found the same spot along the stone wall where a now missing grad student had dug a sample a few weeks earlier. Chase did the honors, then sealed it in the container.

In no time, they were headed back to Luxembourg City. "With any luck, even with a quick stop for breakfast, we'll be back in Antwerp by lunch," Simon said as they drove through the scenic area.

"I think you live your life from meal to meal," Wen said, smiling.

"Partially true," Simon admitted. "Also snack to snack. Hey Chase, are there any of those almonds left?"

Chase handed him the bag of multicolored Dragées, grabbing a few and winking at Wen.

Minutes later, Simon found parking space on the side of an old cobblestone road in the historic district of the city. They ordered pastries, breakfast bagels, coffee, and tea.

"What is that Castle over there?" Wen asked. "It's incredible."

"Oh, that's the Bock Casements," Simon said. "Some Count, I forget his name, had that built in 963."

"Truly incredible," Wen said, continuing to look over at the fortifications.

"Luxembourg was a very strategic site located between the kingdom of France and the Holy Roman Empire. It was really one of the most important and fortified areas in Europe during the sixteenth and seventeenth centuries . . . actually even into the first half of the nineteenth century.

The Bock Casements are now a UNESCO world heritage site."

"Once again, you impress with your historical knowledge," Chase said. "She must be some girl."

"She is *the* girl," Simon corrected. "But even before I met her, I'd heard about this place in the Peace Corps. All UNESCO sites are cool, but this one has had a long network of casements actually built *into* those rocky cliffs above the River Alzette, which surrounds it on three sides. I think, stretched out, it would be like twenty-three kilometers."

Chase loved stats like that. They finished eating and once back at the car, Wen immediately noticed it had four flat tires. Two African men appeared from behind a van. Another approached from behind Chase.

"Car trouble?" one of them asked in a thick African accent. He moved around to the other side so that they were surrounded.

"Need a lift, perhaps?" the other one asked, patting a barely concealed pistol.

Chapter Forty

Tess wasn't doing the Capitol Hill break-in and planting evidence as a favor for Chase, although obviously it would tremendously assist his goals. CISS had been watching Gravacon's growing influence for years, and the pending legislation that would have given it unbridled power simply made what needed to be done more urgent. CISS had been formed to prevent any single corporation from becoming so wealthy and dominant that it would rival governments. Controlling the bulk of the world's food supply, or, for that matter, the dangerous idea that seeds would be the subject of bioterrorism, either by modifying and gene editing in viruses, or other terrifying mutations, certainly classified Gravacon as an extreme threat.

A CIA study, "The Weaponization of Food," showed everything from mind control to slow, almost undetectable, weakening of population segments and deaths, attributed to disease and viruses, were possible. By changing the makeup of seeds and, therefore, the resulting plants, terrorists would be able to hack into the process and inflict incalculable damage. And, what if Gravacon *itself* decided to further manipulate things for its own despicable purposes?

"GMO is a damned Pandora's box," she said out loud.

It just so happens that, once again, Chase's and her objectives were aligned. *I might be able to help you stop Gravacon, Chase,* she thought, waiting for the FBI director to come on the line. *I just might not be able to save your life this time . . . but I will definitely try.*

"We can't go forward with the raids today," the FBI director said.

"What are you talking about? You have to." Tess bit into a pear.

"Even before people got caught, it was going to be risky."

"Why? No one got caught."

"You kidnapped a Capitol Police officer."

"So? We let him go."

"They found him wandering in a field in Virginia with his hands tied and blindfolded."

"Like I said, we let him go." She sat back in a chair, amused.

"There's going to be investigations as to what the hell happened here. This isn't some convenience store that got robbed—hell, it isn't even the Democratic National Committee offices in a private building getting broken into. It's the United States *Capitol*. Senators and Congresspeople are going to go crazy."

"They're never going to know."

"This is Washington, it'll open up all over the place," the director said. "The media is going to eat this up."

"It's not *in* the media. They don't have it. It's contained."

"Nothing is contained in Washington."

"That's a myth. There are plenty of secrets kept in this city, more than anyone can imagine." Tess said, knowing the majority of them herself. She tossed the pear's core into a wastebasket.

"We're not going in."

"You have to. It will be fine."

"Let's just say I'm not as confident as you are."

"You *have* to go in," she repeated.

"I'm not doing anything on this unless you get me written orders from the president."

Tess closed her eyes. "That is not an option here. The president must be insulated on this."

"Why? You just said everything would be fine. That means the president has nothing to worry about either."

"How the hell did you get this job?"

"By being cautious and not doing anything stupid."

Tess lost her cool and started pacing. "Sometimes, you need to put on your big boy pants, muster up a little courage, and do the right thing, even if it scares you."

"This is *your* mess," the director said. "*You* clean up."

"I'm trying, but I don't run the FBI." An assistant tried to get her attention. She cut him off with a zip line of her finger across her throat.

"Look, Tess, in a few weeks, if this all blows over, like you claim, then we'll go in."

She gathered herself, and spoke like a mother to a naughty boy—a mother who loves the boy, but the boy definitely had done something wrong. "We don't *have* a few weeks, you know that."

"Get them to delay the vote."

"It's a continuing spending authorization bill. That's not going to be delayed."

"Get a senator to tack an amendment onto something else, have your political people over there figure it out."

Tess sighed. "Keep your agents on stand-by. I'm calling you back in thirty minutes."

"Unless you get the president on board, don't bother."

Calmly removing the treasured turquoise bracelet she wore every day, Tess slammed her fist against the nearest wall and walked out of Secure.

After the call, Tess wondered if there was any way they could get the Gravacon amendment off the bill with the promise of attaching it to a "better" one. She would check with the senator.

Her assistant, finding Tess standing in the main hall, gave her an update on the Capitol Police captain. "Turns out he was just covering a shift. I got a call from his phone to a co-worker asking, and him saying yes. Then a text to his wife telling her he would be home late because he was covering the beginning of somebody's shift."

"Of all the lousy luck," Tess said. "Why couldn't he have been having an affair with a congressional staff member, or doing something illegal?"

CISS people were already tapped into the capital camera network, and had replaced the surveillance footage taken during the time the IT-Squad was inside the office buildings with footage expertly spliced together from prior nights. They were even able to replace images of the Capitol Police captain with shots of him taken at other times, and through great technical wizardry, had shown two middle eastern looking men abducting him after coming out of a senator's office unrelated to the Gravacon bribes. Once Tess reviewed the footage, she called the FBI director back, told him what the surveillance videos would show. She pressed hard, and finally he agreed to consider resuming the raids later in the day, but was still unwilling to commit absolutely.

"He'll do it," Tess said to her assistant after the call.

"How do you know?"

"Because there's something he's more afraid of than getting caught."

"What?"

"Me."

Chapter Forty-One

Wen looked at the four African men surrounding them, then to Chase. This was not a good place to fight, but without a vehicle, their escape options were limited.

"Please, allow us to help," one of them offered again. "Get in, we'll give you a lift, anywhere you want to go."

"No thanks," Wen said. "We've got to RUN!" She yelled the last word as if it were a battle cry. Chase and Simon bolted, following her across the street.

"Where to?" Chase shouted as they dashed up the other side of the narrow lane. "They're right behind us!"

"They won't shoot," Simon yelled. "Luxemburg has some of the strictest gun laws in the world."

A bullet ricocheted inches from Chase's head, shattering an ancient stone brick of a close building.

"I guess they aren't as well versed in Luxembourg's firearm ordinances as you are!"

"We have to get out of the road," Wen yelled, pulling out her Glock and firing back. The move put some distance between them as the Congolese all went for cover.

"Up here," Simon yelled, pointing. "It's the entrance to the Bock Casements."

"We'll get trapped in there," Wen said.

"No, there are multiple ways we can get out, and it's got miles of tunnels. I've been in there. I sort of know my way around."

"*Sort of?*" Chase echoed, panting. "Sort of like you knew they wouldn't shoot?"

"It's a damned military fort. There are a million places to hide and defend ourselves. They've even got cannons!"

"The cannons don't work anymore!" Chase yelled.

"Let's try it," Wen said, looking back and seeing the men gaining on them. She knew they still needed to find a vehicle, and that this time there wasn't going to be a helicopter to steal. Or maybe there was. "How did they get here so fast?" she asked as they peeked into the entrance, its low ceiling already making it very obvious they were heading into a cave.

Simon, having been there before, had a credit card ready and quickly swiped it through the automatic admission system. A seven foot high spinning pedestrian gate unlocked, and they all squeezed through.

The world that opened up before them was entirely different than the one they had just left. The beautiful autumn morning and the picturesque European historic village, with its modern skyline in the distance, was all but a dream. They had traveled back in time to medieval battles of centuries before. The gray caves and narrow paths, carved out of the massive cliffs, twisted and turned, descending into the earth like a place out of Tolkien.

"Look, a cannon," Chase said, motioning up a short flight of stone steps to the antique weapon. It was pointing out a small opening, cut and finished in rough stone blocks, aiming at the city and long forgotten approaching enemies.

Wen knew the men chasing them would approach the cave with caution, expecting them to be waiting with guns, but it would only take them a minute to realize there was no ambush. Then they would have to figure out how to get in, *would they even have a credit card, or local currency?*

Meanwhile, Simon led them deeper into the catacombs.

Some parts were especially dark and narrow, making them stoop and walk single file. The dank smell of dampness pervaded in other sections. The curving walls were an impressive display of stone cutting and craftsmanship from more than a thousand years ago. If they weren't fleeing for their lives, they could've easily been caught up in the eleven centuries of history—battles between the armies of the Burgundians, Habsburgs, Spaniards, Prussians, French, and others who had triumphed in one of the most strategic strongholds in the world at that time.

They heard running steps coming toward them.

Chapter Forty-Two

Gravacon had converted a small warehouse at their headquarter campus, outside of Cologne, for their legislative command center. Krauss authorized making final bribes and offering other incentives to lawmakers. The firm employed dozens of lobbyists and spent millions each year on "legal" advocacy. However, it was their dark funding which really moved the needle for them. In the lead-up to getting the bills passed, they'd spent nearly $90 million from a secret slush fund, which had all but secured passage in every country other than the United States. Gravacon's largest market was proving the most challenging as they faced petitions, demonstrations, and other backlash.

Yet none of that bothered Krauss. He'd been dealing with it for decades. It was the Antwerp scientists' secret String-Continuum that kept him on the edge of panic in his good moments, and absolutely terrified in the times of doubt.

"We're trying to hold these votes together," the head of

the effort reported to Krauss. "We've got fifty-one votes in the US Senate. We can't afford to lose anyone."

"How many in the House?" Krauss asked, fully versed in the system.

"We need two hundred eighteen to pass, we have two-twenty-five."

"It's going to be close, but we're there. And, of course, the President will sign it."

The man nodded.

Walking back to a private office in the command center, Krauss once again was immersed in the one worry that kept him on edge. *As long as those crazy women in Antwerp don't finish their String-Continuum and make it public before the votes.*

Krauss worked the phones while several assistants continually handed him printouts and pointed to digital readouts, charts, and graphs on various computer tablets they would place in front of him while he was talking to lawmakers in different parts of the world. Although confident, the votes were going to be close everywhere. They had managed to quell demonstrations in many parts of the world, greatly reducing opposition by utilizing tactics ranging from simply denying permits to assemble, to more sophisticated means of manipulating social media by changing meet-up sites and having posts removed that mentioned Gravacon. Krauss's favorite trick was to have social media sites have one profile unfriend another without their knowledge so other posts were made invisible inside the friend's feeds. "Nothing can be trusted in the cyber world," Krauss said, laughing, when told of various other schemes.

Basically, Krauss was confident that the measures would pass; a former Gravacon director was the head of the US Food and Drug Administration; he also had the Deputy

Director of the US Department of Agriculture—and it didn't stop there. Many on the USDA enforcement staff were former Gravacon employees. Even two current judges on the US Supreme Court had been one-time Gravacon attorneys, having worked for law firms representing Gravacon in hundreds of millions of dollars of class-action suits and product liability suits.

Senator Greenley, as a key member of both the Appropriations and Agriculture committees had assured Krauss they had the votes to get the bill passed. "Recent billion-dollar jury awards against your company's *GET-EM®* product has made it tougher to keep the votes in line," the senator told an infuriated Krauss. The US Environmental Protection Agency was also headed by a Gravacon sympathizer, and the woman's executive staff contained several people with either past Gravacon employment or deep connections to the company. In fact, the next in line to be EPA Commissioner, when the current one retired, had also been a Gravacon director.

Krauss's main enforcer was a spindly looking man who kept secret dossiers on lawmakers and journalists around the world, which they regularly used to influence those people to write or work favorably toward Gravacon and its products. The company maintained a massive slush fund, used to pay bribes and the fines incurred when caught, which had happened previously in Brazil, Spain, and the Ukraine. They generally charged these off as consulting fees. Their biggest expense, a medical promotion fund, paid or gave trips to hundreds of doctors and scientists worldwide to review and endorse studies and research which had been funded entirely by Gravacon, and showed that their products were safe and could not be linked to cancer.

"Is it definitely coming to the floor tomorrow?" Krauss

asked, having been promised that it would on numerous occasions, but knowing that last-minute shifts in the political winds could, and often did, change any scheduled congressional act.

"We're still on track. I think everything is going to go our way," Senator Greenley said. He'd received so many donations from Gravacon and Gravacon funded PACs that if anybody looked too closely, they'd see, one way or another, he'd violated most all of the campaign-finance laws.

"Good. This is critical to ending world hunger. Everything we've done as a company, all these decades, comes down to this."

"Your legacy," the senator said, not really sure if Krauss was going to solve world hunger, or even could. But he didn't care either way. It was just another day at the office, and Senator Greenley had products to sell by way of influence, bills, and other proposals. "Keep the donations coming," was his mantra, and whatever he had to do to make that happen was just fine with him. He'd started out in the house years ago and found it too annoying having to run every two years. "It felt like I was on a treadmill—get the money, convince the voters, get in office, get the money, convince the voters . . . " At least in the Senate, he had six years and a whole lot more power and influence.

"I don't care about my legacy," Krauss said. "I truly want to see the suffering end. We're too rich, too smart, and too connected to allow our fellow humans to suffer."

"I know this is the important one for you, Lars. And I'm impressed with all that you're doing. I'm going to get those votes for you, you can count on it."

Lars didn't trust politicians. He'd bought too many over the years to know one could never rely on them, but

Greenley had always been pretty good at taking care of things, and Krauss had been lining this up for years. Everything was in place from the regulatory side and the legislative sides—hundreds of studies and research showed everything Gravacon was doing fell within safe parameters and safety guidelines. Even the president was set to sign the bill. Krauss had donated big to his campaign, but also paid several people in the White House, who had the president's ear, with pockets full of cash.

"I've got to take another call," Krauss said. "I'm counting on you, Senator."

An assistant informed Krauss that a European Union official was waiting on hold. Krauss picked up and, speaking in German this time, began to charm him. The command center was humming. Krauss smiled as the man from the EU gave him more good news.

Nothing can stop us, Krauss thought, having already given orders to kill Kali Garodia, Paloma Boulet, and Chase Malone.

Chapter Forty-Three

In the bowels of the Bock Casements, Simon, Chase, and Wen ran across a metal grated footbridge only about twelve inches wide. It spanned a surprisingly deep chasm, dropping into the forgotten depths. They went single file, with Wen going over last. Reaching the other side, she wondered if there was a way to destroy the bridge behind them, but time constraints forced her to abandon the idea.

Chase came upon a heavy metal door and tried it, but it was locked.

"Keep going," Simon said, "I think we only have two more floors to go."

The narrow passage split in two directions, and somehow they'd lost the Africans—or at least could no longer hear them. They followed the one lit by blue and purple light. Many shorter offshoots opened to the outside, still high above the ground. Others were merely air vents, impossible to squeeze through. They ran into the twisting maze of passageways, knowing time was short before the men caught up.

"I'm already lost," Chase said.

"We need to keep going down," Simon said.

"Why?" Wen asked as they came to a modern metal spiral staircase that took them down ten feet.

"We can get out down there. The entrance for tourists is at street level, and the other side is all the cliff, but eventually we'll reach the bottom, and there are exits."

Getting to the bottom of the current set of steps, there was only another ramp leading up a flight of stone steps.

"Up again," Chase said, as if it was a swear word.

The ramp took them to an observation point with a view out. Wen considered scaling down the rocks, thinking she could do it, and knowing Chase could. He'd acquired superior climbing abilities and experience working for his brother's skyscraper window cleaning business in San Francisco a decade earlier. However, if they were halfway down and the Africans spotted them, they'd be shot off the wall as easy targets. The entire mental debate took less than a second, and they were already moving up another set of stone steps, which Simon assured them would eventually lead to yet another staircase going back down.

A chamber opened wide enough that they could walk side-by-side for the first time. This allowed them to sprint through the dimly lit cave.

"You gotta go up to go down, these passages twist round and round," Chase chanted. "It's like a maze, that leaves me in a daze, I don't know if we'll be found, as we go deeper and deeper underground."

"Quiet!" Wen hissed.

They reached the promised stairs that descended at a startling steep rate around a corner and opened below in a much narrower passage. Thankfully, the stone floor was smoother, but it smelled like a damp basement in a two hundred-year-old house. At the end of that passage, an opening to the outside, catching early sunlight, temporarily blinded them after the long close darkness. Wen cursed, worried that if they abruptly encountered their pursuers, they could not effectively fight back.

She felt along the wall and moved as cautiously as they dared, following the sloping passageway downward.

"How much farther?" Wen asked, second-guessing the decision to ever come into this tomb, although she would never say so out loud. Wen had been trained in the MSS, and by her parents, to never complain—simply adapt.

"I'm not sure," Simon admitted.

They suddenly heard footsteps again. These were coming behind them too fast to be tourists. Wen pulled out her Glock and tapped Chase on the back twice—their signal to get his gun and be ready. One thing Simon had been right about—the Casement was filled with nooks, alleys, concealed passageways, arches, steps, and protrusions, giving her an entire menu of defensive positions and ambush points to choose from.

Simon, unarmed, would not be much help, but he could be utilized if she could find a spot where he wouldn't be noticed as they ran past looking for Chase and Wen.

"Another cannon," Simon said. Wen now knew better than to look at the cannons, since the antique artillery pieces were all positioned on the outer walls and would subject her eyes to the sun again. Now was not the time for another dose of blinding light.

"Don't look at it," Wen snapped, stopping. She whispered for Simon to go back and hide by the cannon. "They won't see you because they won't risk looking at the light either."

"Good idea," Chase said.

"Hide there until they go past, then you can either sneak back out the way they came, or try to attack them from behind if you can find a loose rock or something to hit them with."

"Wait, what?"

"*Go!*" she barked.

Wen and Chase ran ahead. Their noise would also draw the men past Simon.

As Wen led them down another level, she found a purple hallway and told Chase to hide there in a little ledge around the light.

"Being in complete darkness, and above eye level, you'll be in a good position. Don't shoot at them unless they see you. Wait and come after you hear shots ahead."

She gave him a quick kiss, and dashed further down.

Chase knew in situations like these that her training and experience usually prevailed, though he felt torn by not going to take a stand against them. Less than a minute later, the men were approaching his alley.

Chapter Forty-Four

Krauss walked through one of the testing fields located inside a giant, hanger-like building on the Cologne campus. All types of chemicals, including *GET-EM®*, were sprayed on various plants. Soils, seeds, and the vegetation itself were all measured at every stage. The constant blend of smells that others complained about were like a favorite perfume to him. He always thought better in the testing areas. *Progress*, he thought.

Then the nagging feeling caught him again, slamming him against a metaphoric wall . . . The String-Continuum.

I have to stop it, but how can I if I don't know what it is?

Krauss stood there a minute, lost in contemplation, the frustration of it all. An aide cleared his throat, snapping Krauss back to the present.

"The world has gone insane," Krauss lamented to the aide as giant sprayers doused a row of GMO corn. "It used to be oil companies were the most hated in the world. What about the good old days in 2009 when everyone despised banks? But now it's us, a corporation trying to end world hunger. Oh, how everything has gone upside down."

He had just watched large screens in the legislative command center showing worldwide protests against his company. None were going on currently, but Gravacon kept meticulous records, and had footage of just about every protest ever staged against them. They identified people and fought back. "Millions have demonstrated over the years," Krauss continued. "*Millions!*"

"It's the fear of GMOs," the aide offered. "OrgriSource and *GET-EM®* have received so much unfair bad publicity."

"I know *why* it's happening, you idiot!"

"Yes, sir."

"The question isn't why. The question is *why?*"

The aide looked confused.

"GMOs, OrgriSource, and *GET-EM®* are the answer. The reason they hate us is for the ingredients to save them. How can they not understand that world hunger, and its associated poverty, is holding mankind back from its true potential?"

"The environmental fringe groups have brainwashed everyone, scared them, lied, used social media, and the internet to spread conspiracy theories," the aide suggested.

"Of course they have." Krauss shot him another dirty look, impatient the man thought stating the obvious made him look smart. "Try an original thought."

"I thought we were discussing—"

"This isn't open for discussion." He kept walking as an area of bright red tomatoes the size of softballs was sprayed with another mix. "What no one seems to consider is that even if it's all true—all the accusations of ill effects of our chemicals and GMOs—wouldn't that be but a small price to pay for a utopian future of peace and tranquility?"

"Yes," the aide said, thinking the answer was easy.

"No!" He let out a stream of expletives in German. "It shouldn't even be a matter of debate. *No* company on Earth is doing more to benefit humanity, and suffering more as a result of those efforts."

"I tell that to people constantly," the aide said. "Whenever I'm dealing with a public relations issue, I also point out that humans have been genetically modifying organisms ever since our earliest ancestors first created agriculture. Nothing consumers buy in today's markets is the exact same plant it was thousands of years ago."

"What do they say?"

"They think we are going too fast. That it took nature and evolution ten thousand years to do what we do in one."

"They are fools. Of course we want to speed it up—we want to save lives. It would take more than one hundred thousand years to get to where we will be in just a few more. Do they really think our species could last that long by relying on nature? It's preposterous!"

Krauss looked at his phone as a text came in from Krieg: *Missed Malone. Will try again.*

"Is everything all right?" the aide asked, seeing a distressed look on his boss's face.

Krauss, holding his side, suddenly felt sick. "More trouble, but I'll handle it." He pushed a button on his phone, waited until the call went through, said two words, and then hung up.

In the Antwerp lab, everyone continued racing to finish the String Continuum in time. They took turns accessing the samples on the lower level when needed, careful not to be seen.

"We need those samples from Billy," Kali said to Paloma.

"He'll be calling in anytime."

"I hope he's okay."

"He's in Iowa. What could happen to him there?" she asked rhetorically. "Mutsu, when is Billy due?"

Mutsu checked the time. "He's still got a couple of hours until his flight. He's getting in late tonight."

"You actually heard from him at the airport, awaiting his flight?" Kali asked.

"No. I'll pick him up and bring the dirt in first thing." Mutsu looked up from his computer and smiled.

"Okay," she said, wishing they had another day.

"Gravacon claims GMOs conserve soil and reduce the need for herbicides," Bull said to Mutsu, after reading up on the company. "They say it helps farmers by increasing crop yields, and providing increased disease and insect infestation protections. The company insists they are improving agriculture worldwide, that genetically modified plants are drought resistant. Are they? Is any of that true?"

"Production yields were increasing for decades. Way before true GMOs were first introduced," Mutsu said. "Gravacon is taking those long standing trends and trying to fit it into their narrative. They are taking credit for other improvements in agriculture."

"What Gravacon is actually doing," Paloma began,

joining the conversation, "is destroying beneficial soil, creating frankenplants with unknown consequences to human health, and poisoning the water tables and oceans with chemicals."

"Maybe you should go work for Gravacon," WH said to Bull.

"I wasn't defending them," Bull said quickly. "I just wondered where this stuff comes from."

"They have a large propaganda department," Mutsu said, wanting to tell WH to take it easy, but with the news about Ryan weighing on all of them, he let it slide.

"Gravacon is also creating strains of "superweeds" resistant to chemicals," Paloma said. "OrgriSource and *GET-EM®* are so widely used that nature has rapidly developed ways around those products. They have no clues as to the long-term consequences of battling both native and invasive species in the farm fields."

"No one really understands the biodiversity of interrelated plant, animals, insects, us . . . nature doesn't generally make mistakes, or waste resources," Paloma said. "By killing the wrong species at the wrong time, we could be killing ourselves."

Chapter Forty-Five

Colonel Kabongo and his men walked briskly past Chase's hiding place. One of them slowed and looked up his alley, but did not see him. The absence of gunfire meant they had obviously also missed Simon.

Wen found the spot where the passageway hit an intersection splitting four ways—one heading slightly upward, the other three continuing downward in different directions. She realized she'd finally almost reached the bottom. Simon had been right—there were exits, there were ways out—but she was not willing to leave Simon and Chase behind, even for a few minutes of outside reconnaissance.

Wen chose the tunnel that she expected them to go in first, believing the men would anticipate their targets would never go into the most obvious passage, but would instead decide to take a different one. She had been trained to think eight moves ahead, as every confrontation was a chess match.

It worked. They each took one of the tunnels, leaving hers alone. She crept back up, deciding this would be the best chance to stop them. Strategically, a street fight was never a good option.

They had been lucky that the Casement had just opened and that no other tourists were there yet on this early autumn weekday morning. She didn't want innocent people to die, and civilians made any operation more difficult. *There are enough challenges in this situation already*, she thought.

Wen snuck around and pursued one of the Africans down a tunnel. Once alone, she was about to snap his neck, just as he turned around. Wen went for his weapon, but his gun was at the wrong angle. Still, she managed to hit his gun hand with her knee before he could fire. Twisting back in a lightning-fast kick, Wen's foot connected with his face, smashing his head against the stone wall. The man, instantly unconscious, fell to the ground. In a single fluid motion, she snatched his gun and never stopped moving, choosing her next passageway in time to catch another one coming back from his failed search. He saw her at the same moment, the distance too great for her to attack by hand. There was no alternative but to shoot. The gun's report and subsequent echo was deafening.

With the second man out of the way, Wen ran, retracing her steps back to the intersection, and raced into the third passage. Raising her weapon, she fired blindly down the dimly lit corridor, knowing it would prevent the final man from coming toward her. Seconds later, Chase and Simon sprinted breathlessly out of the upper tunnel.

Wen fired into the passage again and then pointed to the first passageway. "Go that way," she shouted, unable to hear her own words. "You can get out!"

"What about you?" Chase asked.

She couldn't hear him, but knew what he was saying. "No!" she yelled firmly. "Go! I'm coming."

Chase followed Simon, who was already jogging down the narrow stone corridor.

Wen sent another burst toward the final man, who still hadn't returned fire. She dashed back to the man she'd shot and dragged his body to the entrance of the passage where the final man was hiding. Propping the dead body up against the wall, Wen fired down the passage again, then bolted out the tunnel Simon and Chase had just taken. The tunnel ended at a cannon. Wen, small enough to slither past it, assumed Simon and Chase would have had to crawl over the top. It didn't matter, glorious fresh air and daylight awaited. The shock of bright light, painful to her eyes, didn't matter—they were free and alive.

Chase pulled up in the Congolese's van, with the back sliding door open. He slowed just enough for Wen to jump in.

"Go!" she yelled.

The van squealed as Chase accelerated, taking a tight curve.

"Incredibly, when we got to the street," Simon yelled breathlessly, "we found their van unattended but with no keys. I grabbed the soil samples from our car, and it only took Chase a second to hot-wire it."

"He's good at that," Wen said, checking behind them, greatly relieved Simon had remembered the dirt.

"Boy is that guy going to be mad," Chase said, as they squealed away. "This is the second time we've stolen their ride."

"Who are they? Where are they from?" Simon asked.

"The Congo," Wen answered, thinking back on the

warning from Tess. "I don't think we've seen the last of them."

Chapter Forty-Six

Colonel Kabongo cursed as he ran out of the Casement and saw them driving away in his van. He made a call to a French connection, who would arrange for a clean-up in Luxembourg. Then he went back inside to check on the man Wen had knocked out. He was just coming to as Kabongo reached him.

"Can you walk?"

Even in his weak and dazed state, the man looked at his superior as if it were an outrageous question. As soldiers, they had been through "the fires of hell and worse." The man, just twenty-one years old, looked around for his comrades.

"No," Kabongo said.

The man, an angry look on his already hard face, pulled himself up. "Where are the murdering westerners?"

In Washington, the FBI conducted raids of Senate and Congressional offices after obtaining search warrants. Capitol Police officers accompanied the federal agents as they collected evidence. The final compromise between Tess and the director came after a CISS report on the Gravacon corruption and influence among US lawmakers was shared with the Director of National Intelligence, who informed the president. Although the president didn't personally read the report, he referred it to the Attorney General, who in turn instructed the FBI to execute search warrants on the suspected senators and congresspeople.

"Thus the president is insulated," Tess told the head of the NSA privately, "much in the same way George W. Bush was several layers away from the weapons of mass destruction lie."

As news of the raids broke, Tess's senate contact, Senator Evans, who sat on the Senate Select Committee on Intelligence, called for an immediate halt to all votes being proposed for any issues until the leadership could determine what effects the allegations and imminent charges would have on pending legislation.

"Just like that, the Gravacon bill is dead," Tess said to her assistant after watching the announcement on television in her private office. "At least for now."

"Congratulations."

"Thank you," Tess said softly, staring at a framed, poster-sized print of the milky way over the Gorge Bridge in Taos, New Mexico, taken by her favorite photographer, Geraint Smith.

Taos, she thought to herself, as she often did in moments of pause. *I wish I was in Taos.* But she wanted a Taos that didn't exist anymore, with someone who was now part of those stars, filling the endless New Mexico sky.

As Chase drove the "borrowed" van toward Antwerp, he and Wen finished explaining to Simon about Congo's food issue.

"It's the reason many smaller countries coping with major hunger and poverty have embraced Gravacon," Chase said. "Krauss is promising them food-independence."

"That's a big deal," Simon said. "When I was in the Peace Corps, I saw so much suffering. Food is everything."

"But with the String-Continuum, the world will be able to cure all these diseases, and addressing hunger will be so much easier."

"I don't know if you realize how many people die every day," Simon said. "These countries have heard promises for decades."

"I saw plenty of hunger growing up in China," Wen said.

Simon nodded.

"Even if they solve their hunger issues in the short term," Chase said as he passed a tractor trailer, "Gravacon's hydenosyn-based products like *GET-EM®* and OrgriSource will give them all cancer and birth defects—the list goes on. And the cruel irony is they won't be able to cure them because the chemicals will have destroyed the only thing that *could* save them."

"Not exactly a great set of choices," Simon said, thinking of all the starving children he saw during his Peace Corps days.

"The countries with the biggest hunger problems also have some of the highest rates of disease and poor health."

"Chicken or egg type thing," Simon said.

"Bottom line," Chase said, "poisoning the soil is dangerous and just plain wrong."

Wen looked down at the soil samples and wondered if the microbes needed to complete the String-Continuum were in them. If they were, the handfuls of dirt they were carrying might just be the most valuable substance on earth.

Chapter Forty-Seven

Wen checked the sideview mirror twice, and then climbed into the back of the van and looked out the window. "This is getting ridiculous," she said. "We have *two* tails."

"Damn it," Chase said. "Which ones?"

"Black sedan, two cars back, our lane. Silver sedan, four cars back, far lane.

"We're going to have to get off the highway. We'll never lose them in all this traffic."

"There's an exit up ahead," Simon said. "City of Hasselt."

"And I need to be driving," Chase said. "I'm kind of a professional at car chases."

"Thus the name?" Simon said.

Chase smiled. "Hey, Hasselt, Belgium, what's the history of the town? When was it settled? What famous battles were fought here?" Chase asked Simon.

"I don't know, I've never been here before."

"Won't your girlfriend be disappointed in you," Chase

said as he checked the mirror and saw the cars following them off the exit.

"My *wife*," Simon corrected.

"Too bad . . . I thought using the turn signal and slowing down to take the exit would have fooled them," Chase said.

"Where do you suggest we stop so you can get in and drive?" Simon asked, ignoring the sarcasm.

"No stopping, I'm just gonna slide in under you."

Chase took the wheel, standing next to the driver's seat, and Simon slid out. Just as Simon's foot left the gas pedal, Chase put his on, but waited until he was in the seat before applying more pressure. Wen stayed in the back, ready to shoot. Simon took the front passenger seat. As they went speeding toward town, a police car got in between them and their two pursuers.

"I'm not planning on stopping," Chase said.

"What if you pull over?" Simon asked.

"Normally that might be a reasonable idea," Chase said. "However, I kind of think the people after us would just assume to kill the cop *and* us at the same time. So the police officer will just have to join in the parade. Hold on."

The police cruiser roared up next to them. Chase sideswiped the car, sending it off the road. With flashing blue lights, the vehicle banked up a sloping knoll rising from the shoulder, flipped, and rolled back down, landing upside down in the road.

"Instant roadblock," Chase said. "See how I did that?"

"Not sure you should be so proud of it." Simon, quite uneasy, gripped the hand hold above him and the side of the seat.

The black sedan plowed into the hood of the police car, spinning it as both pursuing vehicles sped past. Chase's increased speed caused another collision in his wake as a yellow delivery van smashed into a red Volkswagen rabbit.

"Yet another roadblock. Red and yellow is a bit flashier, don't you think?" Chase asked. "I hope nobody was hurt."

Traffic ahead was blocked, so he turned into an underpass area, snapping a parking barricade gate as pedestrians dove out of the way.

"You're going the wrong way!" Simon yelled. "You're going the wrong way!"

"This is the only way that was moving," Chase said.

"But the cars are all moving *at* us!"

Traveling against traffic, in a one way two-lane tunnel, Chase blared the horn, trying to warn oncoming drivers as he wove the vehicle in and out of them. The black pursuing sedan appeared from another on-ramp as they exited the tunnel and crossed through thickening traffic.

"How'd they get around the tunnel so fast?" Simon asked.

"I don't know, maybe *his* navigator has been to Hasselt, Belgium before," Chase said. He thought he actually heard Wen laugh, but couldn't be sure.

Still going the wrong way, but parallel to the other lanes separated by a cement highway barrier, wasn't protection enough, as one of the men in the black sedan began shooting. The back window obliterated in a shattering blast of crystal.

"You okay?" Chase yelled back at Wen.

"Good. I'm just glad they got this glass window out of my way so I can shoot back at the bastards." She fired her MP7 submachine gun. "That'll keep them honest."

Simon, now on the floor behind the front seat, yelled to Wen. "How do you aim at this speed?"

"I don't. My machine gun does all the talking."

The silver sedan raced up behind them as the passenger in the black car continued shooting, pitting the van with bullet holes.

Chapter Forty-Eight

Billy, a twenty-four year-old grad student from Kansas, checked in with Paloma to finalize the range GPS coordinates where he could collect the samples. They had recently accessed satellite data, allowing them to pinpoint soil-type regions. The United States was critical to the String-Continuum project not just because of its size and soil concentration, but because it also had some of the richest, most fertile soil on earth—at least before the Gravacon sterilization had begun with widespread use of hydenosyn and the compounds which had preceded it.

"Ryan is dead," she told him. "You should not continue."

Yesterday, Mutsu had told him about all the missing sample takers, and Billy had believed some of them might have been killed, but hearing the news made him more angry than sad. Billy's father had been a farmer and died of cancer caused by Gravacon products.

"I'm not ever going to stop until they're out of business," he said.

Billy's mission was to locate original soil still in an organic state. Although he didn't always have permission, Billy had used his boy next door looks and aw shucks personality to talk his way out of many prior trespassing situations when collecting samples. He figured the only risk was a slap on the wrist or something like a parking ticket, nothing he couldn't handle, but now Gravacon was *killing* his colleagues.

The fields in Iowa went on as far as the eye could see. Considered some of the best soil on earth, the farmers could grow almost anything—although many favored corn, one of the earliest and most genetically modified crops.

The initial samples Billy needed were easy to get. He simply pulled to the side of the road, walked over to the fields, bent down, scooped up some soil into the sample boxes, GPS-stamped the labels, and put them back in his rental car. He knew those samples were going to be devoid of any meaningful microbes since the entire area was under the influence of hydenosyn-based OrgriSource. The challenge was the next two samples, and as he looked out to the horizon in all directions, seeing nothing but cultivated fields, he wondered if it would even be possible.

Paloma had been optimistic, he thought. *How am I supposed to find dirt that hasn't been subjected to hydenosyn?*

After driving several miles he saw a sign for a town up ahead, Heckabon, Iowa.

Strange name.

The farms went right up to the edge of town, a place so small there wasn't even a post office, or a school. But there was a church, and behind the church was a graveyard. Billy checked the GPS coordinates again and smiled. He was still within range of her specified sampling area. Billy strolled casually up to the little wooden fence that surrounded the cemetery and opened the gate. Looking at the gravestones, he saw that the most recent date was January 19, 2017. In another corner, farthest away from the church, in the most open area, he kneeled down by a gravestone with the date November 17, 1957. Taking out his little shovel, he began to dig beneath the grass.

He looked around to make sure nobody was watching, not sure how he would explain this if he got caught, and filled the sample box with what he hoped was pure organic soil. Walking out, he noticed the stone with his last name and the date August 30, 1975. He latched the gate behind him, pleased with his work, and was just about to get into his car when somebody tapped his shoulder.

Billy turned around, half expecting to be shot, but instead looked into the confused face of a minister. "Excuse me, son, can I help you?"

"No sir, just getting on my way."

"I saw you in the graveyard. You mind telling me what you're up to?"

"My grandfather is buried there, and I wanted a little bit of the dirt as a keepsake."

The minister's eyes softened a little, but he still looked at Billy skeptically. "Who's your grandfather."

"William Beale."

"He was buried there before my time," the minister said. "His sister lives back in Virginia now, but I think he's got a nephew here."

"I don't really know much of this side of the family."

"You mind showing me your ID?"

Billy look surprised. "Is there a law against taking dirt from the cemetery?"

"Why yes," the minister said. "I believe there is, when you don't ask, and it doesn't belong to you."

"Terribly sorry, sir." He took out his driver's license and showed it to the minister.

"William Beale. I guess you were telling the truth."

Billy smiled. "I really should be going."

"Okay," the minister said, handing the license back. "Staying in town?"

"No, just passing through."

"Safe travels."

Billy drove off, strangely shaken by the event. Although not a churchgoer, he still didn't like the idea about lying to a minister. But it was for a good cause, no harm done.

Forty minutes later, just on the edge of Paloma's range, he still had to get the final sample. He hadn't seen any other towns, but he pulled over to a spot where he could see trees not too far away that looked like they might be bordering a creek. Paloma told him that the soil around creeks, even contaminated areas, was often good. He left his car, climbed over a rusty barbed wire fence, and hiked into a cornfield. Eventually he made it to the creek, which had a surprisingly wide grassy bank.

Billy dug in the grass close to the water, pulled up a nice thick sample, filling the container, then sat in the shade for a few minutes, tired from his day's adventures, but happy to be done and ready to drive back to the Des Moines airport.

Walking faster back to his car, now less afraid of attracting attention with the job completed, Billy opened the trunk, unzipped a duffel bag, and added the new sample to the others.

Making a U-turn, he headed back toward the airport. Hungry, and still with enough time before his flight, Billy stopped at a chain restaurant. Forty minutes later, he was on his way, glad he'd stopped for food. He decided he'd phone Paloma once he'd reached his gate at the airport.

At the rental car return lot, he walked to the back to get the duffel of samples and his carry-on bag. As he opened the trunk, the last thing he heard was a series of three quick clicks.

The explosion killed him instantly.

Chapter Forty-Nine

Chase hit the brakes, causing the silver sedan to turn into a delivery truck.

"See if you can get the Astronaut," Chase yelled as he veered. "I want to find out who's after us."

"I'm a little busy at the moment," Wen said, firing back at the black sedan.

"It's called multi-tasking, but whenever you get a chance."

"How can someone do that?" Simon asked.

"There are traffic cameras all over the place. He can tap into them, maybe get a facial ID," Chase said, cranking the wheel hard, taking a last second turn onto a side street. "Welcome to the future. Cameras watch everything." Chase purposely drove through the center of the old town, knowing there would be more cameras. The silver sedan had recovered, and now both cars were behind the van again.

"I've got the Astronaut on the phone," Wen said.

"Okay, I've got your phone on GPS," the Astronaut said

over the speaker. "I see you're in Hasselt, Belgium. Looks like a nice little town. Apparently they have the largest Japanese garden in all of Europe."

Chase glanced back at Simon. "Your girlfriend might like that fact."

"Once you get rid of those bothersome people after you," the Astronaut continued, "maybe you could make a visit. Wen, I know how much you enjoy natural beauty."

"Yeah, that sounds like a great idea," Chase yelled from the front seat. "Is there a bakery around where we could pick up some cupcakes on the way?"

"Ignore him," Wen said.

"Ignore who?" the Astronaut replied.

"Anything?" Wen asked.

"Yes, I just got a hit, and can see you. Where'd you get that clumsy van?"

"Long story."

"Good thing he doesn't bill by the hour," Chase said.

"Seems the police have been alerted to the game. You can expect some company, at any moment. Did you force a police car off the road?"

"I'd rather not answer that question without an attorney present," Chase said.

"I got a match," the Astronaut said. "The driver and passenger in car number one, give me a second . . . the monitor had facial ID'd Eric Granholm as the driver. Seems he is employed by, surprise, Gravacon. Oh, and the passenger is Erhard Krieg, remember him? He's the head of security and safety for Gravacon, scary looking man, wears an eye patch, must think he's a pirate."

"We remember, Wen said.

"Turns out his grandfather was none other than Alton Krieg, prominent SS commander."

"So we're being chased by Nazis?" Simon asked. "Wonderful."

"What else can you tell us about the evil Mr. Krieg—hold on!" Chase yelled back as he pulled the emergency brake, forcing the van into a rapid one-hundred-eighty degree spin, nearly tipping as they slid through a busy intersection, miraculously getting clipped by only one car. Chase then released the brake and stomped on the accelerator, charging back for Krieg. But Krieg's car sailed right past into the intersection, where they were mashed into a multi-car pile-up, police already descending on the scene. Krieg jumped out of the black car, knocked a man—who had just slowed to avoid the pile up—off his motorcycle, jumped on, and rode after them.

"The Nazi doesn't give up," Chase said.

"It seems his three friends have carjacked another vehicle," the Astronaut reported.

Simon, gripping the handhold with white knuckles, yelled, "Why are they after us?" His feet had gone numb from pressing them so hard into the floor.

"They want to feed the world," Chase said, spinning into a turn, jumping a curb, and driving down the sidewalk in order to avoid a red light.

"The carjackers have cut across and appear to be attempting to anticipate your moves," the Astronaut said.

"I can't stand people trying to anticipate my moves," Chase said. "Especially when I'm driving." He pulled the wheel around, drove down a wide set of stone steps from another century, and barely avoided careening into an ancient looking fountain at the bottom.

"I think I might be sick," Simon said.

"Should I pull over?" Chase asked. "Maybe you could catch a ride with Hitler back there." Chase indicated over his shoulder. He had just seen Krieg riding his motorcycle down the steps. "Nothing more annoying than a Nazi who thinks he's Evel Knievel." Chase made a face at his own joke, with its perplexing double meaning.

"You have avoided the carjackers," the Astronaut said. "But I'm afraid you are about to steer into more police."

"Oh, the police are stealing my moves now, too?"

Wen cleaned the remaining glass from the shot-out side window and fired at the motorcycle, missing him, but making him swerve into a street-side café where morning diners, still finishing coffee and croissants, jumped and scrambled out of the way as tables, chairs, dishes, napkins, and cups flew in all directions. Krieg, somehow maintaining control, rode out the other side, back onto the street.

"Where are the police you promised me?" Chase asked.

"You should see them about now," the Astronaut said. "There is a makeshift roadblock with officers actually pointing guns just ahead."

Simon threw up out the window.

Wen moved to the front beside Chase.

"I see it!" Chase yelled. "That's a whole lot of guns!"

Chapter Fifty

Chase prepared to blast through the roadblock, thinking the van had the heft to move the smaller police vehicles.

"I think they want me to stop," he said.

"There," Wen yelled, pointing to a narrow alley.

Chase stomped the brakes and wrenched the wheel at the same time.

"No, it's too tight, we'll never get through!" Simon yelled, bracing as if he were on a plane, about to crash.

"I thought you've never been to this town?" Chase said. "So how do you know we can't fit?"

"Chase!" Wen said, in a combination of a whispered shout. She was nervous about making it, but knew his driving skills were almost as good as her shooting skills.

The van scraped into the cobblestone alley, ripping paint, grinding metal with sparks on both sides. The side view mirrors tore off. Stray trash cans and boxes got pushed ahead of the van as if it were a snowplow moving garbage. The van continued pushing through with the sheer force of its V6 engine, barely winning out over the centuries old buildings.

"We're making it!" Simon yelled.

"So far," Chase said. "These building practices weren't exactly strict code enforcement three hundred years ago, or whenever these relics were constructed, because the walls were farther apart at the beginning of the alley."

Within a few more seconds, the van ground to a halt, wedged, as if melded into the walls.

"Great, now we're trapped!" Simon said. "We can't open the damned doors. I told you this was going to happen—you should've *listened* to me!"

"Hey, Simon, no one likes to hear 'I told you so,'" Chase said, sounding amazingly calm.

Wen was already heading to the backdoors of the van. Chase climbed over the seat and followed her. "Look," Wen said. "They had extra guns back here. You don't think they'll mind if we use them, do you?"

"The motorcycle is turning into the alley," the Astronaut said, still on the line.

Wen fired some shots toward him. Krieg stopped the bike, used it to shield himself, and returned fire.

Chase climbed up onto the roof of the van and gave Simon, who had grabbed the soil samples again, a hand up. At the same time, Chase, carrying a bag of extra guns slung over his shoulder, shot a burst toward Krieg to give Wen cover to climb up onto the van. She managed to put enough bullets into the bike that it was no longer drivable. Its fuel was leaking everywhere, and after a couple more shots, the motorcycle burst into flames.

Chase, Wen, and Simon dropped down in the front of the van and ran out the other end of the alley, down the street, where a florist delivery van had just pulled over. They jumped in.

"Another van?" Wen said.

"I would've preferred something sportier," Chase said, squealing away from the curb as the delivery man ran out, yelling after them. "But at least you can't say I never got you flowers."

"You did? How nice, where are they?" Wen asked.

"Look in the back," Chase said. "I picked them out just for you. Sorry I didn't have time for a card, but you know I love you."

Wen smiled as she lowered the window, checking back just as Krieg came running out of the alley.

"Astronaut, are you still there?" Chase asked.

"Still here."

"Fastest way to the highway, if you please."

"I would recommend *not* getting on the highway until you change vehicles again," the Astronaut said. "The police have just gotten a report of the stolen van you are in."

"Okay, but that takes all the fun out of it," Chase said.

"I'm not having as much fun as you are!" Simon yelled from the back as he rolled into an arrangement of flowers congratulating a couple on their twenty-fifth wedding anniversary.

"Somebody smarter than me once said, 'never complain, never explain'," Chase said, and added, "Take time to smell the flowers." He smiled back at Simon.

"Take a look at that, will you?" Chase said, pulling into a small train station. "A nice parking lot full of great cars to choose from."

"It's a commuter lot," the Astronaut said. "Good choice. By the time somebody notices you borrowed their car, you should be safely back in Antwerp."

"How about that van?" Wen said, trying to suppress a smile as she pointed to a brown minivan.

"I think, given the choice, always take the Mercedes," Chase said, stopping next to a sporty, blue, recent model. Wen quickly broke out the back window and unlocked the doors. The car alarm wailed as Chase crawled in the front and disabled it before anyone would've noticed the all too common modern sound. Within seconds, he had the vehicle hot-wired. He handed three long stemmed red roses to Wen.

"How?" she asked, inhaling their scent.

Chase just winked and pulled out of the parking lot with Simon, the precious dirt, and the gun bag, safely snug in the backseat.

"I'll erase all the security cameras in this lot and the neighboring streets," the Astronaut said, "so they won't be able to determine which vehicle you borrowed."

"That's very helpful, thanks."

"Try to drive gently," the Astronaut said.

Gently? Chase thought smugly, as he soon had them back on the highway and Hasselt was just a memory.

"I would like to get back to that Japanese garden someday," Wen said, checking the sideview mirror.

Chapter Fifty-One

Wen and Simon went up to the Antwerp lab while Chase stayed outside to make a call. They'd abandoned the Mercedes several blocks off campus.

Chase waited to be put through to Krauss, wondering if the man would have the guts to take the call.

"I hope you have a good reason for bothering me again," Krauss said, still reeling from the news that the US Congress had delayed the vote. "I thought we'd said all we needed to say. I'm busy saving the world, while you're making mud pies."

"Is that how you're going to play it?" Chase asked. "Because I just left your attack dog, pirate Krieg, back in some little town where hopefully the local police have read him his rights about now."

"Krieg?"

"I expected you to have a better line of excuse."

"I'm just confused. What are you whining about?"

"I'm saying that next time you send somebody to kill

me, you make sure that they succeed, because if you think I was upset before, you haven't begun to see fury."

"Ah, big scary Chase Malone . . . Aren't you a software engineer? Or, I'm not even sure if you're *that* anymore. Stop wasting my time with idle threats."

"This isn't about wasting time," Chase said. "This is about—"

Krauss coughed. "I'll tell you what this is about . . . food. Food for the people of the world. And you've been warned. I will *not* be stopped."

"You're going to prison, Krauss. I'm going to prove that you've known all along about how dangerous hydenosyn is."

"You can't prove anything. And even if you do, it'll be too late. I'm untouchable."

"Really? You'd better look over your shoulder, because we're coming."

"It's people like you who screwed up this world. You look at me, and judge me, you lay this corporate greed trip on me, but it's your arrogant, sanctimonious attitude, thinking you know what's best for the people in the poor countries, a man who has benefited from all the riches of the world being stolen and siphoned by America. You stand in judgment, with the audacity to proclaim what is right and what is wrong, what the truth is . . . " He coughed again. "When what you really are is afraid. You're afraid to see what will happen if everybody is on an equal playing field."

"No, that's not me," Chase seethed through gritted teeth. "You're projecting your distorted, twisted self-image onto me. But you're wrong. *You're* the one trying to jam your poison down the throats of the world, the desperate who can't say no, who will do anything for the chance of feeding themselves, consequences be damned. You're a pariah.

You're even worse than that—you're a parasite, because you're feeding on the weak, the injured and dying."

"Don't talk to me about dying in hunger. You go to those places, and then you come back, and if there's anything left of you, *then* we can have a conversation, but otherwise, you can burn in hell." Kraus was spitting he was so upset, his face red and puffy and bloated. He coughed uncontrollably.

"I'll meet you there any time."

"You won't be meeting me. You've got a bigger problem now. Krieg rarely misses, and he never misses twice, so *you* look over *your* shoulder!" The line went dead.

Storming to a window of his large tower office, Krauss's coughing turned to hacking and wheezing. "Chase Malone!" he screamed as he looked out toward Cologne, a view that always calmed him. He wished he could visit the mighty cathedral right then, but he just didn't have the time or energy.

He tapped the button to connect him with Krieg, furious that Malone was still walking on the planet and threatening his every plan, the grand design, his legacy.

His head of Security and Safety did not answer, further enraging him. Krauss made another call. When the person answered, he said only three words before disconnecting.

"Finish it tonight."

Chapter Fifty-Two

Chase walked into the lab, still fuming from his conversation with Krauss. Wen hadn't wanted him to make the call, but he couldn't let the attempt on their lives go by without pushing back.

Wen and Simon had already been introduced to WH, and the three of them were helping Paloma set up the new samples. They needed to get the process started quickly, and then move the Luxembourg and French dirt to the relative safety of the lower floor office.

Wen looked at Chase, reading his face. She whispered, "*Breathe.*"

"How's the String-Continuum coming?" Chase asked, taking a deep breath.

Bull looked up from a chart depicting the twelve soil orders overlaid on a map of Europe's eco-zones and waved to Chase.

Chase smiled at the hacker he and Wen had saved from the depths of the dark web, where she'd discovered secrets no one was ever supposed to see.

"The dirt you brought will help a lot," Mutsu said. The lab manager then introduced Chase and WH.

"What does WH stand for?" Chase asked.

"William Howard."

"With two fine names like that, you couldn't find one you liked?"

WH laughed. "I don't know, everyone just always called me WH."

"He almost got taken out in Congo," Mutsu said.

"Sorry," Chase said. Paloma had told them about Ryan when they called in from the road.

"We just got word that Billy Beale, one of our sample-collectors in the States, missed his plane in Iowa."

"Have you tried calling him?" Chase asked, wanting to get Krauss back on the phone to ask him if killing college kids was just another cost of ending world hunger.

"He's not picking up. We've contacted the local authorities."

"WH is our hero," Paloma interrupted. "The dirt from the Congo has the highest concentration of cross-section microbes of any we've tested so far. That poor little country may be the Saudi Arabia of cures."

"Congratulations," Chase said. "What's a cross-section microbes?"

"They are very unique in that they connect to most other microbes. When we try to complete the String-Continuum, microbes only join certain other ones."

"Like a specific sequence?" Wen asked.

"Exactly. And that's why it takes so long, and why the missing ones from the US are so critical. It's called the String-Continuum because it's all connected—that's where the curing power comes from—but they go together in different models. And the ones from the Congo are kind of like a Rosetta Stone."

"They can talk to almost any microbe?" Wen asked.

"Yes!" Paloma clapped her hands. "We're going to do this!"

"In time?" Chase asked.

"Maybe . . . Depending on what the programs do with this soil, and if they can fill in the many blanks. I think we have a great shot now."

"I just got off the phone with customs in Brussels," Mutsu said. "They've got a container of soil they're holding from Ryan. It needs to be signed for by either Ryan or WH, since they're the ones on the original manifest."

"We need that dirt," Paloma said.

"I'm on my way," WH said. "Just tell me where to go."

"It's too dangerous," Kali said. "How many do we want to lose?"

Paloma looked at Kali as if she'd just smashed her microscope. "That dirt could be enough to finish," Paloma said.

"I'll be fine," WH said.

"We'll take him," Wen suggested, looking at Chase.

He nodded. "Sure, I'm happy to drive a few more hours, as long as we don't have to take a van." He looked at Simon and raised his eyebrows. "Come along for a ride?"

"You can take my car," Paloma said. "If you can handle a Mercedes."

Wen laughed. "You said the magic word."

"Then it's settled?" Paloma asked, looking at Kali.

"Okay."

"Dude, if you're riding with them," Simon said, "I hope you've got a barf bag, and good life insurance."

Chapter Fifty-Three

Halfway to Brussels, Chase reluctantly pulled over and let Wen drive, as a call came in from Tess.

"The US vote is delayed," she said as he picked up.

"Are you kidding me?"

"Does that sound like me?"

"No, it doesn't," Chase admitted. "How?"

"Don't ask," Tess said, watching the story continuing to unfold from CISS Mission Control. "We're still working on the EU and others, but I'm not as optimistic."

"Still, without the US . . ."

"Remember, it's only a temporary reprieve. It might still get messy."

"Gravacon on the ropes," Chase announced to the others in the car.

"You underestimate them. You're really in it deep this time," she said, taking a sip of her Caffè Mocha, making a disappointed frown, as it was made with almond milk this time. Her dairy allergies flared during high stress, but the extra shot of espresso and dose of chocolate helped prepare her for another late night. "And I'm not even sure how much I can do at this point. Lars Krauss is a powerful man, and collects politicians and influence the way others collect art."

"He wants to end world hunger."

"I don't believe that for a minute. I learned a long time ago that it's not important what a person says, and it doesn't even much matter what they do. What's important at the end of the day is what happened," Tess said. "In this case, what's going to happen is that Gravacon holds the patent on seeds and the process for growing food to the exclusion of all other current methods. That means, sooner or later, ultimately one man will control the food supply for most of the world."

"If that does come to pass, as frightening as that prospect alone is, we have no idea the ramifications of their chemicals, the long-term impact, and I'm not even talking about the health of producers and consumers, I'm talking about the environment . . . Gravacon's chemicals could easily end up sterilizing the planet."

"Our concern is the food control."

"So that's why you're helping me?" Chase asked.

"We're working our own angles against Gravacon. As you know, that's what we do—keep the corporations in line from getting too powerful, tipping the balance. You should know enough from what you saw in the tech world to know how close the corporations are to completely taking over." She paused. "But the reason I'm helping you doesn't have much to do with any of that. I've always been impressed with you and Wen, but I'm more impressed with my IT-Squads, large staff of technicians, analysts, and our network of operatives around the world—so, no offense."

"Then why?"

"Flint Jones."

Chase hadn't heard the name of his former head of security for quite a while, and it felt like getting punched. A good man, Flint had saved his life several times, and in the end, there were still circumstances surrounding his death that Chase didn't fully understand. "What about Flint?"

"He asked me to make him a promise before he died." She paused again, getting lost in the image of Flint dying in her arms. Her eyes filled, yet she swallowed the emotion, steadied herself, and walked across the busy Mission Control into Secure, a room where no one could overhear or see her calls. *New Mexico Rain*, a favorite song, sung by Michael Hearne, that she and Flint used to dance to, interrupted that tender image and played abruptly in her head. Tess closed the door, sat down, and took a deep breath. "Flint asked me to protect you." Her voice was a little shaky.

"Why?" Chase asked, genuinely stunned, softening his voice.

"I don't know."

"Then why did you say yes?"

"Because he asked."

"So?"

"Do you love Wen?"

"Of course," Chase answered, confused at the question.

"If she asked you to do something, would you do it?"

"Absolutely."

"*Anything?*"

"Yes, I have many times."

"And if she was dying, and she made one last request to you?"

"I would make it my mission to do nothing else until it

was done," Chase said, understanding, even though it surprised him. "You loved Flint Jones?" he whispered.

"More than you could ever know."

Chase was momentarily speechless, as a hundred thoughts and questions flew through his mind. Dozens of moments between him and Flint, between Chase and Tess, replayed in a montage of confusion and clarity that made his head hurt. This was a woman he did not trust. If he were the main character in a novel, he knew Tess Federgreen would be his antagonist, and yet she was making the unbelievable claim, like a fairy godmother, that she was working to protect him at the behest of her now deceased great love.

He shook his head, and, still not knowing what to say, opened his mouth for the first words to stumble out. "I'm sorry." As he said it, he wasn't sure why, or what he was sorry for, but he had sounded sincere, because, somehow, he meant the words.

"Thank you," she whispered, the strain of loss and maybe a trace of odd forgiveness lacing her tone.

Chase wanted to ask her how long this promise was good for. Surely there was an expiration date, maybe until she met another man, or married, or he did something she *really* didn't like . . . he didn't know.

"Be careful, Chase," she said. "I can only do so much."

Chapter Fifty-Four

It took under forty minutes to get to the Brussels airport, and almost that much additional time to clear customs, before they were finally heading back to Antwerp with yet another precious cargo of dirt.

"I do like this car," Chase said as they merged into traffic heading north. "Mercedes-Benz C63—Paloma has good taste. Not sure how she affords it on a researcher's salary."

"Her husband is a big shot surgeon," WH said.

"Nice ride," Chase repeated, thinking about the call from Tess. With all their history, he knew he shouldn't trust her, but she had stopped the vote, she had warned him in France. Yet, at the same time, the CIA, *her* CIA, had given his location to the Congo militants.

His thoughts were interrupted by a familiar refrain from Wen.

"We're being followed," she said. "Green Jaguar."

"Unbelievable," Chase moaned. "I feel like we've been chased all over Europe."

"We have," Wen agreed, readying her MP7.

"Let's try not to get Paloma's beautiful Mercedes all shot up," Chase said.

"I guess Simon was right about the life insurance," WH said from the backseat. "I thought once I got out of Africa, I'd be safe."

"Don't worry," Chase said. "I'm a professional race car driver. We won't let anything happen to you." He hit the accelerator.

"This is why we didn't let you go to Brussels alone," Wen assured WH. "We're good at this."

The driver of the Jaguar sped up and rammed their back bumper.

"This guy means business," Chase said, flooring the gas pedal. "Let's see what this Twin Turbo Premium V-8 can do."

Chase managed to put some distance between them while Wen checked the magazine in her gun.

"Maybe I should've taken the train," WH said, only half joking.

"There's probably people also waiting for you on the train," Wen said.

"The Jag is coming up again, faster," WH said, watching out the back window.

"I'd like to find an exit," Chase said, as he veered onto the shoulder, tearing past a line of cars.

"That's probably what they want you to do," Wen said. "We're safer on the highway."

"Not if they start shooting." Chase maneuvered back onto the road, weaving in and out of other cars.

"You just passed a Porsche," WH yelled.

Chase barely missed clipping a Toyota as he swerved between it and a BMW.

"How fast are we going?" WH asked.

"Not fast enough!" Chase snapped without even looking at the speedometer, which was exceeding two-hundred-twenty kph, which was around one-hundred-forty mph, as they roared toward two slowing semitrucks ahead of them.

"Chase!" Wen yelled.

"I see them, I see them." Instead of hitting the brakes, Chase took his foot off the gas for only a moment, and then slammed it back on again, swerving onto the loose shoulder, spraying gravel, fishtailing, sideswiping the guard rail, and then whipping back onto the highway in front of the trucks. Chase whooped. "Four hundred sixty-nine horses and four hundred seventy-nine pounds of torque!" He opened it up again, taking the one clear lane like a runway, hoping to lose the pursuers still behind the semis.

It didn't take long before the Jaguar came screaming up between the now separated trucks, horns blaring from the big rigs.

"Where are the cops when we need them?" WH asked.

"I just prefer we handle this ourselves," Wen said, knowing she and Chase were traveling under false passports and with illegal weapons. The last thing she wanted was Interpol, or worse, any intelligence organizations, looking into her true identities, backgrounds, and past.

Traffic began stacking up ahead of them, and this time the shoulder was blocked by a tow truck. Wen looked ahead to see if the police had arrived yet, and was relieved they had not.

"Here they come!" WH yelled.

"Hold on," Chase said, expecting the Jaguar to ram them again. Instead, it stayed back.

"Why aren't they hitting us?" WH asked nervously.

"They know we're armed," Wen said.

"Aren't they?" WH asked.

"It's safe to assume that they are, and they've decided a traffic jam isn't the best place for a gun battle."

"You should get down on the floor anyway," Chase said to WH.

"I'll get carsick."

"I think you'd rather throw up than get shot up. Do it!" Chase yelled.

WH complied.

They crept past the tow truck and the traffic flow started to pick up slightly. Chase cranked the wheel hard, and tore up the shoulder once again, breaking away from the Jaguar, but the lead didn't last long as the Jaguar flew onto the shoulder and pulled within one car length of them. A man came out of the sunroof and began firing.

Chapter Fifty-Five

Bullets ripped into the sleek, sapphire-blue metal of the Mercedes as Chase tried to find a way to put more distance between them.

"Damn it!" Chase yelled as another four bullets hit. "You okay back there?"

"Still here, but there's a bullet hole three inches from my head," WH said.

"All good," Wen said. "Paloma is not going to be happy."

"She'll be less happy if we don't get there alive with the dirt!" WH yelled.

The Jaguar was gaining. Chase jerked the wheel, knocking them into another lane where the Jag sideswiped a pickup truck. The collision with the Jag had ripped and smashed the side of Paloma's car.

"Now maybe she won't notice the bullet holes," Chase quipped.

The Jaguar recovered quickly and pulled parallel, with only two feet separating them and the Mercedes. Chase was about to slam them again when a slow moving car ahead forced him and the Jaguar to veer around it. Chase looked up and saw a line of three semis and knew if they didn't time it right, they could get trapped again. He punched it just as the Jaguar was coming close, clipped them in the corner, sending him into another car that careened off the road, taking two more vehicles with it. The Jaguar stayed on the road and swung out in front of them.

A man emerged from the sunroof again and began firing—taking out the headlights and both passenger side windows of the Mercedes.

"This guy really wants these samples," Chase yelled to WH. "Where did Ryan get that dirt? Some mafia guy's garden?"

Chase raced past one of the semis. The Jaguar came in, trying again to ram them. Nearing the second semi—a new car transport hauling seven Volvos—Chase knocked a minivan out of its lane. The minivan crashed and flipped into the carrier, breaking the chains, and releasing a car. The violent collision, twisting and rocking caused such a reaction that more chains snapped, sending multiple cars off the carrier. Some remained, chains dragging and flipping until their bonds snapped.

A red Volvo bounced directly over the Mercedes. Chase steered around the streams of sparks and spinning vehicles. The new cars wrecked, flipped, and rolled, exploding bumpers and doors as the cars twisted into oncoming traffic and the unforgiving pavement at seventy miles per hour. The scene in his rearview looked as if a giant toddler was dumping out their collection of Matchbox cars.

The pile-up and chaos forced Chase off the highway, over a guard rail, down across the median, where, somehow, for a moment, they were facing oncoming traffic before

Chase forcefully got the car back under control and bounced over the grassy median again. But the embankment betrayed them, and the Mercedes launched into the air, flying nearly thirty feet before slamming back onto the right side of the highway where they mashed into a Smart Car, sending it pin balling into a couple of other vehicles.

Chase stomped the gas pedal, having no idea where the Jaguar was, and fishtailed around a line of cars, back out onto the shoulder.

"They're still with us," Wen shouted, checking the side mirror. "About two hundred feet back.

"How do they do that?" Chase asked, unable to mask his admiration for the Jag's driver, yet frustrated at the same time.

"Maybe you should take that on-ramp," Wen yelled as they passed a merging lane coming into the highway. "We've done enough damage here. I don't want any other innocents getting hurt! This is crazy!"

"That would be pretty tricky," Chase said, as it was now in the rearview mirror and he'd have to turn around while they were going over one hundred miles per hour.

"I thought you could do tricky."

"Normally, but I don't want to risk getting in an accident with Paloma's nice Mercedes."

WH had stopped being shocked by the dialogue around him, realizing that the more intense the situation got, the more Chase joked. He just hung on, second by terrifying second.

Chase sped up, taking the speedometer past three hundred kilometers per hour—more than 190 mph—the growl of the engine and roar of the wind coming in through the shot-out side-windows making it feel and sound as if they were in a fighter jet. He managed to increase the distance between the Jag until, once again, traffic bottle-necked and Chase had to slow to under one-hundred.

A minute later, a new car rammed the back of them.

"Where'd that Mustang come from?" WH yelled, now off the floor.

"Looks like they took Wen's on-ramp idea," Chase said.

"Now there are *two* of them after us?" WH said. "Can you handle that?"

"For a smart guy," Chase said, "you sure ask some silly questions. Maybe I should just pull over and give them the damn dirt. The question is, WH, can *you* handle this?"

The two pursuing cars fought to sandwich the Mercedes. Chase saw his chance up ahead—an RV in one lane, and a large pickup truck towing a boat in the other. Neither seemed willing to let the other pass. Chase waited until the last instant as the Jaguar and Mustang were about to attempt to crunch him from both sides. Chase hit the brakes, spun the car in a full one-eighty, and sped back down the shoulder. The two pursuing cars smashed into each other and then plowed into the back of the RV. The Jaguar impaled into the outboard motor of the cabin cruiser, bringing the entire boat flipping over on top of it. The pickup pulling the boat caught a piece of the RV, which tipped over and slid forward as the Mustang crashed into it. The cluster of vehicles was immediately joined by a dozen others as the horrendous pile-up burst into flames.

Chase took the Mercedes screaming down the shoulder, then flew up the on-ramp and turned onto the overpass. They stopped to view the spectacle and confirm the Jaguar and Mustang were not going to ever drive again. WH pushed out the broken door and vomited. Police cars appeared on the highway from both directions. Chase yelled at WH to get back in while giving him his most winning smile, and turned onto a backroad.

"Hey, I'm two-for-two with passenger's losing their lunch," Chase said. "I wonder if it's my driving."

"It's definitely your driving," WH said. "And you're going to tell Paloma what, exactly? She really loves this car."

"I will simply ask her what color would she like her new Mercedes to be."

Chapter Fifty-Six

In the Antwerp lab, they had pulled the shades from the strong afternoon sun, which always heated the room just prior to sunset. It was going to be another all-nighter. Other than a few smoking breaks, Bull hadn't left since she'd first arrived at dawn. Knowing their mutual hunger and wanting to chain smoke, Bull volunteered to go get dinner for everybody. Kali, also wanting some fresh air, offered to show Bull where to go, and the two of them headed out together, promising to return with an incredible feast of Chinese food. Simon left with them, having to meet his wife at a previously scheduled function.

Mutsu, Paloma, and three other lab workers continued sifting the data, trying desperately to achieve three objectives: summarize the cancer-causing and other health risks of hydenosyn, continue the trials against their first four major diseases—including two types of cancer, Alzheimer's, and diabetes—and, most important, complete the String-Continuum.

The votes were still taking place Wednesday in most of

the world, and it seemed impossible they could complete the enormous undertakings within so short a time, but as Paloma reminded them, part of the way might be good enough. She had just sent the most complete String-Continuum to the offsite and in-lab backups.

We have it, she thought, looking at the 3D illustration.

"If our data is convincing, we should be able to buy more time."

Bull and Kali had been gone for nearly an hour, so no one bothered to look when the door to the lab opened. Hungry, and assuming it was Kali and Bull with the food, one of the lab assistants turned, smiling, anticipating dinner.

She was shot immediately. And although the killer's gun had been fitted with a suppressor, silencers were only silent in the movies. In the confined space of the lab, they all instantly knew Hell had just arrived.

Mutsu grabbed a chair and flung it back toward the gunmen, then dove under a table. He thought there were four intruders, maybe more.

Paloma also hit the floor behind a heavy counter. Seeing Mutsu throw the chair gave her the idea to toss a microscope. It hit one of the gunmen in the chin, an angry looking guy with an eye patch. It left a bloody gash, and Paloma was shocked that he didn't scream in pain. Krieg turned toward her, disgusted that a black woman and a Japanese immigrant were interfering with his mission.

In the initial moments, the two remaining lab assistants, cowering in different sections of the lab, were shot by the men. Only Paloma and Mutsu remained, unarmed against four assassins.

Chasing Dirt

As Mutsu crawled on the floor to try to get to Paloma, he saw the man with the eyepatch storming toward her. Mutsu managed to kick a table over right in front of Krieg, causing him to trip. Another one of the gunmen rushed to help Krieg untangle himself from the table and other equipment that had also toppled. Paloma sent a digital scale zipping through the air, which bounced off the back of one of the men's heads as he was bending down. At the same time, Mutsu found the ultimate weapon—a swiveling wood and metal stool that he used to charge the enemy like a knight going after an opponent with a lance. He smashed it into the face of one of the men. Blood burst from his nose as he went reeling backward. That's when the first bullets cut into Mutsu. He collapsed onto the floor, writhing in pain for only an instant. There was more to come.

Mutsu intuitively knew he was never going to leave that room alive, but there was a slim chance he could save Paloma, if he could somehow get a gun. The bloody-nose man had dropped his. Mutsu, abandoning all instincts of self-preservation, dove for it. He desperately hoped he could reach the gun and then figure out what to do with it. He'd never shot one before. Even as a kid, his parents had not let him or his siblings play with them. And not being a fan of violent movies, he didn't have much to go on.

Krieg got up and went for Paloma again. It no longer seemed as if he wanted to shoot her. She saw the look in his eye as he came at her—a man filled with rage, enjoying his work. A career-killer who meant to hurt her with his bare hands. Once he was close enough, she kicked as hard as she could between his legs. Her foot connected and brought him to his knees, but there was still no cry of pain, and even with half his strength sapped by the blow, he was strong enough to reach out and grab her hair, pulling her down hard onto the floor.

He squeezed her neck. Frantically, she got four of his fingers into her mouth and bit down—pulling and chewing, grinding her teeth until bone crunched and blood squirted in her mouth, then spewed out. The torture elicited a muffled groan from Krieg, and he thrust an elbow into the side of her head, leaving her ears ringing and disengaging her vicious hold.

Mutsu took another bullet into his buttocks just as his fingertips reached the gun. Using every ounce of concentration to ignore his wounds, he extended his arm.

Just get my hand on that gun . . .

Suddenly, as if by magic, it slipped into his palm. He gripped the gun like a savior. A bullet caught him in the abdomen as he rolled over and wildly fired three quick shots in the direction from where the shooting had come. One of them hit the man and dropped him to the floor, just like in the movies he had never seen. Stunned that he'd actually hit something, Mutsu swung the gun around and fired at a blur he thought was another man. Bullets came back at him. One nicked his shoulder, and he went down.

Who shot me? How many are there? Three, no four . . . Could there be five?

Weak now, he found cover behind a heavy worktable, mounted on top of five-foot wide map drawers, and wondered if there could be any escape.

Chapter Fifty-Seven

Krieg ripped the rest of his left hand out of Paloma's mouth and thrust it back into her face. His bloody fingers clawed at her eyes as he tried to pull her nose off. She screamed, kicking and hitting, frantic to free herself, or at least to do as much damage to the monster as she could. The rage in her unleashed a fury of strength.

The bloody-nosed man stumbled to his feet and started firing blindly toward Mutsu's worktable, but his shots did nothing more than announce his exact location.

The lab manager stood, ignoring the dead bodies of his coworkers, and fired two shots at close range. By some incredible stroke of luck, both bullets hit the man's chest. Before it even registered to Mutsu that he had just killed two men, he turned to find the pirate attacking Paloma, and lined up a shot. Shaking and afraid he might hit Paloma, he fired anyway. *Click, click, click.* The gun was empty. Mutsu panicked and threw the gun at Krieg's back. Krieg wrenched backwards at the blow, giving Paloma a very brief reprieve.

Mutsu didn't stop to see where the gun went. Instead, he scrambled toward bloody-nose-man's, body hoping his guns still had ammo. He never made it. The third man came from behind a desk and shot Mutsu from just four feet away. He crumpled to the floor, a fallen hero.

Paloma, taking advantage of Krieg's reflexive jerk from being hit by the gun, got both hands to her face and finally disconnected the pirate's claws. It was her turn to swing an elbow, just like Krieg had taught her seconds before, but before she could jam it into his ribs, he caught her arm with his bloody left hand, gripping it like death. He grabbed her throat with his other hand, shook her violently, then shoved her back against the wall.

She landed hard and woozy. Trying to get up, her legs like jelly, she took a breath, trying to clear her mind. But he was there again, picking her up and slamming her down on the table, as if he was going to rape her. Instead, he laid on top of her with his mouth only inches from hers. With both hands squeezing around her throat, he said to her, "Good night sweetheart. Your nightmare is over now," and he kissed her as the last breath escaped her quivering body.

Krieg got up, straightened his clothes, looked at his bleeding hand, and then back at her. He ripped open her blouse and spit on her dead body.

"These guys are pretty bad," the other man said, checking the bodies of the two downed Gravacon men, "but they're still breathing."

"They aren't going to make it," Krieg said, expertly pulling two computer drives out.

"White's really not too bad," the man said. "I'm not sure if he can walk, but—"

"*They are not going to make it,*" Krieg repeated firmly.

"We've been in here too long. We've got to go before the police show up."

Just inside the door, Krieg's men had brought in two twenty-liter cans of gasoline and an incendiary device. Krieg pointed to them. The reluctant man picked up one of the cans and started spreading gas around the room, then through the hall and down the steps. The lab building was part of the annex, and appeared deserted, as everyone had left for the day.

Krieg poured some gas on Paloma, tossed the can across the room, toward the former dirt storage cabinet, then joined the other man on the lower level where he'd just finished applying some pyro-putty to the maintenance room electrical panel. The two Gravacon men walked quickly to the exit next to the stairwell. Krieg sparked a small flare and dropped it on the floor, watching for a moment as the flame rapidly climbed the stairs and another moved down the hall to the maintenance room. They left the building.

"We'll have to get Kali Garodia, the other scientist, at her home later tonight," Krieg said, wrapping a handkerchief around his bleeding hand. "Hope she's more fun than this one."

Chapter Fifty-Eight

Wen looked at Chase's phone. "It's Tess."

Chase pulled over again to take the head of CISS's call. They were just outside of Antwerp, and needed to get the dirt to the lab. Wen took over driving.

"The president just screwed us," Tess said. "He cut some sort of deal with congressional leadership, and they're going to vote on the continued spending resolution tomorrow morning, which still includes the Gravacon addendum."

"What? Whose side is he on?"

"It's complicated."

"It always is."

"What I mean is, it is entirely possible he's in Gravacon's pocket, but he also may not be. They need the continued spending resolution to avert a financial crisis. Ultimately, it doesn't matter why the vote is going forward, we just need to figure out a way to stop it."

"We're fifteen minutes from the lab. They may have proof."

"Some science experiment isn't going to cut it.

We need irrefutable proof of Gravacon's corruption, bribes, payoffs, kickbacks, falsifying studies, etcetera. Nothing else is going to stop the vote," she said, thinking about all the efforts of the congressional break-ins and raids. In the long run, they could still be useful, but it was Washington. It could all get buried. "We need something to feed the worldwide media."

"What are you suggesting?"

"You need to go inside Gravacon headquarters."

"That's crazy," Wen said, looking at Chase.

"Count me in," WH said from the backseat.

"I can help," Tess said. "My people can't go in, but they will offer advance support and intel."

"Sounds risky," Chase said.

"It's the only way," Tess pushed. "And there is another reason to go."

"What?"

"Dirt."

"What's that mean?"

Tess laughed. "Aren't you people running around the world scooping up buckets of dirt?" She didn't wait for an answer. "And you're missing good samples from the United States . . ."

"How do *you* know this?"

"Never mind. What if I told you that Gravacon took before soil samples."

"Before? Are you saying what I think you are?" he asked, still trying to figure out how she knew this much about their secret quest to complete the String-Continuum.

"Yes. They have soil samples, from all over the US, taken *before* they started using OrgriSource and other hydenosyn-based products."

"Incredible . . . and these are inside their headquarters?"

"They are."

"Then we need your help."

But is this the set-up? Chase wondered. *Is she using Wen and me to do her dirty work, leaving us to take the fall?*

"I'll call you back," Chase said.

The discussion between Chase and Wen, with WH interjecting comments in favor of the expedition, didn't last long. Wen called her contact for a grocery delivery, their code for guns and equipment. A man was already in Antwerp for their scheduled drop off in the morning. They moved it up, and would meet in a little used park near the river in twenty-five minutes.

WH called Paloma. "It's going straight to voicemail," he told Chase and Wen. "She turns it off sometimes when's she's pushing a deadline."

"This certainly qualifies," Chase said.

"I'll try Mutsu."

"Forget that," Chase said. "You'll be there soon enough. Simon's at an art opening with his wife, right up here. We'll drop you and the dirt there, and you both can take it to the lab. Have Paloma call me once she looks at these samples and tells me how close they are to String Continuum."

"Then you'll pick me up to go to Gravacon?" WH asked.

"Yeah," Chase agreed. "We'll need you and Simon."

"Are you sure?" Wen asked WH, but it was also directed to Chase.

"Yes," WH said. "I have to go."

When Kraus learned earlier in the day that Congress was not going to vote on the Gravacon Addendum, he implemented an all-out assault on lawmakers using everything in the Gravacon arsenal—cash, blackmail, and favors, chief among them. The mounting stress had been taking its toll on the seventy-three year-old. His doctor had called with recent test results, and warned him to take it easy.

"I'm trying to end world hunger," Krauss told his longtime doctor. "Any idea what that entails? Particularly when I'm up against idiots and bureaucrats!"

"Aren't they the same thing?" his doctor said dryly.

Krauss laughed so hard he started coughing. "Why, yes, they are," he finally spat out between coughs. He then promised he'd try to relax more.

At least after I make sure Chase Malone is dead, he thought.

Checking to be sure they had not been followed after taking several different roads and circling the block three times, Chase and Wen dropped WH off at the gallery. Simon met him outside, and they went immediately to a friend's car he'd arranged to borrow.

"This dirt," WH began, patting the containers, "has already gotten someone killed. My friend Ryan."

"Sorry, man."

"I'm just saying, I don't want his death to be in vain."

"And we don't want to be next," Simon added.

"Right. So let's get this to the lab, and then go meet Chase and Wen."

Krieg and the other man from the lab attack waited in a van outside Kali's home. The man watched the house while Krieg cradled his hand, swollen and bruised from Paloma's bite, and worked on the computer drives he'd taken from the lab. He'd sent word to Krauss that Paloma Boulet was dead—along with most of her staff.

"Finally, some progress," was the response.

"We'll have Kali Garodia soon."

"Excellent. I have reason to believe Malone will be taken care of within the hour."

"Good," Krieg replied, sorry he wouldn't be the one to kill him, and knowing that Krauss had been greatly disappointed by his failures. "Let me know if there is an issue. If I can assist."

"Just get into those computers and tell me what the String-Continuum is. Then shut it down."

"I'm on it. But if Boulet, Garodia, and Malone are gone, doesn't that mean the String-Continuum is also dead?"

"I sure as hell hope so, but we need to know for sure. And anyone who can complete it needs to go away. Understand?"

"Of course," Krieg said, looking at Kali's house. "No survivors."

Chapter Fifty-Nine

Mutsu woke coughing, his body screaming in torment. He looked about the lab, now an alien world filled with the worst horrors imaginable. Paloma's body was in flames, the room choked with toxic smoke and burning flesh. His own skin felt as if it were melting from the intense heat radiating from flames only a few feet away. He mustered up his dwindling strength and somehow got to his feet. A fresh blast of heat and fumes nearly knocked him back to the floor. He staggered toward the door, tripping over one of the men he'd killed.

I killed two people, he thought, realizing it had not been a nightmare.

With the flames closing in, Mutsu made it out of the room as it transformed into a total inferno.

Thankfully, there wasn't nearly as much fire in the hall. The line of burning gasoline, which had ignited the lab, had scorched the floor and wall, but was mostly out. Yet the heavy smoke increased with each choking step.

It never dawned on him that the gunmen could still be

waiting. Mutsu no longer cared about his own survival. His only thought was getting the soil samples out of the lower office before the whole building burned.

"Must save dirt," he muttered as he slid down a few stairs at a time, clinging to the railing. It seemed to take him hours to make it all the way down, leaving a trail of blood in his wake.

Flames raged along the walls, emanating from the elevator and maintenance room. The corner office, where the glass jars were secretly housed, was near an exterior exit door. With great effort, he pulled the keys from his pocket and pushed one into the lock. Suddenly he thought of the pirate, and looked to make sure the killers weren't in sight, terrified he might reveal the location of the samples. Once in the room, he closed the door and sat down for a few seconds.

"I'm not sure I can live long enough to get them out."

Hearing his hoarse words, Mutsu got back up and went to the dolly, still stacked with boxes of sample containers.

The relief that the samples were still there gave him the strength to push the first load out to the parking lot. Sweating, shaking, and bleeding badly, he made it to within ten feet of his pickup truck before he collapsed.

Kali and Bull ran up. "Oh, my God!" Kali screamed. "What happened?"

"Gravacon," he whispered.

Bull dialed emergency services.

"Where's Paloma?" Kali asked, looking at the flames pouring out of the upper lab windows.

"Paloma . . . dead . . . Gravacon killed her."

"No!" Kali wailed.

"What happened?" Bull asked, kneeling beside him.

Chasing Dirt

"Freak, pirate, kill her, burn the lab." He winced from the pain. "Got to . . . get dirt."

Bull saw the dolly, amazed he'd brought it out with his injuries.

Kali ran to get the second load of dirt.

"I had to. . . kill people."

"They deserved it," she said bitterly.

"Go get . . . dirt," he said.

"No." She said, cradling his head in her lap. "I'm not leaving you."

"I'm okay."

She laughed. "You're a mess, Fukushima."

"A good time ask . . . you dinner?" he painstakingly raised a hand. It thumped onto his heart and stayed. "With me?"

Bull looked at the cardboard containers of Chinese food she's dropped, their contents spilled all over the grass. "You'll have to take a shower, put on something clean . . . " She realized his eyes were closed. He had slipped unconscious.

Paramedics arrived with equipment and began commanding orders. Pulling Bull out of the way, they immediately went to work on Mutsu.

"Is he alive?" Bull asked the EMT as they got a gurney under him and lifted him up.

"He's breathing."

"Will he make it?"

The EMT made eye contact with her, and then repeated, "He's breathing."

A fireman caught Kali trying to go back in for the last load of dirt and stopped her. She pleaded and pointed through the window. The room was still relatively smoke-free. "It's right there. Two of my friends died trying to protect that dirt, please!"

"No."

Simon and WH ran up as the fireman headed inside. Kali relayed the frantic series of events that led to the crumbling world before them. The two of them smashed the windows to the lower office and went in for the samples, handing them out the window to her. They loaded everything into Mutsu's truck. Kali had found his keys, still in the door to the office, when she'd first gone in.

"We need to get the dirt out of here, in case Gravacon comes back," Kali said.

"Chase is coming to pick us up," WH said. "You and Bull should take it."

"Okay. I'll hide it at my house," Kali said.

Bull walked over after the ambulance took Mutsu away. Although she hadn't shed a tear, she had the look of someone who had been crying for days. "I don't care what you say," Bull said, looking at the three of them, "but he sacrificed everything for that dirt." She pointed to his truck. "We have to protect it."

Kali nodded. "Let's go."

Chapter Sixty

Anxious to pick up the weapons so they could get to Gravacon's headquarters two hours away in Cologne, Germany, Chase and Wen waited in an old park, overgrown and seemingly forgotten, along the edge of the Scheldt River. They had learned, since spending so much time in Holland, that the river flowed into the Port of Antwerp, Europe's second largest, which had been essential and thriving since the Middle Ages. Tienen Park seemed the perfect spot to meet an arms dealer.

However, almost twenty minutes past the designated meeting time, they knew something was wrong. These people, who delivered "groceries," were known for their precision.

In the fading daylight, they began walking back to their car, taking a different path, trees and a steep ravine on one side, boulders and the edge of a small lake on the other. Chase had left a message for WH and Simon to meet them in the parking lot, and hoped they would already be there waiting.

"This is the first time the suppliers haven't showed up with our groceries," Wen said. "I'll call our connection and find out what went wrong."

They walked briskly across an earthen dam between the lake and a ravine as Wen placed the call.

The arms dealers told her that they had been followed.

"There's no one here," she said, turning to Chase. "He says someone followed—"

A man stepped out of the trees, pointing an AK-47 at them. "Hands in the air," he said in a thick African accent.

The only weapon Wen had on her was her Glock. There was no way she could reach it without getting killed, so she would have to wait. Before she could even consider their next move, another man grabbed Chase from behind and took his pistol.

"What about you, Missy. Do you have a gun?" Colonel Kabongo asked, motioning the man holding Chase to check her.

Wen could see in the colonel's eyes that he had killed many times—many more times than she had. He held the AK-47 perfectly, too far away for her to make a move, and close enough to easily cut her in half.

The other man took her gun.

Wen could also tell the colonel was a man used to sizing people up. He looked at Wen as a formidable opponent, having seen her damage in France, watching her pilot the helicopter, and knowing she was the one who had killed two more of his men and escaped from them at the Bock Casement. She could try to challenge him, but all her experience told her it would be the last move she'd ever make. Instead, she would wait.

Wen quickly assessed their surroundings, cataloging every detail of the area, what could be used as a weapon, a distraction, a way to escape. How far each was. How many seconds, how many steps . . . every option. A thousand scenarios whirled through her finely tuned militaristic mind.

"You are Chase Malone," Kabongo said, more as a statement than a question, aiming his weapon at him.

The other man tossed their pistols into the murky lake, and now he had his AK pointed at Wen.

Chase considered denying the charge for a moment, but quickly decided this would only anger the colonel more. *It's never a good idea to anger a man pointing a gun at you,* he thought. It was fairly obvious as he and Wen stood there, alone, in the middle of an old, tired park, in a remote section of Antwerp, in the early evening hours, that these men *knew* he was Chase Malone.

"Yes, I am. And you are?"

For some reason, this made the colonel laugh. "I am the man who is going to end your life. And yours, I suppose," he said, turning to Wen.

"I can't imagine that you have a good reason for this," Chase said. "So why don't you just tell me your reason instead."

"You're an arrogant, selfish man," the colonel said, no longer smiling. "The president of my country has sentenced you to death for interfering with the internal affairs, and put in jeopardy—"

Wen suddenly knocked the man guarding Chase backwards, forcing him down a steep ravine. At the same time, she dove for the colonel.

The colonel flew backwards into the lake, his gun firing as he fell. The seven-foot drop knocked the wind from his lungs. Kabongo's boot filled with water, and in the struggle to get out of the lake, his machine gun slipped from his hand and sank to the slimy bottom. The colonel reached the shore and ran after Chase and Wen. The other man climbed out of the ravine, having also lost his gun in the fall. Chase stumbled and fell over a protruding root. Wen, slowed to help him, and the two Africans overtook their fleeing victims.

The colonel shoved a pistol against the back of Wen's neck. She spun with a fisted-rock in her hand, flinging it toward him. The gun went off, its bullet lodging somewhere in the dusty trail. Wen's rock connected and smashed into his gun hand, sending the pistol flying.

The other man got on top of Wen, pinning her face down in the dirt, holding her arm in some kind of lock, his weight and muscle overpowering. Chase flew into the colonel, knocking him back to the ground, his knee landing on Kabongo's injured hand.

The two of them wrestled, rolling and fighting, until the colonel managed to get the advantage. He straddled Chase's chest, wrapped his large hands around the billionaire's neck, and squeezed.

Chapter Sixty-One

Chase arched his body and got enough power into both his knees as they struck the colonel's back that his grip broke, and he rolled off.

"Why are you trying to kill us?" Chase asked breathlessly, continuing to wrestle the colonel down.

"Why are you trying to destroy my country? My people need to eat."

"We're trying to *save* it."

"That is always what rich white men say," the colonel said, landing a blow to Chase's rib cage. "Gravacon can give us food security."

"No," Chase said, biting back the pain. "Gravacon will destroy your soil, and that's what's so ironic. The Democratic Republic of Congo can become very wealthy from its soil."

"You lie."

"It's true!" Wen yelled. "There are rare microbes in your soil that can cure diseases."

"What microbes?"

"There are scientists in Antwerp working on this. They have discovered the cures for most major diseases can be found in *your* dirt . . . The soil contains microbes, and Congo has some of the best, most important ones."

"This is a lie!" the man holding Wen shouted. "Nothing grows in our country. That's why we need Gravacon."

"We took samples from your country. The cures are real, and Congo will become the Saudi Arabia of natural medicine. The key to curing these diseases is in your soil."

"Where did you get this magic dirt?" Kabongo asked, momentarily pinned by Chase again.

"Ditu, Dipaki, Shula, and some other villages," Chase said, surprised he remembered the names.

"Are you telling the truth to me?" Kabongo asked, obviously surprised Chase actually knew the names of obscure places in his little country.

"Yes," Chase said, looking into the colonel's eyes. "You can forget about growing food. Congo will make so much money from the microbes that you can buy all the food you want."

"I don't believe you."

"I can prove it to you. I've got the data in my pack. Let me get it."

"No, you have a gun in your pack."

"If I had a gun in my pack, this would already be over."

"Kill her," the colonel said. "If he tries to go for a gun."

"There's no gun. If I let you up, you can go to the pack, pull out the tablet, and see for yourself."

"No!" Wen said. "Chase, don't let him go."

Chase met the Colonel's eyes. "I'm telling you the truth."

Colonel Kabongo squinted at Chase, as if trying to read his soul.

"Gravacon is going to poison your soil and kill your people slowly with cancer," Chase said carefully. "It won't matter if they have food, they'll die in the end anyway."

"What about the dirt?"

"If you don't let Gravacon in, then the soil will give you great riches."

Kabongo stared at him.

"I'm telling you the truth." Chase thought he saw a flashing glimpse of recognition in his eyes. Not total trust, but it might be enough. "I'm going to let you go. I'm trusting you, because I want you to trust me."

"Okay," Kabongo said.

"I'm going to let you up. Go to my pack, and pull out the tablet. Turn it on. I'll tell you the password, you click on the red icon. Then scroll down to Congo, and you will see for yourself."

Kabongo and Chase battled momentarily with their eyes.

"I'm telling you the truth," Chase repeated. "I'm trusting you with my life."

Chase stood up and freed the colonel.

Kabongo sprang to his feet as if ready to attack. Chase did not flinch. Instead, he took a slow step back with his hands up—not in surrender, but in a calming gesture.

Wen, believing it was all over, but still unable to move, searched for another option. *I have to kill this man, or we'll be dead as soon as he reaches the pack.*

Chapter Sixty-Two

Colonel Kabongo walked to the pack, unzipped it, and felt around. Finding no weapon, he pulled out the tablet. "Turn it on," Chase yelled, giving him the password.

The colonel backed up a few feet, not wanting to be surprised by Chase as he concentrated on the screen.

"Click the red icon."

Kabongo saw that the icon was labeled *Microbes*.

"Scroll down to Congo."

The list was arranged alphabetically by country. He found Congo under "D" for Democratic Republic of Congo. He began reading, not knowing what it all meant. He could clearly see a list of diseases and references to microbes that have destroyed them, and then he saw column labeled "World Rank," and his expression turned angry.

"This says we are sixth in all the world. You said we were the Saudi Arabia!" Although he yelled this comment, he was also impressed the Congo was so important. He'd never seen Congo in the top ten of anything good. Not even the top one hundred.

"Click on that column. It will sort by ranking, and look at the first five. Three of them are tiny island nations, one of them is Afghanistan, and the final is the United States, but look at the next tab. The US has lost its place because we ruined our soil using chemicals produced by Gravacon."

The colonel could feel he was telling the truth.

"The Congo is the largest country with soil microbes remaining intact," Chase said. "We have the samples to prove it. I will take you there, if you still don't believe me, because it's not just about us surviving here today. It's about your people surviving. You've gone to a lot of trouble to get rid of us because you think we are threatening your people, so I know you care deeply about the people in your country. Don't throw their future away."

Chase certainly fit the bill for "Buddha billionaire," as his cool, even voice, unguarded, sky blue eyes, and Zen smile not at all attached to anything, entranced the Congolese.

The colonel stood silent for a moment, staring at the screen, then up to the sky, then finally back to Chase. He held his stare. "Let the woman up!" Kabongo shouted.

"But colonel, this is a mistake," the man said in French.

Kabongo said nothing. He just turned and glared at the man.

Slowly, he got off Wen.

Once free, she desperately fought the urge to spring to her feet and kill them both. Instead, she backed away cautiously from the man, hostility still in his eyes.

"I would like to go and see the lab," the colonel said.

"We can't take them to the lab," Wen said.

"If he sees the lab, he'll understand there's no reason to kill us. We are not his enemy," Chase said.

All of Wen's training and experience were screaming at her to kill the man, but Chase was so sure.

"Let's go," Chase said.

They reached the parking area. Their vehicles were next to each other.

As Chase and Kabongo were discussing whether to ride together or follow, Simon and WH pulled into the lot.

"The lab's been destroyed," Simon shouted as he jumped out of their car.

"Gravacon killed Paloma," WH added.

"Damn, damn!" Chase said, agonized. "We never should have left them there."

WH went on to explain everything that had happened.

"I'm sorry," Chase said to Kabongo. "There is no lab to take you to. But everything I told you is true."

"I believe you, Chase Malone."

"WH, what country has the best microbes in the world?" Chase asked him. "The most valuable soil on earth?"

"Congo," he replied without hesitation. "Why?"

"I'll explain later."

Kabongo held out his hand. "I am glad we met, Mr. Malone. I am sorry for all the trouble."

Chase wrote his phone number on a slip of paper. The colonel gave him his contact information.

"Someone will be in touch with you, Colonel. People who will help. People you can trust."

"Thank you."

With Simon and WH in the backseat, Chase pulled out of the park. Someone would have to pick up their vehicle later. He watched the rearview mirror, happy that the Colonel did not follow them.

Wen told Chase she was amazed how he'd handled the situation, and hugged him over the steering wheel, practically running them off the road, tears held in her eyes.

"Sometimes it's about understanding and forgiveness," Chase said sheepishly.

"We don't always have to kill people," Wen said, smiling.

"Not always," Chase said. "But sometimes. And in one-hundred-fifty minutes, someone is going to die."

Chapter Sixty-Three

Krieg, still waiting with his cohort in the van outside Kali's, found the String-Continuum on the drives taken from the lab.

"Oh my God," he said, after studying the data and realizing what was missing. "I know where they went."

"Who?"

"Malone and the Chinese woman," he snapped, as though it should have been obvious. "Drive."

"What about the scientist?"

"Forget her, damn it, we'll find her later."

"Where am I driving?" he asked, starting the engine.

"To Cologne . . . Gravacon headquarters."

Krieg called his staff and warned the security gate, sending them Chase and Wen's photos.

"If they try to get in, detain them until I arrive."

Chase drove into a small shopping center parking lot about ten miles from Gravacon's headquarters, and noticed the time. They were early. Wen, sitting in the front passenger seat, checked the sideview mirror while simultaneously scanning the area.

"Let's go over the plan once more," Chase said, looking in the rearview mirror at WH and Simon.

"This is kinda crazy secret-agent stuff," WH said after again hearing the explanation that they'd already heard at least seven times on the way there.

"Hopefully we're in and out with no bloodshed," Chase said, glancing at Wen.

A large, white, unmarked tractor trailer truck pulled in and parked perpendicular to them. A petite woman got out and waved at Chase. He nodded.

She looked him over carefully, determining if he was the person she was supposed to meet. "Chase Malone?"

"Yeah."

"You can call me Susan. I don't suppose your ID matches that name, does it?"

Chase shook his head.

"Okay, guess I'll just have to take your word for it," Susan said, tapping a button on her phone. A second later, Tess was on the line. The woman handed the phone to Chase. They exchanged a few words. He handed it back to her.

"It's him," Tess confirmed to Susan.

"Come on then," Susan said to Chase as she put the phone away. Chase and Wen followed her into a door located halfway down the truck's enclosed trailer while WH and Simon waited in the car.

A silver Mercedes was parked inside the truck at the back.

Two armed agents—one in the front, one in the back—said nothing when Chase waved. Two more women, in white coats and jeans, looked like they could have been sisters.

Wen had noticed that the driver and another man had remained in the cab. She counted five agents, plus the two women, who were definitely not field agents. Wen began making contingency attack and escape plans.

The interior of the trailer looked more like a cross between a doctor's office, a beauty parlor, and a computer repair shop.

"Let's begin," one of the two women in the white coats said.

He and Wen sat in side-by-side barber chairs. Masks were applied to both of them while Susan briefed them on the situation in the Gravacon buildings, and what they could expect. Next, Chase was fitted with a microprocessing voice-simulator, which in addition to transforming his voice, would also convert it to German.

"Try not to say too much," Sue warned. "It'll translate your words in real time and match it to a tone similar, but not exactly like Krauss's."

"The less I say the better."

"Exactly. It's after hours, so you shouldn't encounter many people. Try it out."

"We're here, and I have colleagues visiting," he said in English, but the words came out in German.

"Good."

"That really is pretty close to how Krauss sounds," Chase said, in English, but it also came out in German.

"I hope so," the woman answered him in German, as fluently as if she'd been born there.

"Maybe you should come with us," Wen said in German.

"Strictly forbidden."

"What about when they respond? I don't understand German."

"Of course," the woman said. "That's next." She withdrew a small metal box from a thin, stainless steel drawer. "This fits into your ear and does the reverse of the voice box. It will translate from German to English."

Forty minutes later, Chase and Wen left the truck with their new identities. WH and Simon were stunned by their transformations. Instead of a thirty-year-old, Chase now looked like a man in his early seventies. Wen appeared as an older Italian woman.

Both had been expertly transformed utilizing a pliable, latex-like material known as Twenty-one-36, in which tiny computer sensors were embedded. One of the lab coat women had told them, "It's not a single mask, it's been built in layers and sections. But once I'm done it will all be connected, and you'll be able to remove it in one piece." She also gave them several plastic guns they should be able to get through the metal detectors.

Ramps were extended and Susan drove the Mercedes out of the truck. "It's an exact replica of the car Kraus drives, including the license-plate. We didn't have enough time to change the VIN number, but that shouldn't be an issue."

"What if it is?" Chase asked.

"Improvise."

Chase laughed, but Wen nodded.

Chapter Sixty-Four

The Mercedes stopped at the Gravacon security gate. WH and Simon pulled in behind them. Wen was driving. Chase just hoped the guard didn't know that the real Krauss was attending the symphony at that very moment.

"Good evening, Mr. Krauss."

"Hello. I've some friends visiting. I'll be showing them around."

"Yes, sir. It wasn't on the schedule."

"No it wasn't. Please wave them through." Chase motioned for the man in the guardhouse to raise the gate.

"Sir, I'm sorry, but we've had to increase security tonight, and . . . "

"On whose order?"

"Mr. Krieg."

"Okay."

"Could I ask you to press a biometric sensor?"

"Why? You don't think I'm me?"

"Of course you are, but it would make me feel better."

"Keep you out of trouble with Krieg."

"Exactly," the guard said, sounding relieved. He handed a sensor pad to Chase, who tried not to appear nervous as he pressed his hand on it.

The readout immediately identified him as Krauss.

"Thank you, sir."

"Happy to help make you feel better," he said in mock charm. "Now." Chase motioned again at the gate.

"Yes, sir." The guard double checked the photo of Chase and Wen on his tablet, saw no match with the two young men in the other car, and signaled for the gate to be opened. "Thank you, Mr. Krauss. Enjoy your evening."

The entrance to the main building featured a biometrics lock override. Chase confidently pressed his palm against the sensor, now knowing it worked. There was no way around the metal detectors, which was why they brought plastic weapons.

Getting past the lobby guards was much quicker, since the main gate had already alerted them that Krauss and his guests were on the way.

"Are you heading to the tower?" the guard asked.

"No, I'll be giving a tour first and going to the farm." They believed the massive indoor growing space was where the samples were kept.

The guard smiled, but couldn't remember the last time Krauss had given a tour.

Inside the farm, they walked through acres of enclosed space filled with crops, high-tech growing stations, monitoring equipment, and agriculture machinery.

Wen kept watching the doors.

"It smells like chemicals," WH said.

"I wonder why?" Chase said rhetorically, then realized it was all in German, of which neither WH nor Simon could understand. He touched a chip embedded in his neck and they heard English instead.

"Look at all these crops," Simon said. "Dude sure knows how to grow food."

They used the information Tess had provided and eventually located the safe, which opened with Chase's handprint.

"There's not as much as we thought," Chase said, seeing the four sealed containers inside.

WH opened one. "It's filled with large-size test tubes. They aren't nearly as big as our samples. I hope it's enough."

"Are they from the US?" Chase asked.

"Yeah," WH replied, reading locations from the labels. "They've even got GPS tags. Paloma will be thrilled."

Everyone went silent.

"Damn," WH said, realizing his error.

"Let's get them and go," Simon said.

"We need to go to the tower," Wen said. "Krauss's office."

Before they could leave the farm, two security guards came in.

"Excuse me, Mr. Krauss, but would you mind coming with us?" one of them asked.

"Yes, I would. What's going on?"

"Mr. Krieg just called, and—"

Wen had both guards disarmed and on the floor before anyone knew what had happened.

Chapter Sixty-Five

They tied up the security guards and now had real weapons.

"We should leave," Simon said.

"Not until we get the proof," WH said.

"You've got your dirt, isn't that enough?"

"We need to get the evidence that Gravacon has been bribing people and knew that hydenosyn causes cancer."

"You see this place? Maybe the guy really *can* feed the world."

"Let's go to the tower," Chase said. "You two can finish your debate on the drive back to Antwerp."

They quickly made their way to the tower, knowing time would be limited. The two guards they had tied up were sure to be supplemented by additional security personnel.

Chase opted for the elevator, even though it was riskier. It would be faster, and no one wanted to carry the dirt samples up the stairs. WH had grabbed a roll of duct tape at the farm and taped the containers together, so instead of four, they now had two bulky ones.

"This is getting very dangerous," Wen reminded them. "You two should go."

"No way," WH said, secretly hoping to find Krauss there, but even without a direct confrontation, the grad student wanted to discover enough secrets to bury the old man and his company.

Simon sighed, but reluctantly stuck with the group.

As the elevator reached the top floor, Wen looked at Chase, still not used to his complete transformation. She thought about how far they'd come. When they'd first started chasing Gravacon, it had been just to find out why the company was misusing Chase's invention. But, as with so many of the things they did, it had quickly become a race for survival. She looked at her own reflection in the mirror doors of the elevator, an old Italian woman, and couldn't help but smile. As if all the killings in her past had not been for nothing, she had to survive to get to this point, to be able to help so many . . .

Karma is a mysterious thing.

Entering Krauss's expansive office, the first thing they noticed were the numbers going around the top of the ceiling—two-foot high digital readouts in various colors with constantly changing numbers.

Current world population: seven billion, seven hundred sixteen million, six hundred twenty-nine thousand, one hundred and twenty-four, twenty-five, twenty-six . . .

Undernourished people in the world right now: eight hundred and fifty-one million, twenty-two thousand, four hundred and thirty-two, three, four . . .

People who died of hunger today: forty-nine thousand, five hundred twenty-six, seven, eight . . .

People who died of hunger this year: eighteen million . .
.

Simon stood transfixed, as if his memories of seeing so many people suffer and die in Africa was being documented and memorialized.

He looked at the other numbers, including tons of food wasted in the world, money spent feeding pets, money spent on ice cream, candy, cigarettes, video games, pornography . . . Simon couldn't take his eye off the ticker showing a child dying every twelve seconds due to malnutrition and starvation.

"What do the colors mean?" Simon asked.

"I don't know, but it's pretty wild," WH answered as they watched.

"That means they're hungry," Simon said, pointing to the undernourished ticker. "Look how many died of hunger this year."

"No," WH said. "That's how many died *today*. More than eighteen million died this year."

"Oh my God," Simon breathed.

"Hey, guys?" Chase said. "We can dwell on those brutal numbers later. Right now, we need to get in and get out."

Wen was already at the computer, talking to the Astronaut. "Chase, we need your fingerprint to access."

Chase went over and put his finger on the biometric sensor in the upper right corner of the keyboard, and miraculously the screen changed from a Gravacon logo to a full and active desktop.

WH and Simon got busy going through his desk and checking behind pictures for safes. Simon glanced up and noticed that more than thirty-five billion dollars a year was spent on ice cream, eighteen billion on facial cosmetics, fifteen billion on perfumes.

"No wonder Krauss is so obsessed with hunger," he muttered to himself. "Looking at these numbers all day would make anybody crazy." *It'll be hard to eat ice cream again,* he thought, *after looking at how much it costs, compared to feeding people.*

"We've lost the Astronaut," Wen announced as his signal went dead. She quickly copied large sections of Krauss's computer onto the portable terabyte drives they'd brought while still looking for the prize. Somewhere he had a file that contained the complete geographic grid of Orgri-Source use, which included the number of gallons of GET-EM® that had been sold to each region. That information would allow them to extrapolate additional data layers and be able to place an estimated overlay of residential usage and ultimate soil contamination. However, they were mostly concerned with the industrial uses in the agricultural lands.

Chase's phone rang. "It's Tess."

"Krieg is coming," she said as soon as he answered. "Get out now!"

Chapter Sixty-Six

Wen looked at Chase's face and knew. "How much time do we have?" she asked quietly.

"Ten minutes."

On a different side of the office, WH and Simon were each rifling through physical files, drawers, and cabinets. "This guy is a pack rat," WH said.

Simon found a drawer filled with folders containing correspondence with world aid organizations about stable donations from Kraus personally, and on behalf of Gravacon. He looked up at the tickers. "The guy is for real with the hunger issue," he muttered to himself.

Wen and Chase both stared at the screen, scanning constant streams of filenames, looking for anything that might fit. There wasn't enough time to copy everything on his computer.

"What about that one?" Chase asked, pointing to a file titled "*OrgriSource Spread*." They had already tried dozens of others with no luck.

"That certainly seems like a logical name for it," Wen said, clicking on the file. "That's it!" A map of the world spread across the screen, showing the regions. "This is pure gold. Paloma would have loved this. Talk about making soil searching easier."

"I think we've got it," Chase said to WH and Simon.

"Then let's get out of here," Simon said.

"You guys go. Get the soil to Kali, along with this file." Chase handed them a drive.

"What? What about you?" WH asked.

"We're going to get as much data as we can here."

"Let's just all get out now," Simon said.

"The important thing is to get the dirt safe," Chase said. "We'll be fifteen minutes behind you."

"Are you sure?" WH asked, concerned.

"Go!" Chase said. "I don't want you two here when Krieg shows up."

"We don't want *you* here when Krieg shows up," WH said.

"Get *out* of here!" Chase barked.

A couple of minutes later, Chase watched from a tower window as WH and Simon emerged from the building's main entrance, carrying the soil containers to their car. Chase watched WH slide them into the trunk, and kept watching until they were cleared through the gate.

"I realize I've been holding my breath the whole time," Chase said, turning back to Wen. "But they're out and onto the main road."

"WH knows we're up to something" Wen said.

"There was no reason to tell them. Especially since we don't even know if we'll find him."

The Astronaut is certain he's at the symphony, and we

have his home address, so it'll be successful," Chase said, smiling. He took another look out the window. "We should get going."

"I know, I just want to check one more subdirectory to see if there's any more cancer data," Wen said. "And look, there is!"

"Really? You got it?"

"I'm copying it now. This is insane . . . it shows their whole scheme of suppressing true scientific data while flooding the media with a steady stream of studies countering the true findings! Here's all the names of the phony labs and services they've set up, plus universities they funneled money into from shell companies in order to . . . And these documents, hold on . . . Gravacon knew hydenosyn causes cancer as far back as the 1990's."

"And they kept pushing it onto the world." Chase joined her at the screen. "Stop world hunger, but everyone dies of cancer!"

"It's outrageous."

"Wait, go back," Chase said. "Does that say what I think it does?"

"Yes, I think so," Wen said, skimming the document. "They had that information . . . Gravacon *knew* that soil contained beneficial microbes. Look at the tests they did."

"That explains the before and after samples." Chase went to the window. "It's Krieg!"

"How many are with him?" Wen asked, not even looking up from the computer.

"Looks like he arrived with just one," Chase said. "Plus how many he ever has on site."

"I just need to get these," she said, as if she hadn't heard Chase.

"We need to *go*!"

"One more . . . okay, done. I wish we could take it all."

"We're going to be lucky to get out with what we have," Chase said. "How *are* we going to get out?"

"We aren't."

Chapter Sixty-Seven

Chase stared at Wen. "What do you mean. We aren't leaving?"

"This is the high ground. We fight them here."

Chase looked out the window. He could see the silver Mercedes with the weapons in the back. *No chance to get to those*, he thought. They did have the pistols taken from the security people, plus, of course the fully functional plastic guns given to them by Susan. But even from the tower, he could see Krieg and the other man were armed with machine guns.

"They won't know exactly where we are," Chase said hopefully. "It's a big campus."

"Where else would we be? He'll come straight here. If we go down through the building, we'll run right into them. I'm not looking for a hallway gun battle against machine guns."

"Let's go out a back entrance onto the lawns."

"We'll be too far out in the open," she said, still tapping the keyboard as more files downloaded.

"I thought you had everything."

"I want it all."

Chase looked up at the tickers still moving . . . how much on pet food, how much on beer . . . He wondered why there wasn't one declaring how much homeowners spent on weed killer.

"What's your plan?" Chase asked, flipping a switch near a bank of monitors in the corner. The screens immediately came to life. "Look, we can watch the entire building from here." Chase pointed to Krieg, yelling instructions while freeing the security people they'd tied up. "He's probably surprised to find them alive." Chase wondered if they did the right thing by not killing the guards now that they were going to come after them again.

"He left nobody alive in Antwerp," Wen said.

Chase studied the man who'd been after them, who had so easily killed an innocent, unarmed, female scientist.

"That's the bastard who killed Paloma and the others," Wen said.

It was true, of course, but Chase knew Wen was trying to feed the fire within her that would be needed to kill Krieg. The only way out was through him. If they didn't kill him and at least injure those with him, he and Wen would die tonight.

"He also ordered all the sample-collecting college kids killed." Chase zoomed in on the camera. "Krieg is an ugly man, but now he's got a fresh gash on his chin and his left hand looks like he's wearing a bloody oven mitt."

"I hope Paloma did that to him."

"By now, he knows that we're in disguise," Chase said, watching Krieg and now five others entering the partially underground hallway that led to the tower.

"You can take that off now. Aren't you hot?" she asked, pulling off her mask.

Chase pealed his off, too. It made Wen happy seeing him young and handsome again. She kissed him passionately, knowing it could be their last time, then looked back at the screen, still searching for more data, but her mind wandered for a moment. They were both young, she just twenty-eight, him only thirty, and other than a few bullet holes in each of them, they were in pretty good shape. They loved each other, he had a fortune, under normal circumstances they'd have a beautiful future ahead, but even if they made it through the night, neither of them would ever be satisfied living a "normal" life. There were too many wrongs in the world that they might be able to right. Too many...

"I think we have about two minutes," Chase said, interrupting her thoughts. Wen stopped her search, ejected the final drive from the computer, and slipped it into her pack, but still kept typing.

"Where are they?" she asked.

"Three of them took the elevator, the other three are coming up the stairs."

"Perfect," she said, keying in a few more strokes, then she got up from the computer.

"What did you do?"

She smiled. "Looks like we'll just have three to deal with."

Chase gave her a confused expression.

"I shut down the elevators."

"You can do that?"

"When I was looking for files, I found the program that controls and accesses the security of the whole place. I also locked the door to the stairs, but I have a feeling that won't hold them too long."

"Nice, but there's still three of them with machine guns. What are we going to do?" He knew she'd have a brilliant plan.

"Want some fresh air?" Wen asked, pointing to a spiral staircase that led to a rooftop observation deck. "I looked at the schematics on the computer. There are benches up there that are concealing ventilation shafts. If you're behind one, bullets aren't going to be able to penetrate. So stay behind there."

"Okay."

"There are lots of viewpoints, so you'll be able to see them come out of the staircase. If they do, shoot them."

"I wasn't going to show them the view."

"Hopefully they won't get that far . . . "

"What are *you* going to do?"

"I will try to get at least two of them from down here."

"So *you're* the decoy this time?"

"Something like that." She blew him a kiss. "Time to go!"

He ran up the spiral staircase.

Seconds later, Krieg and two others came blasting their way out of the door from the main stairs.

Chapter Sixty-Eight

Wen waited until Krieg and his two agents were visible through the double glass entryway, then fired. A single shot hit one of them in the face. He dropped to the floor, instantly dead. Krieg and the other survivor dove for cover while two shattered glass walls spilled sharp splinters and shards around them.

She ran back into the office, shut and locked the executive-bathroom door, then slipped into an incredibly tight cavity behind the corner credenza in the main suite.

Krieg and the man approached the room cautiously. Knowing the office so well, when Krieg saw the open door to the observation deck and the locked bathroom door, he assumed he had them. Just to be sure, Krieg fired a few shots under the desk and several rounds into a closet, then more into the bathroom door.

"Check the bathroom," he barked to the other man, then headed up to the tower.

Wen counted, guessing it would take four seconds for him to climb stairs to the observation deck. *One, two, three* . . .

The other man found the bathroom door locked, and kicked it in. She shot him, leaped out of her hiding place, and followed Krieg to the tower. Reaching the top of the stairs at the observation deck a couple seconds after Krieg, Wen fired, but he was moving so fast the bullet only caught his leg.

I should have waited, she thought, but had been worried about Chase.

Krieg rolled and took cover behind the row of benches on the far side of the deck. She knew Chase would be nearby. Now that Krieg knew she was up there, Wen fired again. There was no way to know the pirate's exact location with the benches blocking her view.

Wen worked her way around the twenty-five by twenty-five-foot deck, figuring Chase was awaiting her lead. Krieg had gone all the way around and was now where Chase should have been. She reached the other side and was stunned *not* to see Chase.

Where is Chase if neither Krieg or I have run into him?

Krieg spotted her through a slight opening in the bench and fired at the same time he advanced toward her. Wen was cornered. She returned fire in an attempt to get cover until the gun came up empty. She tossed it off the tower and reached for her plastic gun, but Krieg was already there.

"You fool!" he said, about to pull the trigger.

Two shots rang out, neither from his gun. Two bullets ripped into the back of Krieg. He fell dead, a bitter expression on his face.

"You okay?" Chase yelled, pulling himself back up onto the deck.

"I am now," she said. "Sometimes I forget how at home you are on tall buildings." She helped him climb onto the deck.

"Two summers spent hanging off the edges of the tallest skyscrapers in San Francisco," he bragged, looking out toward the parking lot. The silver Mercedes was still clear. "We need to go before more trouble comes. Unless you need to check Krauss's Facebook page, or maybe copy his browsing history or something?"

"Grab his gun," Wen said, already starting down the stairs, where she collected two more machine guns off the bodies.

They made it to the parking lot without running into anyone, but getting out of the area and through the security gate was not going to be as easy. Wen headed off on foot while Chase drove the vehicle.

The shooting lasted only a few seconds, and left the four security guards injured. She could have easily killed them all, but decided it wasn't necessary. She'd also taken their cell phones and, while still in Krauss's office, had shut down all land lines coming into and out of the facility.

"If they didn't get a call out," Wen said as Chase steered the Mercedes onto the highway, "we might just make it to the symphony."

Chapter Sixty-Nine

Simon kept within the speed limit, nervous every time they passed another car.

"I hope Chase and Wen got out of there," WH said as they rounded a long curve, the full moon bathing the countryside in diffused light.

"Yeah, you don't have to worry about those two. They can take care of themselves," Simon said, recalling their adventure in Luxembourg. "The CIA arranged all that high tech masks and voice-changing tech . . . they got some friends in high places."

"They need them against Gravacon."

"It sure seems we're spinning out of whack in this world . . . what we decide to use money on instead of feeding people and taking care of basic medical needs."

"Tickers got to you?"

"We buy weapons instead of medicine, ice cream instead of feeding the hungry. We spend close to twenty *billion* dollars a year on ocean cruises instead of cleaning up the oceans."

"True, our priorities are a mess, but Krauss is insane, trying to go about solving world hunger by destroying the planet."

"Is he?" Simon asked. "Because of what we helped do tonight, hundreds of thousands of people are going to die, millions hungry . . . how many are children?"

"That's not on us," WH said as a black Porsche raced around them.

Those ticker numbers blazing around the ceiling of Krauss's office were now blazing around Simon's mind.

"Do you think Chase and Wen are really heading back to Antwerp?" WH asked.

"I don't know. They did seem to be acting a little strange. What do you think they're doing?"

"When I texted them where we were, all he texted back was, 'good, see you soon.' But I think they might be going after the CEO of Gravacon."

"Krauss?" Simon asked, surprised. "You mean to his home or something?"

"I'm just guessing, but why else wouldn't they have been able to leave with us?"

"They wouldn't kill him . . . would they?"

They were both silent for a few minutes. WH wondered how Chase and Wen would go after Krauss and what they would do with him. Simon was still unable to stop thinking about the numbers from the tower. WH finally broke the mood with an upbeat comment.

"I can't wait to give these samples to Kali. She's going to be so happy they can complete the String-Continuum."

"Yeah," Simon said absently as he pulled the car over.

"What are you doing?" WH asked, looking around. "What's wrong?"

Simon parked under a streetlight on the side of a low highway bridge.

"I hear a noise back there," Simon said, getting out. "I'm just going to check it."

"You need help?" WH yelled, as he tried to get out. The car was so close to the rail that his door wouldn't open all the way.

"No, sit tight, I got it . . . It's nothing," Simon yelled. "I'll be right there."

Suddenly, WH saw one of the containers of dirt fly over the rail into the river. And then the second one went sailing off the bridge.

"What the hell!?" WH pushed his door open, crunching the paint into the concrete wall supporting the round green steel rail. "What did you just do?"

Simon came back into the car as WH, wrestling his door against the wall, was still trying to get out.

"I just think all the starving children are more important than curing cancer?"

"You're crazy!" WH finally squeezed out the door before Simon could pull away. Without even a thought, WH slipped out of his shoes and jumped into the water. The river reminded him of one back home, where he'd swum many a night, with less moonlight than this. The row of streetlights on the bridge also added to the illumination, and he could see the two containers floating about twenty feet in front of him, separated from each other by about eight feet. He swam hard in the cold water, wishing he was in shorts, but he was still in the slacks and dress shirt from the Gravacon tour. He kicked and struggled. A strong swimmer, who'd grown up on the banks of the James River in Virginia, he was able to close the distance quickly, and soon had the first container. It appeared to be airtight, and the internal containers were sealed with rubber corks. The harder job now was catching up to the other container while holding onto the first one. It meant essentially swimming one-handed.

The fast moving river swept him along with the current.

WH caught up to the second batch of dirt and managed to hold onto both slippery cases while kicking toward the shore. He looked back at the bridge and was surprised by how far away it was. That's when he saw Simon swimming toward him.

"Get away from me you crazy jerk!" he yelled breathlessly, trying to swim harder toward the shore, worried that Simon would try to sabotage the containers again. "These are irreplaceable!"

Simon, also apparently a strong swimmer, caught him, and began wrestling one of the wet containers from WH.

Chapter Seventy

WH fought back, landing a kick into Simon's stomach.

"You've lost your mind!" WH yelled. "Get away from me!"

"I've been there, you haven't!" Simon yelled. "I've *seen* these starving kids! We can't stop the only chance they have!"

"What are you talking about?" WH shouted back as he wrestled the container away.

Simon grabbed the other one, trying to push it under, while they continued moving farther downstream.

"Gravacon is the only hope to end world hunger."

"What about the hope to end *all* disease?" They were now only about fifteen feet from the shore, but at least a quarter mile from the bridge. WH swam around and got the container back, and somehow separated himself from Simon. He began kicking toward the shore again, but Simon lunged and grabbed him by the neck. WH, still shocked that Simon had thrown the containers in the first place, couldn't believe that he was resorting to violence.

WH slipped under the water, causing Simon to lose his grip. When WH surfaced, he swung, landing a punch on Simon's face, but floating in the water with nothing to push off from, his blow didn't carry much force. Simon swung back. WH ducked. One of the containers was now floating four feet away. They began wrestling over the container WH still had. Simon stuck an elbow into WH's ribs, causing him to momentarily release. Instead of going for the container, WH swam hard into Simon, riding on top of him, using Simon's body as leverage. WH punched him repeatedly, landing a few face shots. This time, he was striking with full force. Simon tried to pull him off, but his arms kept slipping. WH hit him several more times, then swam to retrieve the now two escaping containers.

WH, exhausted, reached shore, hoisting both containers out of the water, then dragging himself up onto the grassy bank. The bridge in the distance where their car's hazard lights were still blinking was barely visible. Fortunately, a bike path followed the river. He walked briskly back toward the bridge, awkwardly carrying the containers.

"Wait!" Simon shouted, crawling out of the river.

"Screw you!"

"Think about it, man! You give them those samples, you'll be putting Gravacon out of business. Those kids will go on starving, *millions* of them!"

WH started to jog now. "I want Gravacon out of business!" he yelled back over his shoulder. "Chase and Wen will have gotten enough evidence back in Cologne to shut them down regardless of this dirt. This is to stop cancer, dude! Cancer and lots of other diseases."

They both jogged along the bank, yelling at each other, until, finally, a hundred feet from the bridge, WH put the cases down, slipped one of the heavy bands off them, then turned around to face Simon.

"I'm sorry about all that back there," Simon said, "but if you'd seen as many hungry people as I have . . . the devastation, desperation, the *hopelessness*, you'd know the dirt is not as important as that."

WH punched him in the jaw. "Gravacon murdered my friends! Killed Paloma, you son of a . . . " He landed another punch on the side of his head.

Simon staggered backward. WH didn't wait for him to recover before tackling him on the ground and hitting him several more times in the face and stomach. Pinned and overwhelmed, Simon couldn't fight back, and just tried to cover his face. WH rolled him over, tied his hands behind his back with the band from the container box, then got the other band from the second container. Before Simon could get up, WH hogtied his legs to his hands.

"That's how we do it in Virginia!"

"Hey! Untie me!" he moaned.

"Forget it," WH said, catching his breath. "Have a nice life." He picked up the containers and trudged off toward the bridge.

"Hey, WH, you can't leave me here! WH? Come on. Fine, take the containers, but don't *leave* me here!"

"You're lucky Chase and Wen aren't here, because they probably would've killed you."

WH made his way to the car, loaded the containers in the back, and drove away.

Chapter Seventy-One

Krauss looked at the two papers in front of him, one from his doctor, one from his investigators, neither good.

It seemed his cancer, non-Hodgkin lymphoma, had finally won. Or it would in a matter of weeks.

Ironic, he thought, *having won so many lawsuits against people who claimed hydenosyn had caused their cancer, when it has almost certainly caused mine.*

Dying wouldn't bother him so much if he could still solve world hunger before his death, but that was far less likely now because of the second paper. He now knew what the String-Continuum was, and it terrified him.

If Kali Garodia, and whatever was left of Paloma Boulet's team were allowed to complete their String-Continuum, he knew that all of Gravacon's products made with hydenosyn would immediately be banned.

Chase and Wen were nearly at the symphony when they were relieved to finally hear back from the Astronaut.

"I've been using satellite surveillance, borrowed from the Russian intelligence service to track Krauss's car in real time," the Astronaut said. "It seems he left the Symphony early."

"Why?" Wen asked, concerned he'd heard about the trouble at Gravacon.

"I have no way to know, but perhaps he was tired," the Astronaut said.

"Maybe the symphony was no good," Chase interjected.

"Hardly possible," the Astronaut countered. "It was the Cologne Philharmonic playing Wagner. The concert hall is one of the best designed in the world. In their quest for perfect acoustics, there are no walls standing parallel, that way all undesired echoes are avoided. How could it be anything but spectacular?"

"Sorry to miss it," Chase said.

"Where is he now?" Wen asked.

"At home. Minimal security," the Astronaut said.

"Minimal security?"

"I've already hacked into their network. And I have sent three of the five member team home. Told them replacements are on their way. Those, of course, are the two of you. I've sent the layout of the grounds and the rough blueprint of the house to your phone."

"What would we do without you?" Wen asked.

"It's hard to say. However, I don't believe it would be a good situation for you."

"That's for sure." Chase laughed. "I know we'd get in more trouble than we already manage to find."

The Astronaut gave the name of the security firm and the serial number code that would let the guards at the house know Chase and Wen were with the company. Luckily, Krauss didn't like uniformed officers. At Gravacon headquarters, none of those guards had worn uniforms either.

Wen drove up to the gate and gave the code.

The guard nodded with a skeptical expression. "Hold on a second while I call in to verify."

As he reached for his phone, Wen pulled the guard into the car and slammed his head down. Chase pushed a machine-gun out the passenger window at the same moment the other guard reached for his gun.

"Don't do it," Chase said in a deadly serious tone, hoping to avoid shooting the man. Both guards were quickly bound and left in the gatehouse.

"Didn't we learn a lesson at Gravacon?" Chase asked. "Never leave the guards behind? If someone comes, we'll just have to take those guys out again."

"Who's going to come? Krieg?"

Using the security guard's pass card, they snuck inside the house—a relatively modest home that might have been able to accommodate thirty guests, each with their own room.

"Can I help you?" a man asked.

Wen pulled a gun. "We're with security. There is an intruder in the house. Where is the rest of the staff?"

There was only one other person working. Chase and Wen quickly had them tied up in the kitchen. After the man told them that Krauss was in the study and where to find it, Wen gagged them.

"They're always in the study," Chase mused. Less than a minute later, Chase and Wen quietly opened the door to a book-walled room, lavishly rugged in plush red and green oval shag atop glossy teak wood.

Guns pointing at the old man sitting behind a large wooden desk, Wen felt instant remorse.

Krauss looked up from his desk and did a decent job at concealing his shock. "Aren't you taking the enforcement of this licensing agreement a little far, Chase?"

"You have no idea how far," Chase said.

"Hands on the desk," Wen said.

"What's this then?" Krauss asked. "Are you going to shoot me?"

Chase shook his head. "You've done a lot of things that ought to get you shot, and you have much to answer for, but we're not here to judge you."

"That's nice of you," Krauss said, his expression a mix of disdain and revulsion.

"We are going to ask you to come with us," Wen said.

"Where?"

"Back to Belgium."

"Why, is there a party in my honor?"

"Because the first of the many crimes you're going to answer for is ordering the death of Paloma Boulet. And the others who Krieg killed a few hours ago."

"I don't know what you're talking about."

"Yes you do. But don't worry, even if you get off for that one, we've got the proof of many more crimes—the cancer causing hydenosyn that you knew about, the coverups, the bribes."

Krauss laughed.

"A real noble man you are," Chase mocked. "How many people do you have to kill so you can save the ones you think deserve saving?"

"You people are so sentimental and naïve. Why is one life more important than millions?"

"Every life is important," Wen said. Her puzzling remorse just a minute ago faded and transformed to fury. "And you don't get to decide if a million are worth more than a certain one, or certain tens of thousands, or all the ones that you inflicted with cancer."

"But *you* get to decide? Chase Malone gets to decide that millions of people have to continue suffering hunger and die . . . children never get enough to eat because you want to save a thousand farmers from getting cancer, or a few hundred lab people from finding special things in the mud?"

"It's more than that."

"Do you know how many ways there are to cure cancer? We're just getting started in the fields of genetics, immunotherapy, adoptive cell transfer, Dichloroacetate, bacterial therapies—it's endless. We're so close to so many breakthroughs, we don't *need* to play in the dirt!"

"It's not just cancer."

"Let me ask you something, how many people have to die of hunger to get your attention? I have the *cure* for hunger!"

"You don't understand."

"Oh, but I do. I've seen the String-Continuum."

Chase was shocked—not because Krauss had found their secret, but that it hadn't changed his mind. "Then you know how incredible the discovery is?"

Krauss scowled and pulled a gun, pointing it at Chase. "I hate your guts, you piece of—"

"Drop it," Wen said, pointing her MP7 submachine gun at him.

"Or what? You'll kill me? I'm dying anyway. I'll be dead before anyone can even charge me with a crime." Krauss steadied the gun, aiming for Chase's chest. "At three meters, even I can't miss. Say goodbye, Chase." He spat the bitter words, then pulled the trigger.

Wen unleashed the MP7. A dozen bullets ripped into him.

"His gun didn't fire," Wen said. She walked around to the other side of the desk and checked his gun. "It wasn't loaded," she said, closing her eyes. "That bastard didn't even have the courage to kill himself . . . he made me do it for him."

Epilogue

A worldwide fraud investigation resulted in the arrest and indictment of more than two hundred officials, including ninety-three from the US. Tess helped cover Chase and Wen's tracks regarding the Cologne episode. Gravacon declared bankruptcy. WOLF severed ties with Simon, but otherwise he went unpunished. The Democratic Republic of the Congo received loan guarantees and assistance to develop its soil and health industries. Chase and Wen vanished again . . .

A year later, WH stood inside the Paloma Boulet Center for Microbe Research—a brand new building on the Antwerp campus donated by Ed Weston and partially funded by an anonymous billionaire.

"Congratulations on the Nobel," he said to Kali.

"It belongs to all of us," she said, nodding to the memorial plaque hanging by the entrance, listing all the names of those who'd died in the quest for the String-Continuum — Ryan, Billy, and the other sample collectors, lab workers, and Paloma. Kali had officially named it the Boulet-String-Continuum.

"Where's Mutsu?" WH asked.

"Here I am," he said, walking into the room, leaning heavily onto a sturdy cane. "I'm giving a TED Talk this evening." Kali had become famous, but the shy researcher preferred staying in the background, letting others educate the world about the Boulet-String-Continuum.

"Want to rehearse it on me?" WH asked.

"No, thanks. Bull is coming by for lunch. I'll try it out on her."

"Oh, so you did wind up with the girl?" WH asked, concerned at Mutsu's still weak voice. They still didn't know if he'd ever fully recover.

"No, not really. We're just friends, but you never know . . ."

"Good luck," WH said, giving him a high-five. "Has Bull heard from Chase and Wen?"

"I don't know, but even if she had, Bull would never tell us. You know, they kind of just vanished."

"Yeah," WH said.

WH couldn't resist going to the live presentation that evening. A couple that he didn't recognize, but seemed vaguely familiar, walked into the auditorium and stood near the back. WH listened for fifteen minutes as Mutsu built his TED Talk to its exciting conclusion.

"By now, almost everyone in the world has heard of DNA and is familiar with the iconic double helix structure that represents it," Mutsu said, pacing the stage of the Antwerp Auditorium, packed with scientists, educators, and grad students. "In molecular biology, the term 'double helix' describes an incredible structure which is formed from double-stranded molecules of nucleic acids, and this arises due to its secondary structure. We once believed the double helix to be unique."

WH smiled, Mutsu was about to state his favorite part.

"Several years ago, when Dr. Garodia and Dr. Boulet first discovered that the world's soil contained the means to eradicate so many of humanity's worst diseases, they didn't realize that much more was buried beneath our feet. But that was soon to change. I still recall the moment they first realized what the Boulet-String-Continuum represented—by combining the properties of the underlying bacteria and microbes from around the planet, they discovered that the surface of earth is a single living organism and creates its own unique double helix."

The room erupted into applause as Mutsu clicked on the slide illustrating the beautiful and complex multi-colored double helix that is the String-Continuum.

WH turned to take another look at that couple, but they were gone.

Next in the Chase Malone Thriller series

vinci-books.com/chasing-life

Tampering with DNA was the one line humanity swore never to cross—until now.

When billionaire fugitive Chase Malone and rogue spy Wen Zhou uncover a secret plot to manipulate human DNA, they stumble into a deadly conspiracy that could alter the course of humanity—forever.

Turn the page for a free preview…

Chasing Life: Chapter One

For five days she hadn't killed anyone, hadn't even thought about guns. Five days wasn't the longest she'd ever gone, but in recent months, it counted as a record.

Wen Sung, a former top Chinese spy, had been trained and employed by the Ministry of State Security, China's CIA equivalent. The MSS had first recruited her as a teenager, and for nearly ten years, she'd done their worst.

She looked over at her boyfriend and smiled. It had been a wonderful break, but now they needed to return to the real world.

"We could stay longer," the tech billionaire said, moving a wisp of shiny black hair away from her beautifully chiseled face. Chase Malone, an inventor and engineer, comfortable in worn, but tailored khaki pants and an open shirt, grabbed Wen around her waist and pulled them together on the rock they perched on, gazing out at a scenic lake. At age twenty-nine, he'd seen the end not of his career, but of everything, and so had dropped out of the Silicon Valley fast track. After creating breakthrough technologies in AI, machine learning, and cognitive-predictive computer applications, he saw that the continual misuse of his inventions, and other advanced technologies, would eventually spell the end of humanity. After reuniting with Wen and dodging the MSS, Chase and Wen had made a decision to use their talents and connections to prevent people from using technology to do more harm—or, rather, the decision had been made *for* them after a series of events which included being pursued by an unknown group for reasons not entirely clear.

"We're almost out of food," Wen said, glancing at their backpacks.

"How about we live off the land?"

She gave him a 'get serious' look. The two of them had gone off-grid and vanished more than a year earlier, only surfacing when something required them to intervene.

"Okay, but we could hike out, get some more provisions, then hit the trail, find another lake . . . "

"Let's go find another island," Wen suggested.

"Deal."

In order to mend their wounds, relax, and spend a few days alone, a luxury they had only been allowed a few times, they'd spent four days camping by a sub-Alpine lake in the Marble Mountains wilderness of California. They hadn't seen another soul the entire time. The solitude and crystal waters of the lake had cleansed them.

Before the backpack trip, they had been in San Francisco, helping Chase's business partner, Desmond "Dez" Jefferson, with some of the technical aspects of Balance Engineering, their increasingly secretive company.

"It was great seeing your mom," Wen said. "I'm so glad we got to visit her before we came up here."

"Me too, so we could borrow all their camping gear. I'm

amazed she saved it. She and my dad haven't been backpacking in years." His expression turned sad. People who had been pursuing Chase and Wen had killed his father not long ago, and badly injured his mother.

"Your mom's looking really good. She seems to be doing okay," Wen said, trying to lighten the mood.

"She's worried about me," Chase said. "She didn't say so, but I can see it's stressful for her."

"Boone said he's talked to her about it. It's not like it's exactly our *choice* to live this way," Wen said, mentioning Chase's older brother, Boone.

Feeling a bit sad to be leaving the wilderness, they talked about how great it would be to build a cabin up there, or somewhere similar, where no one could find them. But they both knew it was a dream that would never come true. They had too much to do, there were too many problems to solve, and somebody would find them anyway. Somebody always did.

A couple hours into their hike out, Wen spotted trouble. "There's somebody out there," she said quietly.

"Are you serious?" But Chase knew she was. He just couldn't believe that someone had found them again. No one knew where they were, *no one*.

"Four hundred yards."

"Where?" Chase whispered as they kept hiking as before.

"Up ahead in that clearing. Tree. Left."

Chase scanned the area without moving his head, his eyes concealed behind his sunglasses, but couldn't find anyone.

"He's going to get us," Wen said, her eyes darting, searching for other hostiles. "He'll have an open shot in another minute."

Chasing Life: Chapter Two

So far, Wen didn't see any other threats, but they were still walking straight into the sniper's trap.

"I've only got my Glock," Wen said, referring to her favorite pistol, a Glock 19. Normally she liked to carry at least three weapons, two of them being submachine guns, but hadn't anticipated needing them. The only threat they had expected was the possibility of running into a bear.

"I'll drop down to the river and go that way," Chase said, knowing already that Wen would be planning to head up into the woods to find the sniper. Even if they could have both escaped without a confrontation, they needed to know who had sent him and why. "I'll see if anyone else is aiming for us."

"I'll head up," she replied.

"I know."

There was absolutely nothing that bothered Chase more than when they had to be strategically separated. He had never liked it, but by now knew not to debate it with Wen because it was the way she had been trained, and, more importantly, it had saved their lives more times than he cared to remember.

She smiled. "I'll see you on the other side. Let's try to meet at the cattle guard, but if one of us isn't there, second spot is where the trail turns back into the wider gravel road." She blew him a kiss.

He nodded, blew a kiss back, left the trail, and hiked down toward Shackleford Creek, which rapidly descended nearly two thousand feet over five miles, with noisy cascades, drops, waterfalls, and rapids making a frothy mix of white water, moss, evergreens, and crystal pools.

Even with her pack, Wen moved through the trees as if invisible, but planned to abandon it once she got closer to the sniper. Counting steps, checking the breeze, watching how the shadows fell, the angle of the ground's slope, movement of the birds, Wen, now on auto-pilot, took it all in, processing the probabilities and ingredients of the fluid situation that was going to end in a death—hers or his.

The sniper cursed. In thirty more feet, there would have been a clear shot and he could've gone home. He had it all visualized—the woman would fall first, then he'd catch the man on the run. If it all went well, two shots would do it, though the man, moving, might take one more. Either way, they would be dead, he'd photograph the bodies, cut off a finger from each of them, and put them in separate Ziploc bags. Based on the time, he might've been able to get paid that night, but now he wouldn't until the following day. The two targets, for some reason, had suddenly gone off trail. He wondered for a second if they had spotted him, but didn't see how that was possible since he was virtually invisible—a special forces trained sniper hidden in a camouflage blind.

He decided to wait a few minutes to see what was going on. There was a good chance they were both going off to relieve themselves. It made sense why the guy had gone to one side and the woman to the other.

He lost sight of them.

Surely they'll return to the trail shortly. He waited. *Never break the blind, maintain the zone.*

When he heard a twig snap in front of him, he immediately looked behind him, but it was too late.

Wen landed on top of the sniper, his Barrett M95 rifle slid away, and before he could reach his Beretta 92SB-F sidearm, she had it. It had all happened in an instantaneous blur. Her Glock pointed at his neck. He thought about tossing her, he was much larger, but the fierce determination in her eyes and something more—she'd been trained, he realized—stopped him. The better chance at survival was to hold still. She hadn't killed him yet. She wanted something.

Wen, her knees on his chest, watched his pupils dilate, saw the muscles in his neck jump and the slight movement of his mouth as she read the thoughts and plans of her prisoner, and knew she didn't have much time. "Who sent you?"

"I don't know."

"If you truly don't know, then I'm going to kill you." Her eyes narrowed. "So, I'm asking you one more time. *Who* sent you?"

"I *really* don't know. It doesn't work that way. I get the job through an intermediary."

"Who's that?"

"I can't tell you."

"I thought you said he was just an intermediary." She pushed the Glock harder against his throat.

"He is, but if I tell you, I'm as good as dead."

"You're as good as dead right now if you don't. I'm counting to three."

"A guy named Miller. He's in Los Angeles."

"You're lying."

"I am not."

Wen pulled the trigger. "Yes, you are," she said, but the man was already dead. For a moment, Wen thought she heard what sounded like the flapping of thousands of wings . . . but instantly, the forest was more silent than before.

Chasing Life: Chapter Three

Wen caught up with Chase for the last half-mile of the trail back to the car.

"I heard the gunshot," Chase said, feeling himself shift, yet again, from intense fear to intense relief.

"Were you worried?"

"Always, but I've learned to recognize the sound of your Glock, so I knew the chances were good that you had been the one to fire."

"Even before you heard the gun, you should've known I would prevail."

"I did," he said, taking her hand. "What happened?"

Wen explained how she questioned the man and that he had lied twice. Chase knew the MSS did extensive psychological training, and that their agents could spot a lie quite easily with a number of tells—such as blinking rapidly in succession, darting eyes, movement of pupils, shaking of the head, and a dozen other indicators.

"Not only was he lying, but he was about to make a move."

"It's too bad," Chase said.

"Yeah," she agreed.

They both lived with the constant threat from people who had been after them for more than a year, and thus far they had been unable to identify or link them to any specific group, company, or government. Along the way there'd been plenty of others pursuing them, but those had belonged to the CIA, the MSS, and companies they'd been involved with at the time. These people—who they called "shadow people"—were something different, and they worried that, sooner or later, their luck, Wen's skills, or Chase's brains, were going to run out.

"The sniper had no ID on him whatsoever," Wen continued.

"So we know nothing."

"I did take both his weapons, and even dug the slug that went through the bastard's neck out of a root."

"Sometimes you scare me," Chase said.

"Sometimes?" She laughed, but then her expression turned sad.

He regretted making the comment. Wen, an efficient trained killer, probably one of the best in the world, didn't enjoy her work. Chase knew how emotionally taxing it was for her to take a life. That trauma was one of the reasons they came to the mountains, hoping for some peace and to escape the violent adventure their life had become. He was angry at the irony that they had been attacked after such a blissful five days, and that she had to kill again. "I'm sorry," he said softly.

Wen knew he wasn't apologizing for the comment, but for another death she'd endured. "Me too."

"He's bound to have a vehicle down here," Chase said, as they were nearing the final gate that kept the free-roaming cattle from invading the parking area for the trailhead.

"And there's a good chance his ID is in it," Wen added.

Just before they opened the gate, while they were still in a stand of lichen covered trees and ponderosa pines, Chase held out an arm to stop her. "You see that silver Jeep Renegade?" he whispered. "There's a guy in it."

"Someone waiting to make sure the hit job got done."

"We'll have to get to the car without being seen," Chase said.

"I think we can get around. He's parked in the front row, we're in the back . . . if we go around these trees we can get to the car before he notices."

"As soon as we start the engine and pull out . . . " Chase began.

"I'll have the gun pointed right at him."

Chase knew it wouldn't be too difficult for Wen to sneak up behind the Jeep and kill the man without even using her gun, and they would be able to have a safer escape. However, if they could avoid another killing, they were going to try.

"If we get enough of a head start . . . "

"And I can shoot out his tires . . . "

While sitting low in the front seat, Chase started the vehicle. Wen, in the passenger seat, leaned out the open door, ready to shoot the tires, still wishing she had her MP7 submachine gun.

The man spotted them right away, but didn't have a gun ready, so Chase steered out of the parking lot before he could respond. Wen fired toward him, but she couldn't get a steady aim while their Subaru Outback bounced over the roots and ruts of the old logging road.

The man slammed the Jeep in reverse, backed over a

small log and into a ditch, and jumped up to the road, fishtailing in a plume of dust. It was impossible for Wen to hit his tires under those conditions.

Chase gripped the wheel tightly as the Subaru blasted down the road that, in most spots, was only six inches wider then its wheelbase. The crumbling, rocky road descended seven miles toward Mugginsville. Chase, who liked to tell people he was a professional race car driver, normally reveled in a good race, but this road was about as treacherous as he could imagine—unless it started to snow, or maybe if the nearby Mount Shasta erupted. The loose surface fell away eight hundred feet down through crags and trees to a sure death. He pushed the car as fast as he could, trying to gain a bigger lead.

The Jeep's only real advantage was clearance, he thought as the Subaru bottomed out on a dip, then bounced along a rare straight stretch of dusty washboard.

"I should've shot him in the parking lot," Wen said. "We've got six miles of this still ahead," she said, looking back at the Renegade, now only two hundred feet behind, "and when we get down to the main road, it'll be nearly impossible to lose him."

"I'm sure not going to worry about that now" Chase said, checking the rearview mirror. The Jeep was barreling toward them. "I think he means to ram us."

"If he hits us at the wrong moment, we'll go careening over the edge." Wen leaned out and fired, pressing her advantage. She could concentrate on shooting while the driver of the Jeep had to concentrate on driving. *On these roads, it's nearly impossible to shoot and drive at the same time.* Yet as soon as that thought came, somehow the man managed to get a shot off. It didn't come close to hitting the Subaru, but that wasn't his intention. It was a warning that he could both shoot and drive.

A minute later, the shooting didn't matter, as he smashed the Jeep's flat steel bumper into the Subaru. The jolt sent them several feet off course, and one of the front tires hung halfway over the edge before Chase righted it and got back on the road, instantly swerving to avoid a fallen boulder. He hit the gas to escape another ramming, and ran across several chunky rocks—one of them tearing through the wheel-well. Chase over-corrected.

"We're going over the cliff!" Wen screamed.

Chasing Life: Chapter Four

The Subaru headed perilously toward the ledge without enough road remaining to make the turn. Chase caught the steering wheel and cranked it back hard, and through a crazy bit of time-stopping magic that he could never explain, the Subaru, with two wheels going over, somehow found enough traction to get around and back on the road.

"How did you do that?" Wen yelled.

"I have no idea!"

"He's coming back!"

"If he gets us on the right turn, next time we're really going over."

"Drive faster," Wen said as he rammed them again.

"Going fast is the same thing as him pushing us off the edge! There's just not enough road."

Wen fired another shot, aiming for the tires, but as the Subaru jostled over the rocks and ruts, the bullet hit the passenger side of the Jeep's windshield. "That'll slow him down a little," she said. "But he's got bulletproof glass!"

Still, the windshield was now hard to see through, and the Jeep immediately slowed.

Chase shouted two words of profanity. Wen turned as Chase slammed on the brakes. A giant horse trailer being towed by an oversized pickup crawled ahead of them.

Chase pounded the horn. "That thing's way too big to navigate this ridiculous excuse for a road!"

"The man in the Jeep will be able to *walk* faster than us." Wen took aim, but the Jeep came up hard and rammed them. Chase alternated between gas and brake pedals, but slid on the loose scree and tapped the back of the horse trailer. It was impossible to know if the trailer-driver even noticed.

"Somewhere the road has to open up," Wen said. "I remember on our way in there were some pull-outs."

"This isn't a road, it's a damned bike path," Chase muttered.

The Jeep was going slow enough that its driver could easily fire at them. Two bullets hit the side and back of the car.

"He's shooting," Wen shouted, "but not very well!"

"Let's hope he doesn't get better with practice," Chase said, checking the speedometer, which was dancing between four and six mph.

Suddenly a pull off opened on the cliff side of the road. The horse trailer should've gone in, but didn't. At the last instant, Chase took it, whipping around the side of the trailer. Wen looked out her window, straight down, as rocks dropped off over the ledge, cascading into the trees hundreds of feet below. The Jeep foolishly tried to follow. The back right passenger side wheel went off the road, hanging in the air, before Chase gunned it and brought the

Subaru flying around in front of the horse trailer. The pickup truck driver hit his breaks at the same moment, causing the Jeep to miss the opening.

Two wheels went over, as if in slow motion. The driver hit the accelerator, spraying gravel, rock, dirt, and dust, as he fought to get traction back on the road. He didn't, and the Jeep rolled off the side.

Wen looked back in time to see the Jeep's driver trying to climb out of his door before the vehicle rolled the rest of the way, crushing his body as it crashed into the canyon, landing in a twisted wreck, crumpled around a giant tree.

"Instant karma," Chase said. "Never pays to be a tailgater."

"His own doing," Wen said, glad she hadn't killed him.

Once back in civilization, Wen inserted new SIM cards into their disposable burner phones, then called to check messages. Chase drove them north into Oregon, where he had a private plane and pilots waiting at the Medford International Airport. He'd long ago given up buying planes that were too easily traced, and instead leased them through a complex series of shell companies and identities managed by a small team of key employees.

Wen put the phone on speaker to take a call from Margot, the leader of WOLF—sometimes simply referred to as "The Cause"—a group of people seeking to bring about more income equality throughout the world. Whenever Margot called, it usually meant trouble of some kind. However, as soon as Margot said she had a message from Mei Lein, a woman who'd helped her escape China, Wen knew this time it was far worse than simply trouble. Her worst nightmare had actually come true.

Grab your copy…
vinci-books.com/chasing-life

About the Author

USA TODAY Bestselling Author Brandt Legg uses his unusual real life experiences to create page-turning novels. He's traveled with CIA agents, dined with senators and congressmen, mingled with astronauts, chatted with governors and presidential candidates, had a private conversation with a Secretary of Defense he still doesn't like to talk about, hung out with Oscar and Grammy winners, had drinks at the State Department, been pursued by tabloid reporters, and spent a birthday at the White House by invitation from the President of the United States.

At age eight, Legg's father died suddenly, plunging his family into poverty. Two years later, while suffering from crippling migraines, he started in business, and turned a hobby into a multi-million-dollar empire. National media dubbed him the "Teen Tycoon," and by the mid-eighties, Legg was one of the top young entrepreneurs in America, appearing as high as number twenty-four on the list (when Steve Jobs was #1, Bill Gates #4, and Michael Dell #6). Legg still jokes that he should have gone into computers.

By his twenties, after years of buying and selling businesses, leveraging, and risk-taking, the high-flying Legg became ensnarled in the financial whirlwind of the junk bond eighties. The stock market crashed and a firestorm of trouble came down. The Teen Tycoon racked up more than a million dollars in legal fees, was betrayed by those closest to him, lost his entire fortune, and ended up serving time for financial improprieties.

After a year, Legg emerged from federal prison, chastened and wiser, and began anew. More than twenty-five years later, he's now using all that hard-earned firsthand knowledge of conspiracies, corruption and high finance to weave his tales. Legg's books pulse with authenticity.

His series have excited nearly a million readers around the world. Although he refused an offer to make a television movie about his life as a teenage millionaire, his autobiography is in the works. There has also been interest from Hollywood to turn his thrillers into films. With any luck, one day you'll see your favorite characters on screen.

He lives in the Pacific Northwest, with his wife and son, writing full time, in several genres, containing the common themes of adventure, conspiracy, and thrillers. Of all his pursuits, being an author and crafting plots for novels is his favorite.

Acknowledgments

Chasing Dirt was written entirely in the wilds of Oregon and California, the scenic areas most devoid of human attention and distraction. It is fitting for the subject matter. Thanks to those who were with me—who are always with me—Ro and Teakki.

The character of WH is based on an actual person of the same name. We lost him this year at a tragically young age. In tribute to him, I tried to draw the character similar to the real man, who was always adventurous, humorous, a friend to be counted on, and one of the coolest guys I've known. Miss you, man.

More thanks—

My mother, Barbara Blair, for adding much to the European color, and for reminding me the dirt was under the bed.

Jack Llartin, for his steady hand at battling typos and such before the readers find them.

Special gratitude to Melanie C. Hansen, for her keen editing eyes and flashing wit. Thank you Sigosaur, you are a rare creature.

And, finally, to Teakki, who patiently waited to discuss politics, play gotcha-last, ask about various movie ratings, or any number of other things that joyfully distract me, until I finished writing each day.

And to you, and each reader, who has explored these

pages, thank you for making it possible for me to support my family by writing. I'm grateful you found my books and took a chance on me. I look forward to going on many, many more journeys with you.